THE PAPER DAUGHTERS

OF

CHINATOWN

OTHER SHADOW MOUNTAIN BOOKS
ADAPTED FOR YOUNG READERS

The Rent Collector:
Adapted for Young Readers from the Best-Selling Novel,
by Camron Wright
ISBN 978-1-62972-985-5

The Orphan Keeper:
Adapted for Young Readers from the Best-Selling Novel,
by Camron Wright
ISBN 978-1-63993-054-8

THE PAPER DAUGHTERS OF CHINATOWN

ADAPTED FOR YOUNG READERS
FROM THE BEST-SELLING NOVEL

HEATHER B. MOORE
ALLISON HONG MERRILL

SHADOW
MOUNTAIN
PUBLISHING

Interior images by lisheng2121/Shutterstock
Map illustration by Sheryl Dickert Smith

This is a work of fiction. Characters and events in this book are products of the authors' imagination or are represented fictitiously.

Visit us at shadowmountain.com

Library of Congress Cataloging-in-Publication Data

Names: Moore, Heather B., author. | Merrill, Allison Hong, author.

Title: The paper daughters of Chinatown: adapted for young readers from the bestselling novel / Heather B. Moore, Allison Hong Merrill.

Description: Salt Lake City: Shadow Mountain, [2023] | Includes bibliographical references. | Audience: Ages 10 and up. | Audience: Grades 4–6. | Summary: When Tien Fu Wu, a young Chinese girl, is sold into slavery by her gambler father, she is rescued by the women of the Occidental Mission Home for Girls in San Francisco, where she befriends missionary Dolly Cameron.

Identifiers: LCCN 2022045921 | ISBN 9781639930944 (hardback)

Subjects: LCSH: Wu, Tien Fu, 1886?–1975—Fiction. | Cameron, Donaldina, 1869–1968—Fiction. | Occidental Mission Home—Fiction. | Human trafficking victims—Fiction. | Women social reformers—California—San Francisco—Fiction. | Chinatown (San Francisco, Calif.)—Fiction. | Reformers—Fiction. | CYAC: Wu, Tien Fu, 1886?–1975—Fiction. | Cameron, Donaldina, 1869–1968—Fiction. | Chinese—California—San Francisco—Fiction. | Occidental Mission Home—Fiction. | Human trafficking—Fiction. | Chinatown (San Francisco, Calif.)—Fiction. | BISAC: JUVENILE FICTION / Diversity & Multicultural | JUVENILE FICTION / Social Themes / Emotions & Feelings | LCGFT: Biographical fiction. | Novels.

Classification: LCC PZ7.1. M6549 Pap 2023 | DDC [Fic]—dc23

LC record available at https://lccn.loc.gov/2022045921

Printed in the United States of America
Lake Book Manufacturing, LLC, Melrose Park, IL

10 9 8 7 6 5 4 3 2 1

For those who have endured the unspeakable.
I see you.
—Heather B. Moore

With eternal love and gratitude
to my husband and our sons:
少凡，語翔，語傑，語邢
—Allison Hong Merrill

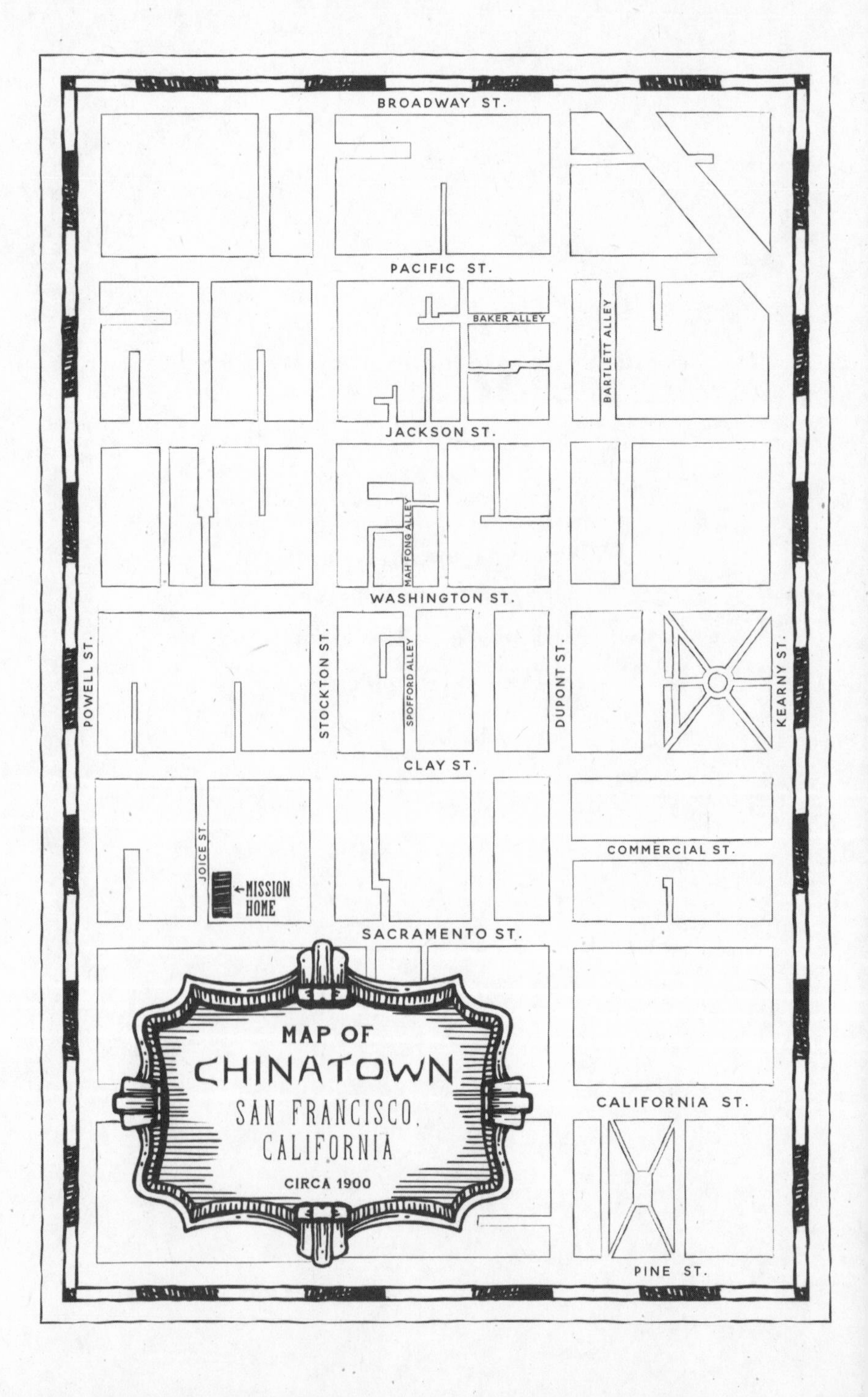
BROADWAY ST.
PACIFIC ST.
BAKER ALLEY
BARTLETT ALLEY
JACKSON ST.
MAH FONG ALLEY
WASHINGTON ST.
POWELL ST.
STOCKTON ST.
SPOFFORD ALLEY
DUPONT ST.
KEARNY ST.
CLAY ST.
JOICE ST.
MISSION HOME
COMMERCIAL ST.
SACRAMENTO ST.
MAP OF
CHINATOWN
SAN FRANCISCO,
CALIFORNIA
CIRCA 1900
CALIFORNIA ST.
PINE ST.

CONTENTS

Introduction ix

Character Chart xi

Historical Timeline xiii

CHAPTER 1: A Locked Door 1

CHAPTER 2: Bound Feet 6

CHAPTER 3: The Mansion 10

CHAPTER 4: A Phoenix Hairpin 17

CHAPTER 5: Paper Daughter 28

CHAPTER 6: Silk Dresses 38

CHAPTER 7: Counting Scars 48

CHAPTER 8: City of Fog 59

CHAPTER 9: Into the Alley 69

CHAPTER 10: A Hard Decision 76

CHAPTER 11: Two Orphan Children 85

CHAPTER 12: A New Roommate 92

CHAPTER 13: One Foot Forward 100

CHAPTER 14: A Birthday Cake 111

CHAPTER 15: Over the Rooftops 117
CHAPTER 16: Sound of the Gong 129
CHAPTER 17: Safe and Sound 135
CHAPTER 18: A Night in Jail 147
CHAPTER 19: Call to Action 157
CHAPTER 20: A Plague 165
CHAPTER 21: The Bridal Bouquet 175
CHAPTER 22: A New Director 182
CHAPTER 23: Lo Mo 189
CHAPTER 24: A Promise 200
Reader Questions & Answers 215
Selected Bibliography & Recommended Reading 220

INTRODUCTION

In 1895, Donaldina Cameron arrived at 920 Sacramento Street in San Francisco. She'd agreed to teach a sewing class for one year at the Occidental Mission Home for Girls. But when she met Tien Fu Wu, Miss Cameron knew she had to join the fight against the human trafficking plague.

Who was Tien Fu Wu?

Tien Fu Wu (伍天福) was a snarky Chinese girl, fiercely courageous in doing what she thought was right, even if it meant challenging tradition and authority. We imagine that, in our day, she would've made a wonderful class president, an interpreter for the United Nations, a bridge between Chinese and American cultures. But really, whatever she chose to be, she would've been successful and a voice for change. Any parents would be proud to have a child like her. But Tien Fu Wu's father didn't celebrate her outstanding talents. Instead he sold her into slavery when she was six years old. Life took Tien Fu Wu on a cruel journey—both physically and emotionally—full of heartbreak, despair, and anguish.

But that happened 130 years ago—why should we care about her story now?

Well, unfortunately, human trafficking still torments innocent victims everywhere in the world today. We hope to magnify awareness of this modern-day plague in the urgent and powerful voice of Tien Fu Wu—a former child slave who grew up to be a brilliant lady fighting this crime against humanity. She not only created a meaningful life for herself but also left behind a glorious legacy of resilience and bravery. Her story helps us understand the reality of human trafficking—through understanding comes empathy; through empathy comes action to end it.

With that, we're humbled and honored to present *The Paper Daughters of Chinatown: Adapted for Young Readers from the Best-Selling Novel.*

—Heather B. Moore and Allison Hong Merrill

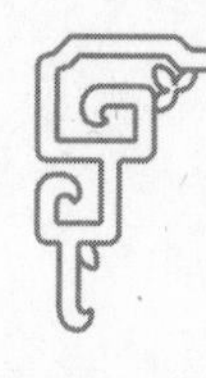

CHARACTER CHART

HISTORICAL CHARACTERS

(IN ORDER OF APPEARANCE)

Tai Choi (Tien Fu Wu)

Kum Quai

Mrs. Lee

Yuen Qui

Margaret Culbertson

Yoke Lon Lee (Lonnie)

Donaldina Cameron (Dolly)

Mary Ann Browne

Eleanor Olney

Dong Ho

Anna Culbertson

Ah Cheng

Mary H. Field

Jean Ying

CHINATOWN POLICE SQUAD:

- Jesse Cook
- John Green
- George Riordan
- James Farrell

Hong Leen

Chan Juan

LAWYERS:

- Henry E. Monroe
- Mr. Weigle
- Mr. Herrington

Chung Bow

Wong Fong

Dr. John Endicott Gardner

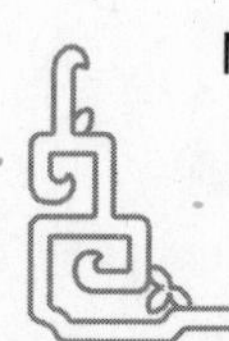

Leung Kum Ching

Hung Mui

Frances P. Thompson

President William McKinley and his wife, Mrs. Ida McKinley

Horace C. Coleman

FICTIONAL CHARACTERS

Yi

Mrs. Roos

Mr. Roos

George Roos

Xiu Gan Lai

Mrs. Wang

Willy Wang

Mr. Wang

Kang and Jiao, children of Hong Leen

Dr. Hall

Jun Ling, husband of Ah Cheng

Huan Sun

Mei Lien

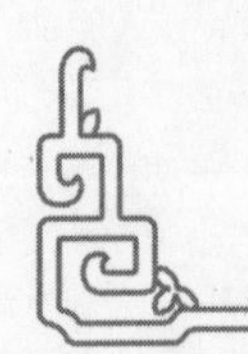
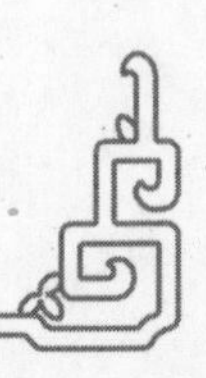

HISTORICAL TIMELINE

1869: Donaldina Cameron is born in Clydevale in Port Molyneux, New Zealand.

1872: The Cameron family moves to California, arriving in San Francisco.

1873: The California branch of the Women's Foreign Mission Society is formed.

1874: The Women's Foreign Mission Society opens the Occidental Mission Home for Girls.

1882: The Chinese Exclusion Act is approved by Congress.

1886: Tai Choi (Tien Fu Wu) is born in Zhejiang Province, China.

1894: The Occidental Mission Home for Girls relocates to 920 Sacramento Street.

1894: Tien Fu Wu is rescued and brought to the mission home.

1895: Donaldina Cameron takes the train to San Francisco in April and arrives at the mission home.

1897: The mission home superintendent Margaret Culbertson dies. Mary H. Field becomes the new superintendent.

1901: Mary H. Field resigns, and Donaldina Cameron accepts the position as superintendent.

1901: Chinatown is scoured because of bubonic plague.

1906: An enormous earthquake devastates San Francisco.

1907: The cornerstone for a new building is laid at 920 Sacramento Street.

1907–1911: Tien Fu Wu attends college in Pennsylvania and Canada.

1908: Miss Cameron and the girls return to 920 Sacramento Street, and the newly built mission home is dedicated.

1910: The Angel Island Immigration Station opens.

1912: Women are allowed to vote in San Francisco.

1916: Tien Fu Wu returns to China to search for her family.

1934: Donaldina Cameron retires.

1935: Trafficked women testify in the Broken Blossoms court case.

1942: The mission home is renamed the "Cameron House."

1943: The Chinese Exclusion Act is repealed.

1968: Donaldina Cameron dies with Tien Fu Wu by her side.

Chapter One
A LOCKED DOOR

ZHEJIANG PROVINCE, CHINA, 1892

Tai Choi pounded her fists on the door and screamed, "Let me out! Lao Ye, where did you go?"

How could Tai Choi's father think of locking her in here? No tourists should travel locked up like prisoners. In this tiny, windowless boat cabin, the mixed stench of body odor and human waste made it hard to breathe. For the past hour or so, she had been feeling along the walls and door in the dark, trying to find a way out. She twisted and pulled at the doorknob once more, but it didn't budge.

"Let me out!" she yelled again, her voice raw. She pounded harder on the door, over and over. Just then, the boat lurched. Dread pulsed through Tai Choi. Her heart rate doubled. The boat was leaving the harbor, and no one knew she was locked in the lower deck alone. Panicked, she kicked the door.

Thump, thump, thump!

Excruciating pain shot up from her foot, nearly dropping her to her knees. Her feet were bound, and kicking the door made her foot feel like it was on fire. Her chest burned with pain too—fear, rage, and confusion all boiled together, but she bit back a cry. She needed her voice and strength to call for help.

The boat was moving faster now, gently rocking, as the engine thrummed somewhere nearby. Her stomach churned with both the stench of urine and the movement of the boat. She was both mentally and physically exhausted. Leaning against the door, she slid to the floor, curled up, and hugged her knees. The butterfly sleeves of her tunic dangled in the air, and the weight of them reminded her of her mother.

If anyone ever asked Tai Choi who her best friend was, she wouldn't hesitate to say, "My Niang." *My mother.*

Earlier in the day, Mother helped her change into a silk tunic, even though Tai Choi was six years old now and didn't need help getting dressed. Then, Mother tucked a washcloth and a toothbrush into a secret pocket in the butterfly sleeves of Tai Choi's tunic. When Father and Tai Choi were leaving for the harbor, Mother was overcome by emotion, unable to do anything else but to give Tai Choi a long, tearful hug.

In fact, she had been crying since last week when Father announced at dinner one night that Tai Choi would travel alone to visit Grandmother in Ningbo. "You're old enough, big girl," he'd said.

"It's not fair!" Tai Choi's older brother slammed his chopsticks on the table. He'd never had the privilege of traveling alone before. "I'm the firstborn and a *boy*!"

Father waved his hand in the air to silence him.

Unexpectedly, Mother burst out sobbing. "Don't—don't let her go," she begged Father. "It's too dangerous."

Tai Choi couldn't believe Mother would dissuade Father. Didn't she know this trip was Tai Choi's dream? Whenever Grandmother came to visit their family, she always brought the most delicious food from Ningbo. This time, Tai Choi wouldn't have to share any treats with her brother. Better yet, she wouldn't have to share any household chores when she stayed at Grandmother's since she had maids.

Tai Choi's family used to have a staff of maids too, but Father let them go a few months earlier, so Tai Choi and Mother had been doing most of the chores around the house. They were both shocked to realize how much effort it required to simply have a cup of hot tea in their hands: walking to the market to buy tea leaves, walking to the community well to fetch buckets of water, climbing up the mountains to chop firewood for the stove, and standing in the sweltering kitchen to tend to the fire that boiled water for tea.

But Tai Choi would gladly do any hard work as long as she could be with Mother. Plus, she enjoyed the process of crushing tea leaves, letting the fragrant herbal scent rise up as they blended them, then measuring out the teaspoonfuls. The memory of the delicious tea blends made her miss Mother right now. The two of them had shared sweet and bitter experiences together.

Like other girls and women in the upper class of society who didn't need to do menial labor, both Tai Choi and her mother had bound feet. A year earlier when Grandmother visited, she declared that it was time to bind Tai Choi's feet—the formality to prepare her to properly reflect the family's high standing.

Despite Tai Choi's crying, squirming, grimacing, and begging for it to stop, Grandmother had managed to bend and twist Tai Choi's feet and wrap them tightly in long cloths so they wouldn't grow with the rest of her body.

Ever since Tai Choi's feet were bound, Mother had dutifully examined the wounds every night and then bound her feet back tighter. Tai Choi couldn't stand the pain but had learned to accept the nightly routine of changing her binding cloths and to appreciate it as a bonding time with Mother. She resented the fact that boys and men didn't have to bind their feet to show their social status. The way Tai Choi's father showed his superior class was spending his days in gambling dens.

It shouldn't have been a surprise—after all, Father's gambling addiction wasn't a secret—but Mother was furious when he gambled away almost all their money and creditors showed up at their house and took away their expensive furniture. Father's gambling not only reduced their family to the peasant class, but it also brought them death threats. Mother had never been so humiliated; she argued with Father all the time. Now this solo trip would be Tai Choi's chance to get away from the sadness at home. What was Mother doing by trying to change Father's mind?

That night at dinner, Tai Choi reached across the table to pat Mother on the hand, her butterfly sleeves dipping in a pot of hot soup that she'd helped her mother cook. "Don't cry, Niang, I'll come home soon."

"You want to go so badly? Go!" Her brother pouted. "Lao Lao will bind your hands too!"

"No, she won't," Tai Choi yelled at her brother. She hated it whenever he teased her about her feet.

"We don't want you here anyway—" her brother continued with a sneer.

"Stop, both of you!" Father roared. "Tai Choi is going. I've made the decision. Whatever happens to her after she leaves is none of your business."

Everyone fell silent. Mother pushed away her rice bowl and chopsticks. She dropped her head into her hands and sobbed. Father's anger seethed red in his face. He slapped his palm on the table and ordered Mother to leave the room.

Now, alone in this tiny boat cabinet, Tai Choi couldn't believe how drastically things had changed within the past hour. When Father led her to the lower deck, she was so excited about the trip, she didn't mind how tight this space was. She'd stretched out her arms to either side like a balance scale, her fingertips almost touching the walls, and called out to Father, "Lao Ye, look, I'm big." She'd giggled. "Get it?"

Her pose reflected the shape of the Chinese character for *big*, the only word she could read. Father had once told her that she embodied the concept of *big*: big attitude, a big heart, and big talent. In fact, that was what her name meant—Tai Choi, big talent.

Father had only nodded. He hadn't even given Tai Choi a simple smile, despite how hard she tried to balance on her shaky legs, her delicate, bound feet inches apart to support her body weight. "Eat your supper if you want to be really big," he mumbled as he headed toward the door, "and do what you're told."

Tai Choi didn't need to hear that; she had always been good. But she was shocked to hear the sound of the lock click, then Father's brisk footsteps thump up the stairs, back to the main deck. She didn't expect to be locked up in the dark as if being punished. Why would Father do this?

She ran her fingers over her bracelet—a strip of silk Mother had torn off her old dress and tied to Tai Choi's wrist. Her eyes stung with welling hot tears, her nose tickled. Mother had the right idea about giving her the washcloth. She brought it to her face to dry her eyes, blow her nose, and breathe through it, believing it would filter out the stink of the room. She wished the washcloth could filter out the hurt too and help her forgive Father for being so eager to leave her behind that he hadn't even said goodbye.

Chapter Two

BOUND FEET

SHANGHAI CITY, JIANGSU PROVINCE, CHINA, 1892

The boat rocked, the engine hummed. Thudding footsteps only stayed on the upper deck, no one came down to help Tai Choi. She'd been drifting in and out of sleep. Now her eyes snapped open. The boat had stopped, and the engine had quieted. Had she arrived in Ningbo?

"Lao Lao," Tai Choi shouted, her voice cracking.

When the door rattled and swung open, Tai Choi scrambled to her feet and squinted at the light coming through. "Lao Lao?"

"Follow me," said a middle-aged man in a long silk robe. Like almost every man in China, he wore a queue—the front and sides of his head were shaved, and the rest of his hair was plaited into a long braid that hung down his back.

"Why?" Tai Choi asked. "Where's my Lao Lao?"

"She's not here, is she?" The man scoffed. "She sent me to get you. Follow me."

Reluctantly, Tai Choi tottered behind him. The early evening sky was deep orange, and the main deck looked like it had been painted gold. She breathed in deep gulps of the fresh sea air. Around her, other passengers talked about Shanghai—some called it *Pearl of the Orient*—and what fun things they would do in the fascinating International Settlement, meeting the residents from America, Britain, and France.

Tai Choi followed the man off the boat, but she sensed something was wrong. She pulled on the man's sleeve. "Is this Ningbo? My Lao Lao lives in—"

"Be quiet!" the man hissed. "Did I tell you to follow me or to question me?" He glared at her, his face flushed and his forehead dotted with beads of sweat. "If you make a scene right now, I'll beat you!"

Tai Choi wanted to yell at him but promptly stopped herself. Before her father left the boat, hadn't he told her to do what she was told? But why would Grandmother ask such a mean man to pick her up? Where did she even know him from? Surely there were nicer people in Ningbo . . .

Wait! If this was Ningbo, the man wouldn't need to be so irritable and defensive as if he'd been caught lying . . .

Lying . . . ?

Oh no!

Could he actually be lying about taking her to Grandmother? If he wasn't doing what he said he would do, what was his plan?

Tai Choi had a feeling she shouldn't trust him. She must find Grandmother on her own. But where was she?

Everywhere Tai Choi looked, people squealed about the new and exciting things in this place they called the International Settlement. The streets were filled with busy people, noisy automobiles, and rare bicycles—she didn't know what to look at first. High-rise buildings stretching to the sky. Vendors with carts filled with culinary delights. Rickshaw runners speeding on, transporting white travelers.

Tai Choi had never seen any white people before and couldn't stop staring at them and marveling at their clothing: men with their tall hats, dark suits, and bow ties. Women with their large flowered and feathered hats, puffy-sleeved blouses with small waists, and skirts that were wider at the hems. Surely Grandmother would've talked about all the fascinating sights and the peculiar people in her city, but she never had. Could it be possible that Tai Choi's suspicion was correct, that she wasn't in Ningbo now? Did that mean what she feared was also true, that she wasn't going to see Grandmother?

No, no, no, no, no! This wasn't supposed to happen. What was going on?

If Tai Choi left her house to visit Grandmother but ended up in an unexpected city among strangers, then she was lost. How did she go from a tourist to a locked-up traveler and arrive in this horrible state of becoming a lost child? Was this Father's plan?

In a sea of people, how could Tai Choi find an honest person to help her get to Ningbo, to Grandmother? But then she didn't know where in Ningbo Grandmother lived; she didn't know where in Zhejiang her parents lived, so even if she somehow managed to find an honest person to help her, how would she get back to her family? What else could a lost child do in this moment except follow this lying man, the only person taking her somewhere?

As much as Tai Choi disliked the idea, it seemed that she didn't have a choice but to obey his command. Tai Choi hoped she was wrong. Maybe this man was taking her to Grandmother. She caught up with him and maneuvered through the streets, where the aroma of garlic, meat, and mushroom wafted in the air. When they arrived at a teahouse, an older woman in a green silk dress greeted the man. While they chatted in Cantonese, the woman fanned her face with a bamboo fan and threw occasional glances at Tai Choi. A few minutes later she seated them at a corner table and ordered a server to bring out steamed meat buns, roasted peanuts, lychee fruit, and tea.

Tai Choi's stomach twisted with hunger. The sweet aroma of the tea reminded her of making tea blends with Mother. She drew in a deep breath and let the comforting smell of the tea calm her. She looked at the woman and asked in the Han language, "Is this all for me?"

The woman nodded with a grin, then she threw a sideways glance at the man. "She doesn't speak Cantonese?"

"Doesn't look like it. Her tongue seems to be bound, like her feet." The man lowered his gaze to Tai Choi's shoes.

"Oooh, will you look at that? She's got bound feet," the woman said. "A girl born with a golden spoon in her mouth—how about that?"

"I know you love a good challenge. Have fun with her bound tongue, bound feet, and all that."

The woman fanned her face again and winked at the man. He stood up and she handed him a pouch. He cupped his hands in front of his chest and bowed, his face split into a wide grin. "Always a pleasure to work with you."

The woman nodded and turned to pat Tai Choi on the head. In the Han language, she said, "Girl, call me Yi. Stay with me and you'll never go hungry."

Tai Choi grunted. She was so busy devouring the food, she didn't even look up when the man left.

Chapter Three

THE MANSION

SHANGHAI CITY, JIANGSU PROVINCE, CHINA, 1892

A rickshaw runner dropped off Yi and Tai Choi at a small house with a red door and a fenced-in garden. Yi handed a coin to the rickshaw runner, then climbed out. She grasped Tai Choi's hand, but the girl tugged away, crossing her arms in front of her chest.

"I'm not a little child."

Yi narrowed her eyes. "Feisty, huh? You better learn to be respectful and obedient to your elders."

Tai Choi was used to this kind of language. It was how her brother spoke to her and she wasn't afraid of it. She ignored Yi and glanced about the neighborhood. Across the road was a park with an exterior wall that had round latticework windows. As they headed toward the small house, Tai Choi said, "You're so lucky to live across from a beautiful park."

"A park?" Yi said, her eyebrows lifting. "No, it's the front yard of that house."

Tai Choi gaped. "This whole park is someone's front yard?"

Yi chuckled. "That's right. The Roos family lives there. Do you want to meet them?"

"Yes," Tai Choi squealed.

"You will soon," Yi said. "But I need to unbind your feet first."

"Why?" Tai Choi was shocked.

"So you can work," Yi said.

Work? What work? Why would any work be a part of Tai Choi's vacation? . . . Wait . . . Taking Grandmother and Ningbo out of the trip, was this still a vacation?

Yi might not be part of the original plan when Tai Choi's father announced the trip, but at least she had the right idea about unbinding Tai Choi's feet. She didn't like the pain anyway. As a lost child with no way of contacting her parents and grandmother, Tai Choi's only option was to do whatever this stranger told her. Thankfully, Yi was nicer than the man who brought her here.

Every morning, before leaving for work in the teahouse, Yi prepared a porcelain basin full of warm salt water for Tai Choi to soak her feet in. Unbinding her feet was saying goodbye to her family's old glory of high social class and bidding farewell to the daily routine Mother had done with her: caring for her feet. Yi had now taken Mother's place, caring for her body. Tai Choi felt she'd betrayed Mother. She didn't choose to be here with Yi, but she could choose to never let Yi replace Mother completely. She would pretend Yi was her aunt.

As she soaked her feet, she closed her eyes and remembered collecting tea leaves, drying them, crushing them, blending them, then sharing the sweet tea with Mother. Every evening when Yi returned, Tai Choi asked her if there were any new tea blends in the market. Then, before she fell asleep at night, she imagined telling Mother about all the new tea flavors she discovered.

During the long hours of soaking her feet alone in the house, Tai Choi looked out the window and wished she could play with the children in the parklike yard of the mansion across the road. About a week after Tai Choi had arrived in Shanghai, Yi declared that her feet were ready. She pointed at the mansion across the road and said, "Want to meet the Roos family today?"

"Yes, yes, yes!" Tai Choi clapped. She couldn't wait to get out of the house.

Yi gave her a pair of sandals to replace her tiny silk slippers that no longer fit. When she stretched out her hand, Tai Choi didn't hesitate to hold it. Together, they crossed the road to the large red gate covered with black half sphere knockers. Even though for days Tai Choi had been watching children play here, she got goose pimples when she stepped onto the grounds herself. When they approached a pavilion with a golden tile roof, she asked, "Why is there a water well under the pavilion?"

"It's a symbol," Yi explained. "It means that once we pass the pavilion, we enter the Roos family's living quarters, where they deal with daily tasks of food, water, and education."

Tai Choi thought it was strange to have a symbol in the yard to remind people they were about to enter some family's living space. Wouldn't the guests know that without the symbol? Could it be that the Rooses didn't know what to do with their vast wealth, so they invented the symbol?

Yi and Tai Choi crossed a bridge over a moat, passed two golden lion statues that guarded tall, red-painted wood double doors, and arrived at the courtyard with a botanical garden, a pagoda, and a lake. Swans glided elegantly across the mirrorlike water, and a couple more rested under a willow tree. *It would probably take two hours to walk around the entire place*, Tai Choi thought.

A stone path under a rose trellis led them to an arched gate—beyond it was a mansion. Tai Choi looked up at the strings of red lanterns that stretched above them and stared in wonder. There was endless marvel in this place—it was like walking through a dream. If she'd said "wow" every time she saw something gorgeous, stunning, or fascinating, she would've been saying "Wow,

wow, wow . . ." endlessly, making her sound like an infant crying, "Wa, wa, wa . . ."

She felt a sense of peace here, so much so that for a brief moment she even fantasized living here.

Yi led her to the grand steps of the mansion entrance. They knocked on the door, and a housekeeper answered.

"Yi," the housekeeper said with a bow, "how wonderful of you to pay us a visit. Please, come in."

Once they entered the mansion, the housekeeper ushered them into the grand hall, where Yi curtsied while Tai Choi bowed to a middle-aged woman—Mrs. Roos. Tai Choi had never seen anyone quite like this lady: pale skin, round, deep-set eyes, and a prominent nose. Instead of wearing traditional Chinese clothing, Mrs. Roos wore a Western dress: a white lace blouse and a long skirt. Tai Choi stared at her high heels. She hadn't realized that a woman in the upper class could choose not to bind her feet. But that wasn't the only thing that set her apart from the rest of the women Tai Choi had ever encountered. After a brief introduction, Mrs. Roos bent down to meet Tai Choi's gaze and—speaking the Han language with an unfamiliar accent—she asked Tai Choi how she liked the mansion.

"The house is so huge and beautiful. I like it," Tai Choi said. She couldn't resist Mrs. Roos's charm; even her accent was fascinating. "Why do you speak like that? You sound different."

Mrs. Roos looked to Yi, who shrugged and said, "This girl is different herself, she just doesn't know it. If she knew who you were, she would be more careful with her words."

Mrs. Roos laughed, then turned to Tai Choi. "My father was a French sailor," she said. "He met my mother in Guangdong but left China when I was little. I speak English, French, Han, and Cantonese. Sometimes I confuse all these languages and dialects in my head. They make me sound strange."

Yi chimed in. "Mrs. Roos is the Empress's goddaughter, Tai

Choi. If you're really good, she might take you to the imperial court someday."

"Someday?" Tai Choi frowned. "More waiting?"

Mrs. Roos gently shook her head at Yi, her expression one of playful disapproval. "Tsk, tsk, tsk, Yi. You disappoint our little guest here."

The two women shared a hearty chuckle before Mrs. Roos became more serious. "Tai Choi, you're welcome to stay with my family. I have some daughters your age, you'll have friends here. If you want, you can attend school with them."

Yi nodded and smiled. "What a brilliant idea."

School? Tai Choi almost jumped up and down and shouted for joy. She'd always wanted to go to school and learn to be as smart as her brother. "Right now I can only read the character for *big*. But I want to learn to read and write my own name and many other words."

Yi winked at Tai Choi. "You're so lucky. Here's your chance to get even smarter than you already are."

"So you'll stay?" Mrs. Roos asked.

"And you'll be good, won't you?" Yi asked.

Of course Tai Choi wanted to stay and go to school in this magical place; of course she would be good. She nodded and smiled at both ladies.

"Class starts very soon," Mrs. Roos said. "Should I take you there right now?"

"Yes," Tai Choi burst out.

Yi curtsied to Mrs. Roos and excused herself. "Enjoy your class," she said to Tai Choi before walking out of the majestic mansion.

Mrs. Roos extended a hand for Tai Choi to hold. Together they passed through the grand hallway, out the back door, and stepped onto a terrace. Across the way stood another building.

"That's the school," Mrs. Roos said. "My husband built it for all of our adopted children."

"Adopted? What does that mean?" Tai Choi asked.

"It means they don't have parents anymore and need a new family."

Tai Choi looked up at Mrs. Roos. "And you are their new mother?"

"Exactly."

Tai Choi wondered what it would be like to have Mrs. Roos as a new mother, but as soon as she caught herself fantasizing about a dream life here, she felt guilty about having pushed Mother out of her thoughts. So instead she imagined what a school was like.

They walked to the building and entered a large room where about twenty-five children sat at desks that lined up in neat rows. As soon as they saw Mrs. Roos, one of the older boys called out in a loud voice, "Attention!" and all the students—as well as the teacher, an old man who sat at a large desk at the front of the room—shot up from their seats in one swift movement, standing tall and still.

The class leader called out, "Salute!" and everyone bowed to Mrs. Roos, saying in one unified voice, "Greetings, Niang!"

Tai Choi was stunned. Were these *all* Mrs. Roos's adopted children?

After Mrs. Roos gave a gentle nod, the class leader ordered everyone to sit back down. Some of the children were Chinese, some were white; all of them wore dark sailor uniforms with gold buttons, complete with white knee-high socks and Mary Jane shoes. Tai Choi noticed that none of the girls had bound feet and none of the boys had a queue, not even the Chinese.

"Welcome, Mrs. Roos," the teacher said. "Who do we have here?"

"This is Tai Choi," Mrs. Roos said. "She would like to come to class. Tai Choi, this is our teacher."

Tai Choi bowed to him. She felt self-conscious all of a sudden. It wasn't because everyone was staring at her, it was because she wore only a tunic and simple cotton pants. The sandals Yi had bought her showed her bruised feet.

The teacher arranged for Tai Choi to sit in the front row. "I'll take care of her," he assured Mrs. Roos and then resumed the class. Only then did the mother of those students leave with a satisfied grin on her face.

Chapter Four

A PHOENIX HAIRPIN

SHANGHAI CITY, JIANGSU PROVINCE, CHINA, 1892

Tai Choi tried to focus on the teacher's lesson, but she didn't understand. What was the earth? What were volcanos? And how had the earth been full of volcanos a long time ago? Soon his voice became a humming white noise. Tai Choi picked her nose, then fiddled with her silk bracelet—a special gift from Mother. After a while, Tai Choi's eyes got droopy. She startled awake when her forehead hit the desk. The class burst out laughing.

The teacher clapped his hands together and announced, "Time for a break."

Chairs scooted and the children all hurried out of the building. Tai Choi followed a group of boys to the courtyard. When they challenged some girls to a race around the lily pond, Tai Choi butted in. "Can I race too?"

As soon as she asked that question, Tai Choi wanted to take it back. She hadn't run for over a year because of her bound feet. Even though they weren't bound anymore, they were still raw and sore. Tai Choi wasn't sure if running was a good idea right now. But how else would she make friends if not by playing with them?

The boys looked over their shoulders at Tai Choi, then

laughed. Instead of including her, they hurried faster to leave her behind.

"Wait," she called out, but no one stopped for her.

Just then, a Chinese girl offered Tai Choi a rag doll. "Do you want to play with this?"

Tai Choi looked up to meet her gaze and was stunned by this girl's exquisite beauty: delicate thin-line eyes, a pointy chin, and sloping shoulders. Her silky hair was pulled into a bun and held by a pair of dragon and phoenix hairpins. She was maybe nine or ten years old.

Tai Choi would rather go fishing or throw a ball like she'd watched the other children do. But this girl was friendly and kind, so Tai Choi could at least be polite. "All right. Thank you." She shrugged. "What's your name?"

"Kum Quai," the girl said. "I'm from Guangdong."

Tai Choi didn't know where that was. "I'm from Zhejiang, but I'm staying here now," she said. It felt strange to make that statement. Saying those words out loud made it real; it made Tai Choi happy and sad at the same time. Would she soon be telling others that Mrs. Roos was her new mother?

"Mrs. Roos is so nice that I'm happy to stay here," Kum Quai said with a sweet smile. "I wish I could be her daughter."

"Don't you have your own Niang?"

"Yes, but she sent me here because she couldn't feed me anymore."

Some people in Tai Choi's village didn't have enough to eat, so sometimes their children were sent away. She wondered if they had all come to a place as nice as the Rooses' house. Could it be possible that, instead of sending her on a solo trip to become a lost child, Father had sent her away to be adopted? Tai Choi suddenly felt it was right for her to be here with the Roos family.

"Maybe Mrs. Roos would adopt me if I didn't have a Niang." Kum Quai looked down at her shoes as if ashamed to not only have the thought but also to say it out loud. "Children like me stay here only for a short time. After all, we still have parents. Mr. Roos says our Lao Ye and Niang should take responsibility."

Tai Choi stifled a gasp. Only a second ago she was comfortable with the idea of being adopted . . .

"Mr. Roos—I haven't met him," Tai Choi said. "What's he like?"

"He's from England, but I don't think he'll go back. His business here is successful. Plus, he and Mrs. Roos have adopted so many orphans, can you imagine taking all twenty-five of them to England?"

Tai Choi shook her head. She had a mental image of a duck leading a line of twenty-five ducklings. She didn't know how any parents kept track of so many children.

Kum Quai interrupted her roaming thoughts. "Mr. and Mrs. Roos really love children, so they built this school not just for those lucky ones but for poor children like me too. My Niang would never be able to afford to send me to school."

Tai Choi hadn't thought of her family as poor before, but Kum Quai's words made her wonder if, from now on, she should tell people she was from a poor family.

"I'm glad your Niang sent you here so we can be friends," Tai Choi said.

Kum Quai's face lit up with a huge grin. She picked up Tai Choi's hands and looked into her eyes. "Yes, we'll always be friends."

Soon the boys returned from the race, panting and laughing. Maybe they would let Tai Choi play with them now. She gave the rag doll back to Kum Quai and approached the boys. One of them pointed at her sandals and snickered. "Look at her feet—"

Tai Choi put her hands on her waist. "What? You've never seen beautiful feet before?"

The boy burst out laughing and slapped his thigh. "You're so backward, it's pathetic!"

The other children gathered around, pointing at Tai Choi and laughing. Kum Quai stood among the crowd. Her brows were furrowed, her lips pressed tightly together.

Tai Choi had never expected anyone to call her "backward." This boy obviously didn't travel much. How could he see her feet and not know she was from the upper class?

"Hey, I don't know why you have a problem with my feet"—Tai Choi pointed at a bonsai tree a few feet away—"I can climb that tree, you know."

"That *dwarf* tree?" The boy shrieked. All the children laughed hysterically—all of them except Kum Quai.

Heat raced through Tai Choi's chest. She clenched her fists and charged at the boy. His eyes widened but he was too shocked to move. Tai Choi pushed him with all her might. The boy stumbled, then tripped and fell into the lily pond behind him.

The other children gasped. A couple of girls screamed and ran off into the schoolhouse. The teacher bolted to the courtyard just as the boy crawled out from the wet bank. He was covered in mud and stank like fish.

"It was her!" Another boy pointed at Tai Choi. "She pushed him!"

Tai Choi's heart pounded. She was filled with bitterness and guilt. Yes, she'd pushed the boy, but he'd asked for it. He'd *made* her do it. If he hadn't been so mean, she wouldn't have punished him. It was *his* fault. Tears threatened, but she refused to cry in front of everyone.

"Tai Choi, I'll have to report you," the teacher said. "Come with me."

Tai Choi dropped her head and followed the teacher to the mansion, all the while reassuring herself that Mrs. Roos was so loving, it couldn't possibly be that bad.

"Wait," Kum Quai called from behind.

Tai Choi turned to see her running toward her.

"If I don't see you again," Kum Quai said, "I want you to know that not everyone laughed at you." She reached up and took out the phoenix hairpin from her hair. "Here, take this and remember me."

Tai Choi was surprised that Kum Quai offered the gift, but more than that, she was confused by the language Kum Quai used. Why did it sound like she was saying goodbye? She must be overreacting. Tai Choi thanked her. It was only proper that she give something back in return, so she untied the silk bracelet from her own wrist to give to Kum Quai. "Remember me too," she said before hurrying to catch up with the teacher.

At the terrace of the house, just before opening the door, the teacher sighed. "George is Mr. Roos's oldest and favorite son. He won't forgive you easily"—he shook his head—"all of this on your first day too."

Tai Choi was the victim here. The other students saw what had happened. Why didn't any of them clarify the truth on her behalf?

The teacher and Mr. Roos had a private meeting. When the teacher came out of the room, he said, "I'm sorry, but you'll have to return to Yi's and never come back here."

What? That's unfair! Tai Choi thought. She wished Mr. Roos could have been just and punished George too—his favorite son or not.

When Yi opened the door, the surprise on her face only made Tai Choi squirm. The more the teacher explained what had happened, the redder Yi's face became.

"Thank you for bringing her back," Yi said. "I'll send the Roos family my apologies tomorrow."

The teacher nodded, then quickly left.

Tai Choi slunk into the house. For the rest of the afternoon she sulked in silence. Why had she become angry so quickly at that boy George? If only she'd stayed with Kum Quai and not tried to play with those boys . . . She gripped the phoenix hairpin in her hand and decided she would make a gift for the Roos family and apologize to George. But before she could tell Yi her plan, an older woman had come to the house to talk to Yi.

As the guest sat on the teakwood chair, she narrowed her eyes at Tai Choi. "Is that her?"

A shiver snaked along Tai Choi's neck.

"Tai Choi," Yi said in a sharp tone. "Go into the bedroom!"

Tai Choi obeyed and shut the door. Then she changed her mind and opened it a crack to eavesdrop.

"What happened?" the guest asked.

"Since Tai Choi is already smart, I thought going to school was good for her," Yi said. "But her intelligence didn't make her a good student. She pushed a boy into a pond."

There was a brief silence before the woman said something in Cantonese. Tai Choi wished the conversation between the two adults could switch back to the Han language. It was unfair that they were talking about her behind her back and she didn't understand everything they said.

"Yes, young children do that," the guest finally said in the Han language.

"I wanted her to help around the house, but I can't keep her now," Yi said. "Not after what she did. She'll now be a target of that boy, and I don't want this to ruin my friendship with Mrs. Roos. What other choice do I have?"

"I understand." The guest's voice was firm.

"I just want a fair price," Yi said, her tone urgent now.

"I always pay the market rate, but I am leaving tomorrow," the guest said. "Do you want me to come back tomorrow morning in case you change your mind?"

"I won't change my mind," Yi said. "I can't afford to."

"Send her in, then," the guest said. "I'll decide what she's worth."

Tai Choi shut the door with a click and hurried to the other side of the room. She slipped the phoenix hairpin in the secret pocket of her tunic where she still kept the washcloth and toothbrush from her mother, then she huddled in a corner.

The person who entered the room was no longer the same Yi she'd known. In front of her was a woman whose eyes burned with determination. She grasped Tai Choi's arm and pulled her up to her feet. "Come!"

In the kitchen, Tai Choi stood still as the guest walked around her in a circle. The woman pinched her cheek and her arm, then lifted her pant legs to examine her feet.

"Twenty-five silver yuan. No negotiations."

Yi merely nodded. The guest handed her a pouch, then gripped Tai Choi's arm and drew her toward the door.

"No," Tai Choi said. "I don't want to leave."

The woman tugged harder until she was dragging Tai Choi out to the street.

Tai Choi screamed for Yi. "Don't let her take me away, pleeeeease! Yiiiii—"

But Yi quietly closed her door, her gaze never meeting Tai Choi's.

By the time the woman and Tai Choi arrived at a different house, it was nighttime. Tai Choi was sent straight to bed in a room with some older girls. Tai Choi didn't ask the woman about dinner. She figured that going to bed without dinner was part of the punishment for having pushed George. She deserved it.

She maneuvered through sleeping bodies on the floor and found a space to lie down. It was shocking that the girls smelled so foul. Tai Choi wondered if the odor came from their breathing or their hair or their pits or their clothes. The more she thought about it, the more confused she was. What kind of punishment was this anyway, sleeping among smelly people? She was sorry for having pushed George, but she was also packed with rage and fear. Why didn't anyone ask her to tell her side of the story? Didn't they care about what she had to say? How long would she have to be stuck here, holding her breath?

She patted the girl next to her on the back. The girl rolled over to face Tai Choi. She was a teenager with a pockmarked face.

"My name is Tai Choi, I'm new here—"

The girl whispered, "Lower your voice."

"Oh, sorry," Tai Choi whispered back. "Do you know how long we're going to be here?"

"We leave tomorrow."

"Where?"

"Gold Mountain. We sail to Gold Mountain in America tomorrow. It's far away."

Wherever that was, Tai Choi didn't want to go. She didn't leave her house in Zhejiang to go to any mountains, with gold or not. She was sick of being passed from one adult to another, going from one place to another. No place truly felt right. The longer she was away from Mother, the more angry she was about the way other adults mistreated her. She wished she was back home with Mother again, even if that meant doing hard work together.

She curled up tighter, closed her eyes, and dug through the memory pile in her head to bring back small moments with Mother: making tea together, cooking dinner together, sweeping the floor together.

When the mean woman came to the room in the morning, all the girls quickly got dressed and gathered in the front room of the house. Tai Choi pulled on the woman's sleeve and asked, "Are you going to tell me who you are?"

The woman gripped Tai Choi's shoulder so hard that it burned. "I am a highbinder agent, and I own you now." She shoved Tai Choi to the ground. "If you dare talk back to me, you'll pay. Understand?"

Tai Choi was furious at how helpless she felt. Turning over on the floor, she screamed, "I want my Niang!"

The woman kicked the side of Tai Choi's head with such brute force that she curled into a ball, clutching her head between her knees. Tai Choi didn't know what a highbinder agent was, but the way this woman behaved, it must mean a *bad person*.

"You're a ghost!" Tai Choi shouted, even though it was more like a wounded cry.

The woman stomped on one of Tai Choi's healing feet. She cried out as sharp pain shot up her shins.

"You think kicking you is bad?" the woman asked. "Want me to cut off your tongue?"

Tai Choi trembled, not in fear, but in rage. She stayed curled up in the fetal position and wept. This woman was the vilest person she'd ever met. Why would Yi choose her as the punisher? Now she really regretted having pushed George.

"Are you ready to shut your mouth and listen now?" the woman said in a grating voice.

Tai Choi didn't answer. Her throat felt tight and dry. Tears pooled up again, and she squeezed her eyes shut. She wanted everything to go away. *Niang, Niang, Niang . . .* she chanted quietly. She wanted Mother with her, not this strange woman.

"Listen to me, you vermin. You're no longer Tai Choi. When you get to Gold Mountain, you'll tell people your name is Tien Fu Wu and you're there to join your father. Do you hear me?"

No. No. No. Tai Choi silently protested. She kept her eyes closed and her mouth shut. She didn't want to go to Gold Mountain and pretend to be Tien Fu Wu. She wanted to go home and be herself.

"Look at me and tell me what your name is!" the woman barked.

Tai Choi wanted to lash out at the woman, but if she had learned one thing from her experience with George, it was that she was in a fight she couldn't win.

The woman slapped Tai Choi's head, then she grabbed a fistful of her hair. "What's your name?"

"It's not Tien Fu Wu," Tai Choi screamed through her hiccup-cries. "My Lao Ye taught me to always tell the truth."

"Oh, isn't that funny?" The woman threw her back to the ground and snort-laughed. "You're here precisely because he lied! Your Lao Ye *sold* you, probably so he could pay his gambling debts."

Tai Choi's stomach cramped. Even though she wanted the woman's words to be lies, somehow she knew they were true. Father indeed had gambling debts, and his creditors had taken away most of her family's possessions. She just hadn't known that wasn't enough and Father had thought of selling her too. Now Tai Choi could see it: Mother had known about Father's plan to sell her. She'd fought for her and failed. She finally understood what Mother's tears meant.

This mean woman was right. Father's promise to send Tai Choi on vacation to Grandmother's was a lie. Just look at where she was now! Far away from home in Shanghai and being sent to Gold Mountain alone without Grandmother, Father, or Mother.

Oh no!

A sudden, painful realization hit her: no one was going to find Tai Choi in this stinking house. No one knew she was being sent to Gold Mountain. If she took on a new name, her family definitely wouldn't be able to find her. But she also understood that Father's plan to sell her had ended her days of being Tai Choi from Zhejiang. She would never see her family again. From now on, she was on her own and had to fight for herself with a new identity.

Ever since the day she left her house with Father to go on

the nonexistent vacation, the adults around her either lied to her or asked her to lie. She knew lying was wrong, but she had to be obedient to survive in this world of ruthless adults.

"Say it," the woman demanded. "What's your name?"

With the taste of blood in her mouth, Tai Choi mumbled, "My name is . . . Tien Fu Wu."

"Good." The woman let out a victorious chuckle. "Get up. We are heading to the steamship and can't be late." As she led the group of girls out of the room, she muttered, "I can't believe I've had to put up with a feisty mui-tsai like you. I should've only paid fifteen silver yuan!"

Tai Choi didn't know what a mui-tsai was, but any words this woman used to describe her couldn't possibly be nice. She slowly got up. Her legs trembled and her feet ached. She felt something under her tongue, so she spat into her cupped hands.

To her astonishment, in her palms was her very first loose tooth.

Chapter Five

PAPER DAUGHTER

SAN FRANCISCO BAY, 1892

Tien Fu Wu.

Tien Fu Wu.

Tien Fu Wu.

Tai Choi let her new name roll around in her head. Tien Fu meant *Heavenly Blessing*, like a godsend. Ironically, this new given name that the highbinder had brutally forced Tai Choi to take almost felt like a gracious gift, a congenial compliment. Would Father and Mother understand that she had no choice but to stop using the name they had given her? Would they approve of the name Tien Fu? Had they ever thought of her as a heavenly blessing? How should she live up to her new name, to be a godsend?

From Tai Choi to Tien Fu, she was becoming a new person. How should she get used to her new self while living a new life in a new country? From now on, whenever people called her Tien Fu, they weren't calling that bound-feet girl from Zhejiang—no. In Gold Mountain, no one would make the connection of her new name with her past or her village or her family. Probably no one cared that she had parents once. There were things she disliked while being Tai Choi. Now that she wasn't Tai Choi anymore, surely she had the freedom to let the qualities she liked represent her new self—strong, brave, and independent.

Tien Fu. Heavenly Blessing. Godsend.

She wanted to feel like she was *that* person; she wanted to feel natural when introducing herself with that name as if it had been given to her at birth. Right now, it was either that or endure another beating from the highbinder, Xiu Gan Lai, who wanted to completely erase Tai Choi from existence. Whenever she accidentally responded to her old name, the highbinder beat her until her arm got tired.

That mean dog only allowed Tien Fu up on the main deck once a day. Tien Fu didn't like the seawater spraying in her face and the cold wind, but she would rather be cold and wet than crammed into the dark cabinet on the bottom deck with stinky girls.

She paced in a circle on the main deck and repeated in her mind, word for word, everything the highbinder had told her to memorize.

"I'm going to join my father in Gold Mountain."

"He's been working in Chinatown for years."

"I'm the only child."

"My mother died last year."

Even though the ship sailing toward Gold Mountain was taking her farther away from home, Tien Fu refused to accept that the physical distance between Mother and her would change her love for her. Lying about her death? Now that was unacceptable. Mother must be heartbroken, missing her every day. Tien Fu couldn't bear the thought of Mother hurting because of her. She wanted to stop the pain both of them were experiencing. Right there and then, Tien Fu formed a secret new plan: return home to her Niang.

One afternoon the mean dog came in the cabinet and barked, "Everyone get ready, we're almost there."

Other girls in the group leapt into action, fixing their hair, changing their clothing, and whispering among themselves about

Gold Mountain. Tien Fu hoped that one of them would help her get on another ship back to Zhejiang, but she also knew that was hoping too much. None of the girls had been friendly to her—not like Kum Quai, who'd given her the pretty hairpin. Plus, like herself, these girls probably couldn't read road signs or a map to go anywhere.

On the day she left her house, Tien Fu's mother had dressed her in a silk tunic with a secret pocket in the butterfly sleeves. Now, the mean dog said the silk tunic was too good for a mui-tsai—whatever that was—and handed Tien Fu a wadded-up cotton blouse. She couldn't tell in the dim light if it was blue or black. She took the blouse and made the mistake of looking at Xiu Gan's face. Her eyes were so mean, a shudder rippled through Tien Fu.

The silk tunic was the most precious thing from Mother. It ate a hole in her heart to hand it over to the mean dog. Her new identity as Tien Fu would start as a six-year-old girl in a plain cotton blouse. All she had to hold on to with the invisible thread between Mother and her were in the pocket of the cotton blouse: the washcloth and toothbrush. She hid the hairpin from Kum Quai in a hole she'd made in the hem of her wide-legged pants.

The hatch to the upper deck swung open. Some passengers climbed the ladder to the upper deck. Xiu Gan turned to Tien Fu and she quickly straightened. She had been careful not to do anything wrong. But whenever Xiu Gan glared at her, Tien Fu couldn't help but think she'd somehow made a mistake. Her heart beat hard, in fear of undeserved, cruel punishment.

"Look down at the floor!" Xiu Gan demanded.

Tien Fu obeyed.

"Do you remember your new name and your new father's name?"

"Yes," Tien Fu said. She hated this woman. She hated that she smelled of onions. She hated that she carried a switch in her pocket to slap at whoever didn't obey her instantly. But Tien Fu had also learned that, most of the time, the one-word answer *yes* wouldn't get her into trouble.

"You stay with me until we get off the ship," Xiu Gan said in a voice so low, Tien Fu almost couldn't hear her. "When the immigration agent questions you, only answer what I've taught you. I'm your aunt. I'm taking you to your father in Chinatown. Understand?"

"Yes." Tien Fu said what Xiu Gan wanted to hear.

"Now put these shoes on," Xiu Gan said. "They're expensive, so don't step in any puddles."

Puddles? Tien Fu didn't care if there was a giant storm. She would be happy to be on land again. She took the soft leather shoes from Xiu Gan. They looked far too big, but she had only worn sandals since Yi unbound her feet. These shoes almost felt like a generous gift from the mean woman.

Tien Fu imagined that when she returned to China, Mother would be unhappy to find out about her feet. She might demand that they be bound again. What a nightmare that would be! But Tien Fu would be so glad to see her, she wouldn't complain or rebel.

Under Xiu Gan's watchful eye, she pulled on the leather shoes. They fit better than she thought they would, even though they were still too big. She wouldn't have known otherwise that her feet had grown since Yi had unbound them.

When Tien Fu straightened, Xiu Gan grasped the back of her blouse and tugged her close. Her onion breath was overpowering. "Remember what I said about the policemen and white missionary women?"

Tien Fu lowered her gaze. "Yes."

"Tell me so I know you remember," she growled, her hot breath on Tien Fu's cheek.

"Don't let the policemen see me," Tien Fu said. "They'll lock me up in jail."

"And?" Xiu Gan urged.

"Don't speak to any missionary women," Tien Fu said. "They'll catch me and poison me."

This was so ironic, having a bad person warn her about other bad people. Did Xiu Gan really have Tien Fu's safety in mind? She doubted it.

"Very good." Xiu Gan sounded pleased at Tien Fu's reply. With a hand still clamped on the back of Tien Fu's blouse, she steered her toward the ladder.

How was she going to escape from Xiu Gan? How was she going to get on a ship that headed back to China? She must act fast and think smart if she wanted to go home. Her heart rate zipped faster and faster as she followed the older girls to wait their turn at the ladder.

Xiu Gan shoved Tien Fu forward. She climbed slowly, trying not to lose her big leather shoes, trying to come up with a practical escape plan. Raindrops hit the top of her head before she could see anything. Tien Fu smiled to herself. Rain was a blessing. This was a good omen. She would find a new ship to take her home.

Everyone crowded at the rails. Beyond them stretched the shoreline of a city—not like Shanghai—no. Rising above the harbor were only gray buildings and gray hills beneath the drizzling rain. "Where's Gold Mountain?" Tien Fu asked.

Xiu Gan smacked the back of her head. "Did you forget my number one rule already? Don't ask questions."

Tien Fu pressed her lips tightly together. She had a lot more questions; one of them was why no one punished Xiu Gan for being so violent.

As their ship drew closer with other ships in the harbor, wagons, horses, and people scurried about, readying themselves to welcome the arriving passengers. Some of the older girls whispered to one another. Some smiled as if they were happy to be arriving in this new country called *Beautiful Nation*—America.

When the ship finally docked, they walked off the ship. Tien Fu looked around for the dangerous people Xiu Gan had warned her about and only spotted one policeman. Tien Fu didn't think he looked nasty though. Not like Xiu Gan.

When a man wearing a blue uniform spoke to the girls in an unfamiliar language, a woman interpreted his words into the Han language and gestured for them to enter a building. Tien Fu was happy to be away from Xiu Gan. Although it would've been perfect if she had not been stuck with the girls who ignored her. Perhaps out of nervousness, one of them burst out crying.

"What's wrong?" Tien Fu asked the crying girl.

"I can't remember—"

Another girl gave Tien Fu a hard, warning look. "Hush! Don't you remember we aren't supposed to speak to anyone else?"

Tien Fu looked down at the floor. She didn't want to get in trouble for breaking Xiu Gan's rules. She didn't want to continue to live in fear of that woman either. She sat on a bench, shivering, waiting, and hoping for a chance to break free.

One by one, the girls were taken into an office and questioned. Some came out crying, others frowning. When it was Tien Fu's turn in the office, she noticed a steaming cup of tea on the desk of the immigration officer. She took a deep breath to calm the jittery feeling in her stomach. The sweet scent of tea reminded her of Mother. Instead of the interpreter, she imagined it was her Niang who sat next to her, helping her cross the border into the new world.

This was the defining moment when she publicly declared she was Tien Fu Wu. As soon as she told the immigration officer and the interpreter that was her name, there was no going back to be Tai Choi from Zhejiang. And once she claimed that new name, there was no other option but to continue to answer the officer's questions with the lies Xiu Gan had told her to memorize. When the officer let Tien Fu go, she could hardly believe it!

Entering America was easier than she'd thought. She hoped it would be as easy to get on a ship back to China.

As she walked out of the office, another interpreter showed her down a hallway. "This way, hurry," she said. "Your aunt is waiting."

Tien Fu wanted to hurry the other way. She didn't want to see her fake aunt ever again. But there were immigration officers and policemen in this building—what would they do if she tried to run away?

The second she entered the next room, Xiu Gan stood from where she sat with the older girls. The men and women in the room looked up at her, some with worried looks on their faces. Maybe they too were waiting for the children they'd brought with them on the ship.

Xiu Gan latched onto her arm and that destroyed Tien Fu's chance to escape. Together their group walked out of the immigration station toward a street of tall buildings. There were all kinds of shops with English signs out front. They passed a bakery, and Tien Fu's stomach grumbled so loudly that Xiu Gan heard it.

"You'll eat later," she said. "After I get my money."

Tien Fu clenched her teeth. Of course Xiu Gan was getting her money. Why else would she bring her to Gold Mountain if not for money? But starving Tien Fu to death and expecting to still make money off her? This woman clearly wasn't thinking straight.

The looks of the buildings changed as they walked farther down the street. Instead of stone and brick, they switched to wood and plaster. The signs changed from English to Chinese. The group passed by an alley that smelled like a fish market. An old man called out to them, saying he was selling hot porridge. This was pure torture. Tien Fu was so hungry that she'd eat anything, but Xiu Gan didn't let go of her arm. She was walking almost too fast for Tien Fu to keep up.

Her short legs weren't a match for everyone's longer legs. She began limping, partly because her feet hurt from all the speed walking, but also because she was trying to not lose her big shoes. She didn't dare complain though. She was so weak and tired, she didn't want to get a brutal beating right now.

They turned a corner. Xiu Gan came to an abrupt stop in front of a two-story building and tilted her head. The top floor had several windows with laundry strung between them. On the first floor, there was a single door and two barred windows painted black.

Xiu Gan knocked on the door three times. No one answered.

From somewhere above, maybe through an open window, a scent sweeter than the sharp smell of tobacco wafted down. Tien Fu knew it was opium—something Niang had yelled at Lao Ye for, especially when he didn't come home at night.

Tien Fu couldn't think about her parents right now or she would start crying. She'd promised Mother that she would return home. She would find a way. She would be patient for the right time to come.

Xiu Gan knocked three more times before a woman finally opened the door. She wasn't much taller than Tien Fu, but her eyes were sharp like a beetle's.

"What do you want?" Her gaze cut to the older girls. "I don't need more mui-tsai. We're full here."

"I've brought a younger girl," Xiu Gan said. "Tien Fu Wu. Six years old. She's strong. She can clean and cook."

The woman scanned Tien Fu from her two braids to her leather shoes. "Do you speak, girl?" she asked.

Tien Fu lowered her gaze and said, "Yes."

The woman's hand darted out and pinched Tien Fu's upper arm. Tien Fu flinched.

"How much?" the woman said, her fingers latching onto Tien Fu's chin.

"Three hundred American dollars," Xiu Gan said.

The woman lifted Tien Fu's chin, then let go. "Two hundred."

Tien Fu was furious that she was being sold again. Her stomach grumbled. Who would feed her? This beetle-eyed woman or Xiu Gan?

"Two seventy-five," Xiu Gan said.

The woman shook her head.

Xiu Gan tugged Tien Fu backward. She stumbled, almost falling.

"Her feet were bound," Xiu Gan said. "I had to pay extra."

The woman's eyes narrowed, then she waved a hand, motioning for them to come closer. "Two fifty. Final offer. She's limping and too young. I'll have to wait years before she earns me real money."

Nonsense! Tien Fu thought. She almost wanted to tell the beetle-eyed woman that, in the past few months since she left her family, several adults had been making money off her. What kind of *real* money did she want?

"You can sell her for double when she's older." Xiu Gan's grip tightened again on Tien Fu's arm. "She has pretty features."

The interaction between these two women reminded Tien Fu of two dogs fighting over a scrap of meat. And it sickened her to think of herself as meat.

The beetle-eyed woman took a step back. "I only have two fifty. Nothing more." She cast a final glance at Tien Fu, then headed back into the building.

"Wait," Xiu Gan said. "Two fifty. But I need it now. I can't come back."

The beetle-eyed woman gave her a forced smile. "Wait here."

She disappeared inside. In a few moments she returned with a sack. Xiu Gan took it, then shoved Tien Fu forward.

"Move!" The woman steered Tien Fu into the building.

Tien Fu looked behind her before the door closed. Xiu Gan was ushering the older girls up the alley. Right there and then,

Tien Fu made herself a promise: someday she would walk out of that door and never come back to this place again.

The woman shut the door, and Tien Fu blinked to adjust to the large, dim room. The painted windows kept out all the natural light. A couple of gas lamps were lit, giving off an amber glow. But it wasn't enough to light the entire place.

Several round tables were scattered about the room. Three young ladies in colorful silk gowns sat at one of them, sipping tea. Their eyelids were caked with heavy makeup, and they stared at Tien Fu in curiosity. She was wondering about them too. Drinking tea in silk gowns; wasn't that a little overdressed?

"This is Tien Fu Wu," the beetle-eyed woman told them.

"Isn't she too young to be here?" one of the girls asked. "The law—"

"I know the law well," the woman snapped. "No children allowed in brothels or gambling dens. That's why you need to hide her behind the trunk upstairs when the men come. You hear?"

All the girls nodded.

"For now, she'll clean and cook for us," the woman said.

Tien Fu didn't know what *brothel* meant, but she knew what gambling was. It was what people did to lose their money. Tien Fu was furious to be reminded of the truth once again. Gambling had made her father lose more than money, it had made him do the unthinkable. He had traded her for money the way he had with their furniture. She didn't choose this. How could all this be her life?

The woman's beetle eyes landed on her. "Call me Mrs. Lee. If you complain or are slow in your work, you'll join the rats in the street. Understand?"

Tien Fu had been trained enough to know she should only say one word: "Yes."

Chapter Six
SILK DRESSES

SAN FRANCISCO, 1893

For many months now, as her daily routine, Tien Fu had been cleaning up after the gamblers. She'd adapted to a schedule that made her stay up most of the night, then sleep during the day until the sun was halfway across the sky. She'd learned to be quick and quiet, stay out of people's way, watch, but not talk or ask questions. She'd also learned to hide behind one of the tables when she heard the first creak of footsteps on the stairs.

Her favorite chore was making tea for Mrs. Lee and the girls. She tried a different blend each time. Mrs. Lee loved it so much, she even praised her sometimes. But it didn't mean anything to Tien Fu. She only did it to honor the memory of being with Mother.

Tien Fu's jobs were different than the older girls'. Each evening, the girls painted their faces with eye makeup, rouge, and lipstick, then they put flowers in their hair and changed into a silk dress. Tien Fu wondered why they sat by the second-story windows until the sun set, waving and smiling at passing men on the street.

Once, a girl was too sick to get dressed and wave at the men. Mrs. Lee yelled at her, "You'll pay with your own money for this!"

Paying for being sick? It was unheard of. Tien Fu didn't have her own money to pay for anything, so she decided that if she ever got sick, she would never let Mrs. Lee know.

Past midnight, the building was mostly quiet. Tien Fu scurried around the gambling room that glowed in the gas lighting. After gambling, some of the men went into one of the older girls' bedrooms on the second floor. Sometimes Tien Fu heard voices murmur from upstairs, or a laugh, or the creak of the floorboard. It only made her work faster. She swept up the litter, cleaned off the tables, emptied the buckets of tobacco juice, scrubbed food stains, straightened chairs, then finally put away the gambling cards into their boxes. About an hour later, the men came down the stairs, fetched their hats and coats, which Tien Fu lined up neatly near the door, and left. Every night, after all the gambling guests were gone, Mrs. Lee locked the door and the windows, then she released Tien Fu from her work.

Tien Fu looked forward to this moment of freedom when she could head upstairs to her bedroom, even though it wasn't much larger than a closet. She didn't mind the tight space. The room was hers alone—so what if her mattress was lumpy or the window grimy?

One night, a creak of the floorboards sounded, and Tien Fu reflexively crouched behind a corner table in the gambling room. She peeled the tablecloth back to peek at a man who crossed the room, weaving among the tables. Tien Fu's gaze followed his shiny leather shoes. He picked up his hat and coat, then a cane—Ah, so he was the one with the cane! He opened the door and stepped out into the night.

Tien Fu stayed quiet beneath the table. A few minutes passed and another man came down the stairs, the last one of the night. After he left, Mrs. Lee's footsteps came, tapping in her heels. She released a heavy sigh as she locked up the place, then she set her hands on her hips.

"Tien Fu," she said. "Come out."

Tien Fu scrambled out from under the table. Mrs. Lee hadn't been as mean to her as Xiu Gan, but everything Mrs. Lee said was stern. Tien Fu clutched her hands behind her back so Mrs. Lee wouldn't see them shaking.

"Tomorrow you'll go live someplace else," Mrs. Lee said, her beetle eyes on Tien Fu. "I need the money, and you're a hard worker, so I'll fetch a good price."

Tien Fu clenched her jaw. This was both bad and good. Bad because she was used to this place. She even felt comfortable here. She knew the routine. She knew how to stay out of sight. Good because she would be able to keep her promise to herself, to walk out of Mrs. Lee's door and never return. Maybe this was one step closer to finally escaping her life of being sold and owned by people who didn't care about her. She was older now and smarter. She could find her way back to China. Mother would be so happy to see her. *Yes, yes, yes!* She could hardly hide her excitement for all the possibilities ahead of her. But just to let Mrs. Lee hear what she wanted to hear, she said a firm and pleasant, "Yes."

The next morning Tien Fu was awakened much earlier than usual. She didn't even have time to watch the first trolley cars of the day start their shift. She loved watching them whenever she had a moment to look out the windows. They resembled little houses going up and down the hills.

Mrs. Lee bundled Tien Fu's few pieces of clothing into a pillowcase, then led her down the stairs. She presented Tien Fu to a stout Chinese woman who looked younger than Mrs. Lee. Her face was wide and her cheeks were red as if she'd been standing in a cold windstorm.

"Is this the girl?" the stout woman asked. "How old is she?"

"Seven," Mrs. Lee said. "She's been no trouble. I need the money since Mrs. Ding's brothel has been stealing our business."

The stout woman stepped close to Tien Fu. Her breathing

was heavy. Tien Fu wondered if this woman's life had been so easy that taking three small steps was too laborious for her.

"Two hundred."

"Mrs. Wang, be reasonable. I paid more than that for her," Mrs. Lee said. "I've trained her well. Four hundred."

Tien Fu was sick of this bargaining process. None of these adults cared that she was a human being, not a thing. She had feelings just like them, and it hurt whenever they criticized her looks, judged her abilities, and tried to set a price on her value and worth.

The women bickered over a price until they agreed upon three hundred and fifty dollars. Just like that, Tien Fu was walking slowly alongside Mrs. Wang to her next workplace. She wondered if this woman also ran a gambling den where she would continue to work all night and sleep all morning.

Tien Fu had only been allowed to leave the gambling den when Mrs. Lee took her to the market. But that had always been in the afternoon. This morning the streets were blanketed with fog, with gray patches clutching to the corners of buildings. Tien Fu shivered in her thin cotton clothing. Her feet were healed now, no longer bent or curved, so she could keep up with Mrs. Wang, whose breathing continued to be heavy.

They headed in the opposite direction of the market toward the ocean. Tien Fu breathed in the salty air as her mind spun with new ideas. If Mrs. Wang's house was closer to the ships, she could run away easier. While working for Mrs. Lee, Tien Fu had gotten used to hiding for hours at a time. She was good at staying small and silent. She would hide and find a way to sneak onto a ship that would take her back to China.

They turned a corner, then another, and walked along a row of shops, everything from a fabric store to a grill house to a bakery. Then Mrs. Wang turned into an alley and tugged her toward a building. They entered through a creaking door. Inside was a kitchen with two ovens, a high stove, and large pots. Steam rose from the pots, and the smells of soup and hot tea reminded Tien Fu that she hadn't had breakfast yet.

A thin man with even thinner hair wearing an apron turned. He shoved his fogged round glasses up his forehead.

"Is this the girl?" His gaze was lighter and softer than Mrs. Wang's, but there was no smile on his face. "She's small. How will she carry the boy?"

"Mrs. Lee said she is strong and works hard." Mrs. Wang's nails dug into Tien Fu's arm where she still gripped her. "You'll work hard or you'll be sent outside to beg for your food."

Tien Fu lowered her gaze. "Yes, Mrs. Wang."

"Today I'll show you how to do everything." Mrs. Wang led Tien Fu past the scowling man and up a flight of narrow stairs. "Tomorrow you'll be on your own."

Tien Fu drew in a deep breath as she scurried up the stairs. The rooms on each landing were so filthy, it looked like this family never cleaned their house. Possibly whenever their living quarters started to resemble a landfill, they moved up to a higher level.

"You'll sleep in the top room on the fourth floor." Mrs. Wang pointed upward at the attic as they paused on the third floor.

"In here is Willy's room."

"Willy?" Tien Fu said. The name sounded strange on her tongue.

Mrs. Wang gave her a sharp look. "Our son has an American name because he'll be an important man in America someday." Her eyes narrowed. "You think it's funny?"

"No, Mrs. Wang." Tien Fu didn't know why Mrs. Wang was offended. She was merely repeating her son's name.

Mrs. Wang stared at Tien Fu for a long moment as if trying to decide if she was lying. She eventually opened Willy's bedroom door.

A wooden crib sat against one of the yellow walls. Staring through the slats was the fattest face Tien Fu had ever seen.

"This is Willy," Mrs. Wang said with pride in her voice.

The boy looked funny with his ball-shaped body, chubby rose-colored cheeks, and his short spiky hair standing straight up. Tien Fu covered her mouth to stifle the giggle, but the giggle escaped anyway. Mrs. Wang curled her fingers into Tien Fu's braid and yanked it so hard that her head snapped back. She was so shocked that she cried out.

"You don't laugh at my son," Mrs. Wang hissed.

Her face was so close to Tien Fu's that she could spot fine hairs above the woman's upper lip and on her chin. Mrs. Wang had facial hair! What if she braided them? That image made Tien Fu want to laugh again, but the pain of having her hair pulled forced her to end her imaginings.

"Yes, Mrs. Wang."

Mrs. Wang let go so quickly that Tien Fu nearly stumbled.

"Now you'll get Willy out of the crib and change his pee cloth." Mrs. Wang folded her arms. "Then we will take him downstairs."

Tien Fu nodded, but she didn't know how she could get the large infant out of the crib. He probably weighed more than she did! Mrs. Lee had told Mrs. Wang that she was strong—this must be why.

Mrs. Wang nudged Tien Fu, and she walked to the crib.

"Hello, Willy." Tien Fu smiled. "Can I change your pee cloth?"

Willy kicked his chunky legs in excitement and grinned at Tien Fu. He had two bottom teeth that looked like tiny white pebbles stuck in his gums. Being this close to the boy, Tien Fu could smell his stinky pee cloth. Her stomach kept turning and turning.

"Come!" Tien Fu lifted her hands. "I'll get you out. Then we can change you and go downstairs."

"Da Ba!" Willy shrieked.

Tien Fu had no idea what he'd said, but Mrs. Wang was still watching, so she stood on her tiptoes and lugged the boy out of the crib. She almost lost her balance and Willy laughed. Tien Fu tried to smile, but she could barely breathe. The air smelled fetid now. She wanted to run out of the room, but Mrs. Wang would probably punish her for that, so instead she knelt on the floor next to a bookshelf that held pee cloths and folded clothing. It would be great if Willy would just lie still, but he kept trying to roll over.

"No, no, stay," Tien Fu said. "I need to change you."

When Willy began to cry, Tien Fu's whole body heated. How was she supposed to get a strange infant to cooperate?

"Step aside! I'll show you how to do it," Mrs. Wang said. "I didn't pay good money for you to make my son cry."

Tien Fu nodded and scooted back. Mrs. Wang cooed to her son. After she changed him, she handed the dirty pee cloth to Tien Fu. "Wash it out in the bucket in the courtyard, then add it to the laundry. That's your job too."

Tien Fu pinched one edge of the pee cloth, trying not to make a face.

"Willy doesn't like to be alone, so you need to carry him as much as possible." Mrs. Wang picked up a long length of cloth. "Turn around. I'll strap him to your back."

Willy was so heavy, Tien Fu thought she might fall over. She grasped the crib slats to steady herself and held her breath as Mrs. Wang worked so she wouldn't breathe in the stinky pee cloth. When the baby was secured on Tien Fu's back, Mrs. Wang said, "Come downstairs. You'll start laundry today. After that, you'll clean the entire house."

Clean the entire house? That would take forever! In her

mind she imagined herself carrying on her back not only Willy but also the entire house. Tien Fu was so distraught just thinking about doing all the daunting work on her own, she felt like fainting. She was glad there was a rail to hold on to as she walked down the stairs. They passed the kitchen on the bottom level, and beyond it was a line of customers waiting to buy soup and tea from Mr. Wang.

Outside, the sun's rays came between the surrounding buildings and made a patch of warmth in the courtyard. The fog was gone now, but Tien Fu still shivered.

"Wash out the pee cloth in here." Mrs. Wang pointed to a green bucket. "Dump the water over the fence. Next, fill up two buckets at the water pump. One for washing, one for rinsing. Then hang the clothes on this line."

Tien Fu looked up to the clothesline. She didn't know if she could reach that high. She would have to stand on something—a bucket maybe.

"Here's the dirty laundry." Mrs. Wang nudged a basket piled with clothing, kitchen rags, and pee cloths.

When Mrs. Wang left, Tien Fu went to work. She wasn't sure exactly how to do everything, but she needed to show Mrs. Wang she was working so she didn't get thrown out to the street to become a beggar.

Earlier when Mrs. Wang was around, Tien Fu didn't dare say anything when Willy pulled at her hair. Now Willy was babbling nonsense and pulling her hair as she bent over a bucket, washing a stained apron.

"No, Willy!" Tien Fu said. "That hurts."

The boy squealed, then pulled again, harder this time.

With one wet hand, Tien Fu pried his fingers off her braid. "Don't pull my hair!"

Willy grabbed her braid again.

"No." Tien Fu reached back to move his hand again, this time with more force.

Willy burst out crying.

Tien Fu straightened her back to bounce the boy. "It's all right. We'll be done and then your Niang will give you lunch." She didn't know if that was true. She hoped it was. In fact, she hoped it was true for her too, that she would have lunch soon. She was so hungry, she could almost eat a pee cloth right now.

Willy quieted down, and Tien Fu picked out more laundry. She plunged it into the washing bucket and swirled it around. The water was cold and her hands became red and cramped.

Willy grabbed her hair again. Instantly, Tien Fu tugged his hand away. Willy screeched, arching his body, which jerked Tien Fu back. She lost her balance and they plopped to the ground. She scrambled to her feet using the bucket to brace against. But the bucket tipped over, and all the water spilled out. Willy cried even harder.

"It's your fault," Tien Fu said. "Stop pulling my hair!" She reached behind her and pinched his seat—not hard, at least she didn't think it was.

"What's going on?" Mrs. Wang charged into the courtyard. Her cheeks were deep red. Her mean eyes were even meaner now. "Did you just pinch Willy?"

Tien Fu could barely hear Mrs. Wang over the crying child. She wanted to lie, but she was sure Mrs. Wang had seen her.

"I'm sorry—"

Mrs. Wang slapped her across the face.

"How dare you hurt my boy, you filthy rat!" She yanked Willy off Tien Fu's back and stormed into the building.

Tien Fu placed her cold hand against her burning cheek. Her tears couldn't be stopped now. Her chest heaved and her sobs erupted. Maybe she could run back to Mrs. Lee. She would work harder. She would go and tell men on the street to visit Mrs. Lee's gambling den.

Tien Fu knew none of those things would happen. It was useless to imagine, so she stopped. Her place was here with the Wang family now, and if she didn't want to beg for her food, she needed to put her head down and keep her hands busy. She pumped more water and washed more clothing, trying to ignore her trembling hands that shook from hunger and fear.

Chapter Seven

COUNTING SCARS

SAN FRANCISCO, 1894

Bruises on Tien Fu's back and arms? Mrs. Wang pinched and then twisted her flesh.

Scars on Tien Fu's arms and face? Mrs. Wang heated red-hot tongs in the oven, then branded her.

Tien Fu had stopped counting how many times Mrs. Wang had hurt her. She had no control over when Mrs. Wang would torture her. It all depended on Willy's mood. On days when he was happy, Tien Fu was spared. But when he was grumpy, Tien Fu became Mrs. Wang's target.

The first time Mrs. Wang seared Tien Fu's face, she howled in excruciating pain and scared Willy so much that he wouldn't stop crying. Furious, Mrs. Wang dragged Tien Fu to the courtyard and locked her out there in the pouring rain while she and Mr. Wang had dinner in the kitchen. The rain helped soothe Tien Fu's physical wound a little, but it couldn't heal Tien Fu's emotional wound. She shrieked so loudly for so long that neighbors peeked over the fence, but they never said anything to her.

It took her hours and hours to clean the house every night after Willy had gone to bed. If he woke up in the middle of the night, Tien Fu had to take care of him so the Wangs could sleep.

The surname Wang meant *king* in Chinese. If Tien Fu's surname had been Wang, she wondered if she could have lived like a king like her owners, making others work for them while they slept and ate.

The kitchen was Mr. Wang's territory, he never let Tien Fu in. So she snuck into the forbidden space late at night to make tea when he was in bed. Tien Fu imagined this as having a secret meeting with Mother, making tea and chatting about the day.

Every day, China seemed farther and farther away. Tien Fu couldn't remember what her village looked like anymore. When she thought of a neighborhood, all she could imagine were San Francisco's tall buildings and store signs.

One afternoon, Tien Fu was on all fours, scrubbing spilled tea off the floor on the fourth level and listening for Willy to wake up from his nap. She liked the smell of tea, so she slowed her pace to inhale the scent. Out the window, the trolley moved up the hills beyond. Tien Fu imagined she lived in the trolley, always moving, never trapped in a house with vile owners. And there was endless tea in the trolley. Mmm . . .

Just then, a wail came up through the floor. Tien Fu leapt to her feet and scurried down the stairs.

"I'm here," Tien Fu said, pushing open Willy's bedroom door. He had a stinky pee cloth again; she almost backed out of the room. "Don't cry," she said instead. "I'll change you, then we can go play outside. The sun is out."

Willy bit his lip as if he knew what she was saying.

Tien Fu was much stronger now. She could easily lift Willy from the crib and change his pee cloth. Balancing him on her back, she strapped him on. She headed down the stairs, past the kitchen, then out into the courtyard. The laundry was piling up again. She would have to do it tomorrow. Right now she walked about the small space, talking to Willy.

"Should we look for a bird?"

Willy yelled, "Da!"

"Or a Da?"

Sometimes it was fun to play with Willy. But most of the time he just wanted his own mother, which got Tien Fu thinking: no matter how terrible a person chooses to behave, there's something good in that person.

"Newspaper," a voice said from the other side of the fence.

The newspaper man came by every evening. Tien Fu's interaction with him was as routine as his delivery route. He handed a folded newspaper to her. She took it and thanked him. Wordlessly, he gave her a kind smile, tapped his hat, and continued on his route. Tien Fu knew to take the newspaper upstairs right away. Since Mr. Wang read the newspaper every night, he didn't want it to sit in the kitchen and get wet or greasy.

With a sigh, Tien Fu headed up the stairs, the weight of Willy heavy on her back. When she reached the parlor on the second floor, she paused before a wall mirror. Her burn scars were red and ugly along her jaw. Since she wasn't allowed to go on the street, not even to shop at the market with Mrs. Wang, no one outside of the Wang family had seen her scars except the newspaper man. Did he care how she got them? Did anyone care about her? Did anyone miss her? What about her mother? Her brother? Her grandmother? Or had they all forgotten about her by now?

A lump pushed against Tien Fu's throat as she set the newspaper on a teakwood side table. She would get into trouble if she lingered in the parlor too long. As she walked down the stairs and reached the landing on the bottom level, Mrs. Wang's voice came from the shop. "There's not a twelve-year-old girl here."

Tien Fu peeked around the corner and was surprised to find a white woman with dark hair standing in front of Mrs. Wang.

"You have the wrong house," Mrs. Wang continued.

Suddenly the white woman moved her gaze and saw Tien Fu. "Who's that?"

Mrs. Wang whipped around, but Tien Fu had already hidden behind the wall.

"Tien Fu is my niece," Mrs. Wang said. "Her father is traveling, so she's staying with us until he comes back."

Tien Fu closed her eyes. She recognized the edge to Mrs. Wang's voice. She wasn't happy. That meant, inevitably, Tien Fu would be punished. Another scar. Another bruise. She strained to hear what the white woman said next, but the sounds of pots and pans clanking in the kitchen were too loud.

"I don't like that woman from the mission home," Mrs. Wang said next. The white woman must have left. "She thinks she can steal girls and use them as her own workers. Who told her about Tien Fu? What's that sow up to?"

No! Mrs. Wang thought Tien Fu had something to do with the white woman. How could outside trouble come to her when she never left the house? Tien Fu hurried out to the courtyard and started the laundry right away. She kept busy to avoid punishment. And speaking of punishment, like Xiu Gan, Mrs. Wang lied about being Tien Fu's aunt, but no one punished them for their deception. How was that fair?

Tien Fu spent most of that night awake thinking about the white woman looking for a twelve-year-old girl. On the ship coming to San Francisco, Xiu Gan had warned her about the missionary women. She was supposed to stay away from them so she wouldn't get poisoned. But the pale lady looked nice and her voice was soft. In fact, she reminded Tien Fu of Mrs. Roos. What did this missionary woman want? And who was the girl she was looking for? Obviously not Tien Fu. But why did Mrs. Wang lie, then get mad at the woman who had accidentally knocked on the wrong door?

The next day it rained so hard that Tien Fu couldn't take Willy out to play in the courtyard. He was grumpy and cried in protest when Tien Fu put him in his crib for a nap, so she put him on his bedroom floor and laid next to him. When he finally fell asleep, Tien Fu didn't dare leave the room. She didn't want Mrs. Wang to find Willy sleeping on the floor. Also, she was so tired now that she could really use a short nap. Thinking about making tea with Mother always comforted her, relaxed her, and helped her fall asleep. In her mind, she dried tea leaves, sorted them, crushed them, blended them . . . but her thoughts were interrupted by arguing sounds downstairs.

"There is no girl here except for my niece," Mrs. Wang said. "Her father is coming soon to pick her up."

A man's voice spoke in English.

Then a woman said in Chinese, "We have a search warrant to look through your house."

"Who's the search warrant from?" Mr. Wang asked.

Within seconds, footsteps thudded on the stairs, coming up. Willy was still asleep on the floor, and if Mrs. Wang saw him . . . Tien Fu scrambled to her feet and bent to lift Willy, hoping he wouldn't start crying. Luckily, she transferred him to the crib without waking him up.

The voices were getting closer. While working in Mrs. Lee's gambling den, Tien Fu had developed a habit of hiding whenever strangers approached. At this moment she instinctively thought of hiding, even though she wasn't the girl they were looking for. She wasn't twelve, and besides, no one in San Francisco knew her or her family. Who would come search for her? Nonetheless, she looked about the room for a place to hide. Under the crib? Behind the dresser?

The door opened and Tien Fu froze. She hadn't had time to get out of sight.

The first to enter the room was a tall man in a police uniform. His skin was pale, his eyes light blue. His rust-colored mustache looked like a caterpillar above his lip.

Two women crowded into the room behind him. One of

them was the same woman from the day before. Next to her stood a petite Chinese woman dressed in American clothing: a white blouse, long brown skirt, and a round brooch at her collar. Her silky hair was pinned up in a puffy cloud.

The man looked right at Tien Fu and said something, but she didn't understand him.

"That's my niece," Mrs. Wang said, her breath huffing as she stood in the doorway, her hands on her hips. She had sweat on her forehead and her wide cheeks were flushed red. Her gaze darted to the sleeping Willy, then over to Tien Fu. It was the first time Tien Fu had ever seen her owner look afraid.

The pale lady stepped forward and asked Tien Fu in Chinese that sounded funny, "What's your name?"

Tien Fu felt Mrs. Wang's eyes burning into her like one of her searing tongs. Tien Fu lowered her gaze and said in a quiet voice, "Tien Fu Wu."

"How old are you?" the white woman asked.

When Tien Fu didn't answer, the Chinese woman repeated the question in fluent Chinese. Tien Fu didn't know her own age. She was six years old when she boarded the ship to San Francisco. She didn't know how long she'd been here.

"Tien Fu is *seven*," Mrs. Wang said. "She isn't the twelve-year-old girl you are looking for. Now, leave my house. My boy is sleeping in here, and we're busy in the shop."

Tien Fu lifted her gaze. Willy had opened his eyes and rolled over in the crib. When he saw his Niang, he grinned and babbled. Mrs. Wang smiled at him, but it wasn't sincere. Behind the smile, her eyes were hard and mean.

The strangers continued to look at Tien Fu . . . no, they were *staring* at her. She was sure that when these people left, she would be punished, even though this entire ordeal had nothing to do with her.

"Take the boy and leave, Mrs. Wang," the Chinese woman said in a quiet voice. "We'll speak with Tien Fu in private."

Mrs. Wang's mouth opened like a fish. No one had ever spoken to her like that.

Tien Fu wanted to hide again because she was sure Mrs. Wang would scream at these strangers. Maybe she would burn them too! But the burly policeman pointed to the door, and Mrs. Wang rushed out with Willy without further argument.

The white woman knelt before Tien Fu and spoke softly in English. The Chinese woman joined her and said, "Hello, Tien Fu. My name is Yuen Qui. This is Florence Worley and Officer Jesse Cook." She paused and gave a small smile. It made her eyes crinkle at the corners. "Can I see your arm?"

What a strange request! Tien Fu stared at her and reluctantly held out her arm.

Yuen Qui touched one of the deep scars. "How did you get this?"

Tien Fu swallowed. Would Mrs. Wang be angry if she told these people? Tien Fu would've happily told them how mean her owners were, but what if these adults were just as cruel?

"I was punished." She wouldn't say anything else.

Yuen Qui walked behind Tien Fu. "Can I look at your back?"

Tien Fu didn't know what to think of this, but she had already shown Yuen Qui her arm, so what was the point of trying to hide her back? She nodded for Yuen Qui to lift the back of her shirt. The white woman joined her while the policeman stayed by the door.

When they lowered her shirt, Tien Fu was nervous and afraid. What would happen now that Mrs. Wang's abusive behavior was no longer a secret?

Finally, Yuen Qui faced Tien Fu. "We're from the mission home that takes care of little girls without families. We can teach you how to read and write Chinese. We can teach you how to speak English. And we can teach you how to sew and cook. You won't have to take care of another child all day or do the Wangs' house chores anymore. No one will hurt you there. You'll be safe."

Tien Fu knew that Mrs. Wang would be furious if she chose to go with these people. If she stayed, Mrs. Wang would definitely burn her again tonight. Why would she give her the chance to continue to abuse her today, tomorrow, and every day after that? How could she decline this opportunity to escape? But then what about Xiu Gan's warning? What if the missionary ladies poisoned her?

At that, Tien Fu shook her head. But Yuen Qui didn't seem surprised. She only nodded, then straightened. Now the two women spoke to the policeman in English, who hadn't taken his eyes off Tien Fu. Then Yuen Qui walked to Tien Fu again and held out her hand.

"You need to come with us, Tien Fu. This is not a good place for you. Mr. and Mrs. Wang have no right to hurt you."

Tien Fu hid her hands behind her back. But Yuen Qui grasped one of her arms and pulled her toward the door. Tien Fu didn't resist at first because she was surprised that this Chinese woman was strong. Before they got to the door though, Tien Fu pulled back, breaking off.

Yuen Qui spun. "We must go now." She held out her hand again, but Tien Fu backed away.

The white woman moved toward Tien Fu and spoke in her broken-up Chinese. "Please come with us, child."

Still, Tien Fu moved backward until she bumped into the dresser and there was nowhere else to go. She considered running past them, out of the room, and up the stairs to hide in her bedroom. But the policeman moved toward her and picked her up. His strong arms held her tightly, and Tien Fu didn't like it, not at all. She kicked and wriggled, trying to break free.

"Put me down!" she yelled over and over. "Let me go!" But

he headed down the stairs, carrying her like she weighed nothing. The group continued out the back door of the kitchen and into the alley.

It was raining hard. The sky was gray, the clouds almost close enough to touch. Tien Fu kept yelling, but the policeman and the two women only hurried down the alley, then onto another street. No one paid attention to Tien Fu's crying and kicking, not even when her shoes flew off and she screeched, "My shoes!"

The policeman kept walking with big strides, moving up a steep hill, up where the trolleys traveled. Finally, they reached a big building made of brown bricks.

It was warm inside. The policeman put Tien Fu down and left. She was faced with the two women who'd brought her, as well as a gray-haired woman wearing spectacles.

"Who's this?" the gray-haired woman asked in Chinese.

"This is Tien Fu Wu," Yuen Qui said. "She's about eight years old."

"Ah." The new woman crouched before Tien Fu and switched to English. Yuen Qui interpreted her words. "My name is Miss Culbertson. I'm the director at this mission home. When is your birthday?"

Yuen Qui interpreted the woman's words.

Tien Fu bit her lip. She knew she had a birthday, but Mother had been the one who remembered it for her. She was embarrassed that she didn't know this important thing about herself.

"I don't—" she said, but she suddenly had an idea. "Um, what's today?"

"January 17," Yuen Qui answered.

"Then today will be my new birthday. January 17," Tien Fu said with the glowing pride only an eight-year-old girl who chose her own birthday could feel.

The three women looked at her like they were pleased.

"I like that idea," Miss Culbertson said.

Yuen Qui nodded. "Yes, now, let's give you a bath and some clean clothes. Are you hungry?"

Tien Fu was always hungry, but she wasn't going to tell these people she was never fed enough food. These women seemed like they might be helpful, but they were still strangers. Even though they didn't buy her or own her, did that really mean Tien Fu could trust them completely? Now that she'd escaped abusive Mrs. Wang, she needed to stick to her original plan to get on a ship and sail back to China. Spending time here at the mission home was only delaying her plan.

Just then, some voices came from upstairs. Tien Fu looked up the staircase at the Chinese girls who were staring at her from the landing. Some of them were teenagers, others were about Tien Fu's age or younger. One of them came down the stairs, smiled at Tien Fu, and said, "Hi, my name is Lonnie."

"That's not a Chinese name," Tien Fu said.

The girl's head bobbed. "My real name is Yoke Lon, but I changed it to Lonnie."

Tien Fu was impressed. Apparently this was a place where girls were allowed to choose their own birthday and name.

"Come, I'll show you our games in the parlor."

Tien Fu hadn't forgotten her plan to get on a ship and sail home. These people in the mission home were distracting her.

"Want to play Tiu-u?" Lonnie asked.

What, Tiu-u? Tien Fu didn't want to be interested, but she was. She'd played that game with her brother before, and she loved it. When she went back to China, she definitely wanted to play with him again. But why wait till then when she could play now?

"All right." Tien Fu rubbed her hands together and said to Lonnie, "Are you ready to lose?"

"Let's give you a hot bath and some dry clothing first. Then you can have supper," Yuen Qui said in a gentle voice. "The game can wait."

Tien Fu made a face at her. Yuen Quai was helping Lonnie to save face, Tien Fu knew it. But delaying the game wouldn't change anything. Tien Fu would still win, like she always did.

"Oh yes, you should take a hot bath. You'll love it," Lonnie said. "Then you can wash your hair and make it shiny."

Hmm. Maybe Lonnie sensed that she would lose the game, so she took advantage of the occasion to get out of the potential embarrassment. Tien Fu didn't mind, though. She hadn't had a bath since she left Yi's house in Shanghai, and she did want to have clean, shiny hair. Also, dry clothing sounded comfortable. And supper? How could Tien Fu possibly say no to that offer?

Gladly, Tien Fu agreed. "I'll come."

Chapter Eight
CITY OF FOG

SAN FRANCISCO, APRIL 1895

Fingers of fog slipped away from Dolly's long skirt as she stepped closer to the buggy she'd hired. That morning she'd arrived on the train in San Francisco. She'd heard about the fog here but didn't realize how heavy and thick it could be. The misty grayness made buildings across the street look sad somehow.

The driver loading her luggage grunted under the weight of her trunk. "Are you staying a while, miss?" He swiped off his cap and rubbed at the perspiration on his forehead. "Moving to San Francisco?"

"For a year." Dolly Cameron's heart did a little leap. She was twenty-five, but this was her first real adventure outside her family's ranch in the San Gabriel Valley. "I'm teaching sewing classes at the Occidental Mission Home on 920 Sacramento Street."

She expected the driver to be impressed. Her family had been impressed when she told them she'd been invited to the big city to teach Chinese girls how to sew.

Instead the driver's thick eyebrows dipped low. "Are you sure about the address? That mission home isn't a safe place."

Dolly blinked, gripping her carpetbag tighter. "What do you mean?"

The driver muttered something as he tied the trunk with a rope. Then he crossed to the door of the buggy and opened it. "It's none of my concern, miss." His pale blue eyes studied her. "Wouldn't be surprised if you changed your mind, that's all."

Dolly tried to decide if she should question this stranger or not. What did he know about a mission home for Chinese girls who wanted to be educated? She moved past him and climbed into the buggy, then sat on the thin seat cushion. The driver shut the door firmly, and soon they were on their way.

She wouldn't change her mind. Mrs. Browne, the president of the board that oversaw the mission home, had invited Dolly to teach for one year and work with Margaret Culbertson. Miss Culbertson helped Chinese girls who had escaped terrible places and dreadful living conditions in Chinatown. The girls had been brought to San Francisco by highbinders, promised a good job or marriage to a rich man. But when the girls arrived, they were instead sold as slaves. Some of the girls were sold to brothels. A shiver skittered along Dolly's arms. She could not imagine living in such a way, but it had only given her courage to leave her comfortable home and find a way to help the girls at the mission home.

The Chinese girls needed to learn how to read and write English and then learn new ways to support themselves, earning money by sewing or cooking. And Dolly would help them.

As the buggy lurched forward, rattling along the cobblestones behind the horse, Dolly peered out the window. The buggy passed by burly dockworkers, arms the size of their necks. The men worked to load crates, barrels, and trunks into wagons and carts, while the large draft horses pawed impatiently at the ground. The dull brown streets and murky gray sky only made her feel homesick. She already missed the green hills and budding trees of home.

Once they left the warehouse district behind, the streets

changed to tall buildings rising from the sidewalks. Multistoried hotels with domes and spires looked like opulent castles. Electric lights glowed along the storefronts of Grant Street, making the place feel like riding through a fairy-tale book. Along the sidewalk, a man and a woman walked together, wearing elegant clothing and stylish hats.

When the buggy reached Dupont Street, the hotels and fancy stores were replaced by tall pagodas and cramped shops. Shop signs scaled the buildings, covered in red and yellow Chinese characters. A woman dressed all in black, her hair pulled into a severe bun, swept furiously at the boardwalk in front of her shop. She looked up at the passing buggy and her mouth formed a grim line, her face mapped with deep lines as if she'd lived two lifetimes.

Two Chinese men stood on the corner, sharing a long pipe, the trail of smoke dissipating into the fog. They both wore loose black clothing and long single pigtails down their backs. The woodsy scent of their pipes reached Dolly, mingling with other sweeter scents of baking.

Turning off Dupont, the buggy started up a steep hill, now passing square brick homes. Below, the city of San Francisco began to brighten with the rising sun. The shadowed buildings warmed to yellows and golds, and smoke puffed from many chimneys. Beyond, the bay's murky gray water sharpened to a deep blue.

Dolly decided that San Francisco was beautiful after all. Excitement swelled deep in her belly, and when the buggy stopped, she was eager to get out.

The driver opened her door, and Dolly craned her neck to look up. The mission home building rose five stories, was made of brown brick, and looked very safe. Except—why were there bars on the lower windows?

The driver muttered again as he unloaded Dolly's trunk and

carried it up the steps to the double front doors. Then he paused to look at her, his thick brows pulled down. "You can still change your mind, miss."

Dolly lifted her chin. "I won't change my mind."

His gaze darted past her, then he nodded. "Take care, then."

Dolly watched him drive away, the buggy wheels clattering on the cobblestones. Then she turned and read the sign above the front door: *Occidental Board Presbyterian Mission Home*. Pride rushed through her. She was really here. Her adventure was about to begin.

She walked up the flight of stairs, then stopped in front of the doors. Raising the knocker, she let it fall, and the sound reverberated with a *thunk* against the wood. Dolly clasped her hands together and waited and waited. When the door finally opened, a young Chinese girl looked out, her dark hair parted straight down the middle with the ends woven into short braids. She wore a long white tunic over white pants. The girl's deep brown eyes focused somberly on Dolly.

"Who?" the girl asked.

"I'm Miss Donaldina Cameron, and what's your name?"

The girl didn't answer, but she grasped Dolly's skirt, giving it a tug as if inviting her inside. Did the girl not speak English?

"I guess I'll come in?" Dolly shifted her trunk through the doorway.

The young girl shut and bolted the door. Then, before Dolly could ask another question, the girl dashed off, disappearing into the depths of the house.

Beyond the entryway, a staircase rose, the walls lined in dark paneled wood.

Above her, something thumped, and Dolly looked up. At the top of the staircase, another young Chinese girl crouched in front of the banister, her dark eyes peering through the slats. The girl had a deep scar along her jaw and more scars mapping her thin arms. She was older than the girl who'd answered the door. Maybe nine years old?

"Hello," Dolly said. "What's your name?"

The girl's eyes widened in fear. She scrambled to her feet and fled, her two pigtails bouncing against her narrow shoulders.

"Well," Dolly murmured, setting her hands on her hips, "a fine welcome to me."

Other sounds reached Dolly. Footsteps pattered on one of the upper floors, and the sound of kitchen preparations came from the back of the house. Did Dolly have to go search for a staff member? Should she take off her hat and jacket yet?

Then a white woman appeared from the corridor beyond the stairs. Her round, freckled face beamed with a smile. "Dolly. Welcome to the mission home." Eleanor Olney strode toward her, arms outstretched.

Dolly had gone to school with Eleanor years ago; she was now one of the staff members who volunteered here.

Eleanor hugged Dolly, then drew back. "How are you doing? I'm so glad you agreed to come."

"Thank you, I—" Dolly began.

But Eleanor started talking again. "Come, let me show you around." They walked into the next room, and she waved her hand. "This is the parlor."

The furniture was elegant but worn, as if it had been donated and not purchased new. A couple of bookcases lined the walls.

Before Dolly could ask any questions, Eleanor led her to the next room. "And this is the Chinese room. Most of the items are gifts from the Chinese Legation and other merchants. We are fortunate to have such a place for the girls to feel connected to their heritage."

Dolly turned slowly to study the area. Intricately carved teak furniture pieces stood in small groups atop thick rugs. Scrolls of Chinese watercolors hung on the walls, showing scenes of China painted in soft blues, greens, and pinks. Tiny figures and even smaller flowers and trees had been painted on vases and bowls.

As lovely as the room was, Dolly wondered if the girls truly felt connected to their heritage in this space. The items might be from China, but heritage was so much more than artifacts. Besides, no one was here. "Where is everyone?"

"The younger girls are in their classes learning to read and write in their native language," Eleanor explained. "The older girls are working in the kitchen, doing laundry, or sewing. Then the age groups will switch places with each other, and the older girls will go to class and the younger girls will do their chores."

"Where did the girl who answered the door disappear to?" Dolly asked. "And another one at the top of the stairs seemed afraid of me. She had terrible scars on her face and arms."

"Oh, that's Tien Fu Wu," Eleanor said with a sigh. "She should be in class with the others. I guess she's too curious for her own good." She paused, her eyes narrowing like a watchful cat. "How much did Mrs. Browne tell you about the girls?"

"She said they've been rescued from dismal situations," Dolly answered.

Eleanor nodded, then lowered her voice. "The girls in your sewing class have deep, dark histories. Some girls can be . . . very difficult . . . like Tien Fu. She was sold over and over and had abusive owners. But please know that we are all here to help you with any concerns."

Dolly's throat had grown tight. The scars on Tien Fu's body weren't because she'd fallen off a bike. They were there because someone had abused her. Dolly felt like crying, even though she didn't know the girl.

Eleanor touched Dolly's arm. "The girls will come to love you, you'll see. Now, if I haven't scared you off, come and see your bedroom."

Dolly exhaled slowly and smiled, although her heart throbbed with a dull ache. "All right."

Eleanor led Dolly back to the staircase, and they climbed to the third floor.

"Your room is down this corridor," Eleanor said.

Inside, Dolly found a small bedroom furnished with only a corner table, chair, and narrow bed.

"You can leave your things here," Eleanor said, "and then I'll take you to meet the director."

Dolly set down her carpetbag, then quickly removed her hat, gloves, and jacket. She could bring up the trunk later, she guessed. She then followed Eleanor downstairs. On the second landing, she caught a glimpse of another Chinese girl whose black eyes watched her like a frightened animal. But the girl ducked out of sight, limping as she went, before Dolly could say anything friendly. Why was the girl limping? Dolly really needed to learn some Chinese.

Her thoughts were interrupted.

"Miss Cameron?" An older woman walked toward her in the dim hallway. "I'm Miss Culbertson, the director of the mission home."

Miss Culbertson's almost entirely gray hair was pulled into a pompadour style. Her brown eyes behind spectacles matched the color of the wood paneling along the wall, and her dress seemed much too big. Had the woman lost weight recently?

"Hello. It's lovely to meet you," Dolly said. "Eleanor showed me around. I haven't met anyone else save for one of the girls who let me in. It seems every girl who sees me disappears."

Miss Culbertson almost smiled, then stopped. "Yes, well, making themselves scarce is a prized skill among our girls."

"I need to check on the kitchen," Eleanor murmured, then left.

Miss Culbertson studied Dolly as if she were trying to decide if she liked her. "Come into my office, Miss Cameron, where we can speak in private."

Dolly followed the director along the corridor. The woman walked slowly, and once in a while, she used the wall for a bit of support. Was the woman sick or injured? Unease filled Dolly, making her stomach feel like it was being pulled tight like a stitch.

Miss Culbertson led the way down the stairs, then into her office. She motioned for Dolly to sit on a faded brocade chair. The director didn't say anything for a long moment. Outside, a cart clattered by, pulled by a horse.

Should Dolly be asking questions? The back of her neck prickled in anticipation and she cleared her throat.

Finally, the director's brown eyes focused on Dolly. "Are you sure you will not be afraid of this work?"

Dolly was reminded of the buggy driver's warning. "I have come ready to work."

"Mrs. Browne was very enthusiastic in her recommendation of you," Miss Culbertson said. "She also said you're an excellent seamstress, but city life is quite different from life in the smaller towns."

Dolly wasn't afraid of hard work. She'd grown up on a ranch. "I am not a young girl recently out of the schoolhouse. I understand the difficult circumstances these girls come from, and I'm looking forward to helping with whatever is needed."

Miss Culbertson's frown appeared, making more wrinkles on her face. "There are dangers, you know."

Did the girls get into fights? Pull hair? Yell at each other? "What sort of dangers?" Dolly asked.

Miss Culbertson walked around the desk. "This morning we were threatened by the tong. Do you know who the tong are?"

Dolly shook her head no.

"They are gangs of slave owners," Miss Culbertson said.

"Sometimes they are called highbinders. They buy and sell the Chinese girls, and they are not happy that we rescue them."

Dolly's stomach did a slow turn.

"One of the girls found a long stick in the hallway," Miss Culbertson continued. "We called for the police to investigate and they declared that it was dynamite."

"Real dynamite?" Dolly's thoughts raced. "An explosive?"

"Yes." Miss Culbertson rested both her hands on the desk as if she needed to support herself. "Our latest rescued girl was worth a lot of money to her owner. Thousands of dollars. We have many enemies, you see, Miss Cameron. The tong gangs want their slaves back. They want to destroy our work." She dropped her voice to a whisper. "The dynamite was strong enough to blow up this entire city block."

Dolly stared at the director and thought of the young Chinese girls she'd seen: their scars, their thin bodies, and their haunted eyes. Those girls had been frightened of *her*—a young woman who had come to teach sewing skills. She thought of the buggy driver who'd warned her to stay away from the mission home. And now Miss Culbertson had told her about how the tong wanted to destroy the work here with dynamite.

Dolly blinked away the sudden burning in her eyes.

"You're very tall, Miss Cameron," Miss Culbertson said. "Your eyes are green, and your hair a deep bronze color. You will stand out in Chinatown. Not only that but your Scottish accent will attract attention."

Dolly swallowed against the sudden rawness of her throat. Her family was Scottish and she'd grown up speaking like them. "Is my accent a problem?"

"It will draw notice from those who wish us to fail," Miss Culbertson said matter-of-factly.

The breath in Dolly's lungs deflated. "I cannot help my

appearance." She touched her hair, then lowered her hand. "And I've never judged others for theirs."

Miss Culbertson eyed her for a long moment. Faint sounds reached through the closed door. A bell rang. Someone called out, "Dinner's ready."

Still, Miss Culbertson didn't speak. Finally, she said, "You will stay despite all that I've told you?"

Dolly thought that stepping off the train had been the turning point in her life. But she'd been wrong. This moment was. The director was more than twice Dolly's age, and yet she was living and working here. Dolly lifted her chin. "Are *you* staying, Miss Culbertson?"

Miss Culbertson's brows jutted up in surprise. "Of course."

Dolly rose to her feet and leveled her gaze with Miss Culbertson's. "Then I will stay too."

Chapter Nine

INTO THE ALLEY

SAN FRANCISCO, 1895

"Miss Cameron! Kicking!"

Dolly spun from the cupboard in the sewing room to see seven-year-old Lonnie pointing a finger at another girl. Lonnie was either giggly or moody. Nothing really in between. She was deathly afraid of fire and refused to go near the kitchen. The burn marks on her arms were a witness to the reason behind her fear.

"I saw Tien Fu kick Lonnie," Dong Ho confirmed. She was a scrap of a girl who also had two moods: sweet or feisty.

"Kicking. Stop her!" Lonnie cried again.

Dolly knew it was only seconds before an all-out fight began. That was something she had witnessed more than once in the past week since arriving at the mission home.

Dolly crossed the room swiftly and crouched before a Chinese girl of about nine or ten years old with horrifying scars along her jaw and arms: Tien Fu Wu. The young girl who'd been frightened of her on that first day at the mission home and who, since then, had shown nothing but defiance. Tien Fu had made no secret of disliking Dolly, although she seemed to tolerate Miss Culbertson. Tien Fu also followed Yuen Qui around a lot.

"Tien Fu," Dolly said in a soft tone, gazing at the girl, "we must keep our hands and feet to ourselves."

As usual, Tien Fu wouldn't make eye contact, but Dolly knew she'd heard because her face had flushed.

"I am *not* kicking," Tien Fu said in good English.

Dolly exhaled. Should she argue with the girl or just ask her to behave?

At least the girls didn't hide from Dolly anymore and she'd learned everyone's names. The younger ones could be very sweet when they wanted to, and Dolly had even received hugs from a few of them.

Tien Fu was intelligent and a quick learner. Despite her pretty features of lovely dark eyes, rose-colored cheeks, and pale gold complexion, the scar on the girl's jaw told a darker story. Yet she didn't seem to care about the consequences of misbehaving.

Still, Dolly wanted to find a way into Tien Fu's heart. Dolly had read the girl's record in the ledger and discovered that Tien Fu had been sold by her father to settle gambling debts. Tien Fu's feet had barely been unbound when she came across the ocean on the ship. Her first mistress in Chinatown owned a brothel and gambling den, and Tien Fu had worked as a domestic slave cleaning the gambling den and other rooms. When her mistress had fallen into debt, Tien Fu was again sold to another woman. There, she'd been in charge of the owner's little boy and she was forced to work day and night. Her new slave owner had been cruel and abusive. Surely Tien Fu still suffered from what had happened to her.

Now Dolly kept her gaze steady and spoke quietly so the other girls wouldn't overhear. "Do you know what *lying* is, Tien Fu?"

"Not telling the truth."

"Correct," Dolly said. "When we lie, we lose the trust of another person. Do you know what *trust* is?"

"I don't trust *anyone*," Tien Fu said, her tone hard.

Dolly wasn't surprised, but it still pinched her heart to hear this from a child so young. "What about Miss Culbertson or Yuen Qui? Do you trust them?"

When Tien Fu didn't answer, Dolly continued. "When you don't lie, other people will trust you. Don't you want your teachers to trust you?"

The girl still didn't answer, but Dolly knew she understood. She glanced about the room. The other girls were bent over their tasks, either trying to ignore what had just happened or they had already forgotten.

"You may get back to sewing," Dolly said with a sigh as she straightened. "Please remember what I told you."

Tien Fu returned to the quilt squares she was piecing together in a row.

Glancing at Tien Fu's work, Dolly saw that the stitches were uneven and sloppy. She guessed that Tien Fu was doing this on purpose because the previous rows were sewn with even stitches.

"Your sewing is beautiful, Tien Fu," Dolly said. "The first rows of stiches are very nice."

Tien Fu said nothing. She tugged another stitch through the fabric, just as sloppy as the previous one.

For a moment Dolly gazed down at Tien Fu's dark hair, parted neatly in the middle and braided. The girl sat stiffly, but her slim fingers trembled. "If you keep working hard," Dolly finally said, "and keep telling the truth, someday *you* could teach this class."

Tien Fu's gaze lifted. The girl's eyes were filled with disdain.

It was like Tien Fu had slapped Dolly with one look.

"I don't want to live here," Tien Fu said in a sharp hiss. She ripped out a row of stitches.

Dolly had pushed too far. Not every girl here liked the mission home, but if they had nowhere else to go, they stayed.

Another staff member named Anna appeared in the doorway.

Anna was Miss Culbertson's niece and her brown eyes were the same color. Since Miss Culbertson had been sick these past two days, Anna visited classrooms to check on their progress.

Anna motioned for Dolly to join her at the door.

"Miss Culbertson is asking for you," Anna said in a quiet voice. "She's in her office now. I'll oversee your class while you're gone."

Dolly nodded, happy that Miss Culbertson must be feeling better. "Just a warning, Tien Fu is not happy with me."

Anna didn't seem surprised. "I'll keep a special eye on her."

"Thank you." Dolly strode to the director's office and knocked on the door, curious as to what Miss Culbertson could want.

"Come in," Miss Culbertson called in a muffled tone.

Dolly stepped into the shadowy office to find the director standing by the window, a small scrap of paper and a red cloth in hand. No lamps were turned on, and the early evening light made everything dim.

Miss Culbertson's expression was serious. "In two weeks, I leave for New Orleans to take one of our Chinese women to begin her married life."

Dolly nodded. She'd heard about the woman who was soon to marry. Chinese men were allowed to court the women at the mission home if they could prove to the director that they had a good job and had converted to Christianity.

"I've been watching you closely, Miss Cameron." Miss Culbertson clasped her hands together. "I've watched your interaction with the girls, and you seem to care for them already."

This was true. Dolly had grown fond of many of the girls. "I grew up in a large family," she said. "I lost my mother when I was five, and I guess I can relate to these motherless girls."

Miss Culbertson looked thoughtful as she scanned Dolly's face. "The girls are growing fond of you as well. Although it seems Tien Fu gives you trouble."

This was true as well. "She's young yet," Dolly said, "and I think it is hard for her to trust adults. They have wronged her so many times."

"Yes, you have been very patient with her. Now, since I'll be gone for a few weeks and the work must go on," Miss Culbertson tapped the paper in her hand, "I need your help tonight so that you can begin your training."

Dolly's brows pulled together. "Training for *what?*"

"We're going to rescue a girl kept as a prisoner in Spafford Alley." Miss Culbertson set the paper on her desk. "This note has the name and location of the girl who has asked for rescue." Next she held up the red cloth. "This torn cloth belongs to the girl, and she will have the other half."

Dolly stared at the note and the torn piece of cloth as questions tumbled through her mind.

"We'll leave at midnight," Miss Culbertson said. "Ah Cheng will translate for us. Yuen Qui is helping with something else tonight. We need to get in and out of the place as quickly as possible. Are you willing to come?"

Dolly nodded, although she had many questions. Going on a rescue would feel like running toward a cliff in the dark with no idea where the drop-off began. Would the rescued slave be sweet like Lonnie or full of bitterness like Tien Fu? "What should I wear?"

"Dark clothes and shoes you can run in." Miss Culbertson's gaze traveled the length of Dolly. "You must be very sure about this since you might be seen by members of the tong. They will know you're from the mission home, and you will no longer be anonymous in San Francisco."

Air left Dolly's chest. The criminal tong were the gangs who had planted the dynamite at the mission home. They were the ones who sold the Chinese girls into slavery. And now they would know *her*. She would become a target. Fear pulsed through her as she thought of how the tong were cruel and abusive to young girls, forcing them into slavery. But if Dolly didn't stand up for these girls, who would? She was here now, and it must be for a reason. How could she say no to a woman like Miss Culbertson, who'd dedicated her very life to this cause? Dolly lifted her chin. "I will be ready."

By the time Dolly returned to her bedroom, the initial shock of the director's request had faded. She shut the door behind her and drew in a shaky breath. Going on a rescue was very different from teaching a sewing class inside the safe walls of the mission home.

Dolly closed her eyes for a moment, wondering what sort of conditions Tien Fu had been discovered in. Surely she'd been too small to send a note on her own or ask someone to do it for her. How had Tien Fu been rescued?

And now Dolly was being trusted to help. She didn't speak Chinese, and although Miss Culbertson took an interpreter with her, could Dolly do what Miss Culbertson did? Go into brothels and opium dens and find slave girls clutching scraps of red cloth?

Dolly paced her small bedroom as she thought about what she loved about San Francisco so far. She'd gone shopping with Anna once at the Chinese market. They'd walked through the bustling crowds, where melons, Chinese cabbage, fresh and dried fish, sugared ginger, and incense were sold. She'd been fascinated with the beautiful satin mandarin gowns, the intricate porcelain vases and dishes, and the highly polished teakwood furniture almost too dainty to use. Dolly loved the decorative lanterns that glowed in the evening, the colorful red and gold signs scaling buildings, and the elegant pagoda rooftops. Anna interpreted for Dolly as they spoke to friendly merchants about their goods and negotiated prices for their purchases.

Tonight Dolly would see beyond all of that—into the underbelly of Chinatown. Somehow Miss Culbertson trusted her.

Dolly slowly exhaled. She'd led a privileged life compared to so many out there. Yes, she'd had her sorrows and losses and disappointments. She'd lost her mother as a child, then her father more recently, and she hadn't married like she'd wanted to. But she'd never been sold, her body had never been abused, and she'd never been mistreated.

What if tonight she helped rescue a girl from a horrible life? What if because of Dolly's actions, a life was made free?

Chapter Ten

A HARD DECISION

SAN FRANCISCO, 1895

Dolly crossed to her closet and pulled out a navy print blouse. It was almost midnight, and very soon, she'd be going on a rescue. She unfastened her underskirt and slipped it off, leaving only the main skirt. Next she picked up the boots that she'd worn around the ranch back home. Why she'd even brought them, she hadn't known at the time. Now it seemed fortunate that she had.

When a light tap sounded at her door, Dolly opened it to see Miss Culbertson dressed in dark colors as well. The director made a quick scan of Dolly, then nodded with approval.

Without a word, Miss Culbertson turned, and Dolly followed her. They joined Ah Cheng, one of the Chinese interpreters, at the bottom of the stairs. They left by the front door, and Anna, grim-faced, locked it after them. Sacramento Street was quiet, the night air was cool, and the breeze made Dolly grateful she'd brought her shawl.

Dolly followed the two women down the hill to Stockton Street. She was out of breath by the time they reached the corner, where three police officers waited. Miss Culbertson made quick introductions to the officers. "Dolly, these men are with the

Chinatown Squad. This is Jesse Cook, John Green, and George Riordan."

Dolly greeted them. Their mustaches, bowler hats, and dark suits made it hard to tell the men apart in the dark. She tried not to stare, especially since two of them carried sledgehammers and one an axe. Where were they going that required such tools?

The officers set off at a brisk pace. Her long legs had no trouble keeping up, though her pulse raced as if she had run for miles. They turned one corner and then another, walking through Chinatown. Officer Jesse Cook switched his sledgehammer to his other hand and moved near Dolly.

"Where are you from, Miss Cameron?" he asked, his voice low as he looked from side to side as if he were trying to see into the dark alleys.

"San Gabriel Valley," she said.

The police officer chuckled. "A mite different from Chinatown. What about your accent?"

"My family is from Scotland, although we lived in New Zealand for many years," Dolly answered. "And you?"

"Sometimes it's better to forget the past and move forward."

Her gaze moved to the sledgehammer in his hand. "Is that why you go on these rescues? You're trying to forget something?"

"I'm part of the Chinatown Squad because those who are trafficked have no chance for justice in this city," Officer Cook said. "I couldn't sleep at night if I didn't try to help."

Yes, thought Dolly. *That is why I'm here too.*

"There's Bartlett Alley up ahead," Officer Cook continued. "If I could burn it down, I would."

What's so bad about Bartlett Alley? Dolly wondered.

"We're almost there," Miss Culbertson said from up ahead in a hushed voice. "Stay by me, Miss Cameron."

Dolly moved quickly to her side and headed down the alley. Although it was dark and quiet, she sensed they were not alone.

She tried not to breathe deeply because the alley smelled like rotten vegetables and burning opium. Officer Cook stopped in front of a heavy door and knocked firmly on the rough wood.

Dolly flinched at the sound.

No one answered the door. No sounds came from within the building. The only sounds were the *drip, drip, drip* of water nearby.

Officer Cook pounded on the door again, calling out in a gruff voice, "Open the door! It's the Chinatown Squad!"

No response. Dolly's heart was beating so loudly, she wondered if anyone else could hear it.

Officer Green moved to a covered window and rattled the metal grating. "Open up!" he called.

Dolly tried to imagine what must be going on inside the dark building. Were people hiding? Fleeing?

"Stand back," Cook growled as he lifted his sledgehammer and brought it down on the door latch.

Nearby, Officer Green took hold of the metal grate over the window and wrested it free.

There was no way anyone within a hundred yards of the place didn't know that police officers were breaking into this building. Dolly wrapped her arms about her torso to steady her nerves as Officer Riordan shattered the window with the axe. Then he climbed in through the opening.

"It's our turn," Miss Culbertson said.

Dolly moved to the window, ready to help. She crouched, her heart thundering in her ears. Whatever room was beyond, it was nearly all dark, save for the flicker of a guttering candle. Perhaps this building had no electricity. Dolly gathered in the fullness of her skirt and climbed through the window, following after Miss Culbertson and Ah Cheng.

It was the smell that hit Dolly first. Her throat squeezed and she clamped her mouth shut to avoid breathing in any more of the rancid air than she had to. A ratty bed stood against the wall, its single blanket soiled, and a basin sat in one corner next to a single lopsided chair missing one leg. A cracked bucket served as a latrine. Someone huddled against the far wall of the room on the dirt-packed floor. At first glance, Dolly thought it was a small child.

But when she stood, the thin girl looked fifteen or sixteen. Her too-large dress hung limply around her body, doing very little to conceal a bruise on her shoulder and scratches along her arms.

Miss Culbertson and Ah Cheng approached her with careful steps.

"Ask her if she sent for us," Miss Culbertson said softly.

Ah Cheng interpreted, and the Chinese girl looked from Officer Riordan to Dolly and Miss Culbertson. Slowly the girl uncurled her clenched fist to reveal a scrap of red cloth.

"She will come," Ah Cheng announced, her voice triumphant.

Miss Culbertson extended her hand, but the girl didn't move. Instead she rattled off several phrases in Chinese.

Ah Cheng interpreted quickly. "She has some jewelry with her mistress. She wants to bring it."

Dolly wanted to tell the young woman no. Shouldn't they hurry out of this dank place? She could hear the other two officers pacing outside, and someone shouted in the distance. What if the Chinese mistress retaliated?

Dolly was doing everything she could not to gag, not to flee this horrible room. She already wanted to scrub her hands with soap and rub these images of filth from her eyes.

"All right," Miss Culbertson said in a gentle tone. "Tell her we will go with her to get her belongings."

They were interrupted by a man unlocking the door to the room from the outside. He burst through the doorway. He was Chinese, his face flushed in anger. "You cannot be here," he barked in English, glowering at Miss Culbertson. "This woman is mui-tsai. She no good. Look at her. Pitiful prostitute."

The words felt like a slap to Dolly. What gave this man the right to call the girl names?

Miss Culbertson didn't back away. "*You* are the one who is no good, sir. You care only about the money she can bring you, no matter the cost to her life."

The man's face darkened another shade of red. He grabbed the girl's arm and shoved her against the wall, then pointed a finger at Miss Culbertson. "*You* stop talking, woman. You will pay for this."

Officer Cook came through the window in a flash.

The Chinese man lifted his hands in surrender. "I will leave. But you will all pay." His gaze sliced to Dolly, and she knew he wouldn't forget her either.

But Miss Culbertson didn't seem bothered. "Ah Cheng, tell the girl to come with us now. We will find her jewelry later."

The young woman's wide, dark eyes shifted to Miss Culbertson. Then she moved to her bed and grabbed something beneath the soiled scrap of a blanket. She brought out a round picture frame and clutched it to her chest. Her nod told them she was ready to go.

Someone shouted somewhere deep inside the house, followed by someone else crying.

"Let's go," Miss Culbertson insisted.

Grasping Ah Cheng's hand, the girl climbed through the window.

Once Dolly was outside, she breathed in the cool night air, thankful to be out of the foul basement room.

Miss Culbertson and Ah Cheng each grasped the girl's arm, and all of them hurried along with the police officers. The poor girl kept up with the pace, but she was trembling, and she kept mumbling something in Chinese.

Dolly's heart felt like it had been ripped in half.

"Are you all right, miss?" Cook asked in a low tone after they'd exited Bartlett Alley.

"I think so," she whispered in a shaky voice.

"It will get easier," Cook said. "You did fine in there, Miss Cameron. I've known the director for many years, and she wouldn't have brought you along if she didn't think she could trust you."

Trust. There was that word Dolly had used on Tien Fu that day.

Dolly glanced over at Officer Cook beneath the light of the moon. He walked with sure steps, his sledgehammer casually swinging at his side. How did he do this night after night?

"I felt so hopeless in there," Dolly said.

"Don't worry, you will have plenty of chances to do more. This war is not over yet."

His words sent a shiver along Dolly's neck. "Will they not come after us for what we have done?"

"They might. Miss Culbertson keeps the girls under watch at all times."

Dolly wondered how many slave girls had been rescued by Miss Culbertson and her staff, and how many others were still out there, living in misery and filth?

When they reached the base of Sacramento Street, Officer Green said, "We'll wait here to make sure you get up the hill. Lock things up tight, ladies. One of us will be around every hour or so to make sure no one is trying to get the girl back."

Dolly's stomach tightened with worry. By the time they reached the mission home and were safely inside, the girl had started crying.

Ah Cheng locked the door behind everyone. "Can you help me, Miss Cameron? We need to get her into a warm bath."

Dolly helped the girl bathe and dress in a clean nightgown.

The girl cried through most of the process, but then she asked Ah Cheng how to say "thank you" in English. Dolly thought her heart would melt, both from pain and relief. The girl was safe and clean at last.

After the girl went to bed, Dolly stood in the dimness of the hallway for a few moments, remembering all that she'd seen in Bartlett Alley. *This war is not over*, Officer Cook had said. His words wouldn't leave her mind.

She also remembered another phrase. *Feed my sheep*, the Lord had said. Sure, Dolly had helped others in small ways. She believed she was a good person. Yet tonight had been the first time in her life that she felt like she'd accomplished something with eternal consequences. She had literally helped change a life for the better. She'd assisted in pulling a young woman out from a very vile place. Dolly had helped rescue another person, but it felt like she'd somehow rescued her own soul.

The tears that burned in Dolly's eyes were not of sorrow or pain but gratitude.

A small cry sounded from the other end of the hallway. Dolly hurried along the corridor until she found someone huddled in the corner.

"Tien Fu," Dolly whispered. "Why are you out of bed?"

The girl scooted farther into the corner, pulling her knees tightly to her chest.

"Did you see the new woman we brought in tonight?"

Tien Fu didn't move, didn't respond.

"She'll be all right," Dolly said, hoping to soothe Tien Fu. "She was very hungry and very dirty, but she took a bath and we gave her food, and now she is safe."

Tien Fu's small shoulders trembled.

Dolly could only imagine the horrible memories Tien Fu had about her former life in slavery. Were they now haunting her again?

"Come, I'll sit with you in your room until you fall asleep." Dolly touched the girl's shoulder, hoping to give some comfort.

But Tien Fu's head shot up and she shoved Dolly's arm away, scratching her in the process with sharp fingernails. Then Tien Fu scrambled to her feet. She ran down the hall and disappeared into one of the bedrooms. The door slammed shut.

Dolly braced a hand against the wall. The sting of the scrape hurt. But Tien Fu's pain was worse. Dolly didn't know if she should report this to the director.

She waited in the dim hallway for a long moment, but no other sounds came from Tien Fu's bedroom. Dolly decided she wouldn't tell anyone about the scratch from Tien Fu, but when Dolly reached her own bedroom, she found Miss Culbertson waiting inside.

"I wanted to see if you're all right," Miss Culbertson said in a quiet voice, her face shadowed from where she sat by the single lamp.

Dolly was too late in hiding her arm.

"Let me see your arm."

"Tien Fu was upset and she lashed out when I tried to comfort her," Dolly explained.

Miss Culbertson clicked her tongue. "I'll speak to Tien Fu in the morning. Sometimes these girls relive the things that have been done to them. But we need to teach proper behavior and respect."

"Be gentle with her. She is hurting too."

Miss Culbertson nodded. "You are generous, Miss Cameron. I hope you haven't been scared off from the mission work."

"No," Dolly said. "But I didn't know they would come from such . . . depraved living conditions. And I didn't know a person could be so . . . abused."

"We are lucky she came willingly." Miss Culbertson folded her hands upon her lap. "Her owner cursed her, and sometimes that's enough to change a girl's mind. Most of these girls have no idea what will happen to them when they leave China. They think they are going to marry rich men or have good jobs in America. Because of the Chinese anti-immigration laws, the highbinders train the girls on a new identity and produce false papers."

Dolly sat on the edge of her bed, trying to soak in all this information.

"Some of the girls are kidnapped, and their families have no idea that their daughters are alive," Miss Culbertson continued. "The girls take on new names in America, so they become paper daughters without a home. Without care or love."

"Paper daughters," Dolly whispered.

Miss Culbertson rose to her feet, then crossed to Dolly and squeezed her shoulder. "Good night, Donaldina. Tomorrow is a new day. The sun will shine through the darkness you've experienced tonight. We must always be grateful for the blessings we *do* have. Tonight one more girl is safe."

After the director left, Dolly switched off the lamp. She was afraid to see her reflection in the mirror and remember what her eyes had seen. As she shed her outer clothing in the dark, tears slipped down her cheeks. How many other abused women and girls were out there beyond the walls of the mission home? Needing to be rescued?

Chapter Eleven

TWO ORPHAN CHILDREN

SAN FRANCISCO, 1895

Tien Fu sat at the landing at the top of the staircase, even though she should have been in class. The noises in the foyer below intrigued her, and Tien Fu was good at staying quiet. Through the banister spindles she peeked at the guests. A couple of hours earlier, Officer Cook had escorted Miss Cameron and Miss Anna to the immigration station. Now Miss Anna had returned to the mission home with a Chinese woman and two small children. Miss Cameron wasn't with them; neither was Officer Cook.

Tien Fu couldn't resist the temptation to find out more about the guests, so she walked down the stairs. The children noticed her first. Their gazes were curious, but they stayed close to the woman—who must be their mother.

"Hello, Tien Fu," Miss Anna said.

Tien Fu eyed the children as she asked, "Are they going to live with us?"

"Yes," Miss Anna said. "This is Hong Leen. She's just arrived with her children from China."

Tien Fu's gaze shifted to the mother. Hong Leen looked frail. The older of her two children—a girl about five years old—clutched the hem of Hong Leen's tunic and clung to her thin frame. The little toddler boy stretched out his arms, stomping in place and whining for the mother to hold him.

If Tien Fu had been younger, and if her mother had been here, she would have asked her to hold her too. By now she had been away from her family for three years, but sometimes at night when she was about to fall asleep, she could still hear her mother's voice in her head. Seeing these children with their mother now made Tien Fu irritated. Why could they have their mother with them and she couldn't? Why did Tien Fu have to be stuck in the mission home?

"Children," Miss Anna said to the young guests, "this is Tien Fu."

Tien Fu hadn't decided if she liked these children or not, so she didn't smile.

"Tien Fu," Miss Anna continued. "Can you find Yuen Qui? Hong Leen needs help to the bathroom. She's very ill."

Tien Fu nodded and scurried to the kitchen, where Yuen Qui was making afternoon tea. When she passed on Miss Anna's message to Yuen Qui, she set down the teacup and rushed out of the kitchen. Tien Fu trailed behind her, back to the foyer. Once Yuen Qui took Hong Leen down the hallway, Tien Fu asked Miss Anna, "Where's Miss Cameron? Didn't she go with you?"

"She's walking back from the immigration station," Miss Anna said. "There wasn't enough room for her in the carriage."

"There isn't enough room for her here either," Tien Fu blurted out.

Miss Anna's brows shot up.

Tien Fu knew immediately she shouldn't have said that, even though she meant what she said. It was no secret that she didn't like Miss Cameron. Tien Fu liked to boss younger children in the mission home. When Miss Cameron gave orders, Tien Fu felt that her authority over the little kids was threatened. She believed there should be a seniority system in the mission home—those who arrived later shouldn't be allowed to be in charge of her. When Miss Cameron came to work in the mission home, Tien Fu had already been here for over a year. Yet Miss Cameron told Tien Fu what to do all the time. A mere sewing teacher acting like she owned the place. Even though Tien Fu hated how cruel her owners had been to her, at least they didn't pretend to like her. Miss Cameron was the opposite. She pretended to be likeable, but Tien Fu was smart enough not to fall for her fake kindness.

Miss Culbertson was in charge though. Tien Fu had no objection to that. It had taken Tien Fu over a year to finally trust Miss Culbertson and respect her as the director of the mission home. She still hadn't found reasons to extend the same courtesy to Miss Cameron.

"Miss Cameron is a really nice lady," Miss Anna said. "There will always be room for her here or anyone else who needs to stay with us."

Tien Fu couldn't stand how Miss Anna was lying to herself. Why couldn't she just admit that there was no room, no room, no room in the mission home? Where did she think Hong Leen and her children were going to sleep? In the dark basement?

Before Tien Fu had a chance to talk back, Miss Anna said, "Do you think you could take the children to the kitchen and get them some food? I should help Yuen Qui with their mother."

Tien Fu was too surprised to answer. She'd never been put in charge of someone brand new at the mission home. But Miss Culbertson was sleeping off a bad headache today, and Miss Cameron wasn't back yet, so who else was there to care for the newcomers?

"All right," Tien Fu said, mostly because the children looked sad and helpless. She could imagine how they must feel. Their stomachs probably hurt from hunger. Maybe they were scared about being in a new country and surrounded by foreigners who spoke a different language.

"Oh, thank you," Miss Anna said with relief in her voice, and she hurried away.

Tien Fu's gaze moved to the little girl. "Are you hungry?"

The little girl nodded, her eyes wide as she looked at Tien Fu. The toddler boy reminded Tien Fu of Willy. She'd made him happy sometimes; she could do the same for this new little friend. She held out her arms to him. "Want me to carry you?"

The boy didn't hesitate. He stuck out his arms. Tien Fu reached for him and balanced him on her hip. He gently traced the scar on Tien Fu's jaw then kissed it. Instantly, something warmed inside of Tien Fu.

Her eyes welled up. Tien Fu carried the little boy to the kitchen; his sister followed them. She set the boy on a chair, then ruffled his soft dark hair. His eager eyes scanned all the pots and pans and baskets of fruits and vegetables.

"What's your name?" she asked the boy.

His sister answered for him. "His name is Kang—he's one year old. My name is Jiao. I'm five. Our Niang lived here before."

Tien Fu looked down at the little girl and frowned. She didn't understand why someone who had a chance to leave the mission home would return.

Jiao continued, "Niang said that my Lao Ye's family is mad at us because we are Christian."

At the mission home, most of the girls took a Bible study class to learn about Jesus Christ. Some of the older girls were baptized. Tien Fu hadn't yet decided if she wanted to get baptized. It made her sad to know that these children's grandparents were mad at them because of their religious beliefs.

"After my Lao Ye died, Niang got so sick that she couldn't take care of us anymore. She said the women here would take care of us, so she brought us here."

"You came all the way from China just to live at the mission home?" Tien Fu asked.

Jiao nodded.

China was a huge country, but Hong Leen couldn't think of anyone else in China to care for her children? Sailing all the way to San Francisco could take months. After they arrived, the children needed to learn a new language, adapt to a new culture, start a new life. People at the mission home must be like family to Hong Leen. That thought somehow made Tien Fu want to be kind—just like Jesus Christ was to the children in the Bible. She wanted to be someone Hong Leen could trust with her children.

Tien Fu measured a spoonful of tea leaves into a teapot, then she poured boiling water into it to soak the leaves. Next, she got four meat buns from the icebox and gave each child two. The buns were cold, but Tien Fu didn't think these hungry children cared.

Someone knocked on the front door. "I'll get it!" Lonnie hollered from another room.

The locks were turned, and Miss Cameron's voice sounded. "Lonnie, where's Miss Anna? Is Hong Leen with her?"

Tien Fu sighed. She didn't want to explain anything to Miss Cameron. But before she could slip out of the kitchen unnoticed, Miss Cameron appeared.

"Oh, I thought Miss Anna was in here." Her gaze swept across to the children, then landed on Tien Fu. "What are you doing out of class?"

Tien Fu couldn't believe she had to answer this question. Wasn't it obvious what she was doing out of class, when there was no one else to tend to these new children's needs?

"Miss Anna asked me to feed them."

Miss Cameron's brows pinched together like they always did when she was thinking. "Well, thank you. I'll take over from here. You shouldn't miss your English class."

Tien Fu spoke English just fine—maybe not good enough to go to the court for a hearing like some of the other girls had to, but she could understand most of what the English staff members talked about. If anything, she spoke better English than any of the staff members could speak Chinese. In fact, wasn't she speaking English with Miss Cameron right now? Why didn't *she* go to a Chinese class, huh? But then Tien Fu remembered she was trying to do unto others as she would have them do unto her, so she stopped her disrespectful thoughts about Miss Cameron and waved goodbye to the children.

That night Tien Fu lay in bed thinking of the sick mother, Hong Leen, and her two little children. She heard a knock on the front door. Someone opened it. Curious, she left her bedroom and crept along the landing until she had a view of the foyer. There stood Miss Cameron in a robe pulled tightly about her, speaking to a doctor in a tall hat and an overcoat. Their voices were so low, they were almost inaudible. Then Miss Cameron led the doctor into the parlor, where Hong Leen and her children were sleeping.

Quietly, Tien Fu crept down the stairs to the unlit part of the hallway so no one would see her there. She listened from behind a wall.

The doctor asked Hong Leen some questions, but she didn't answer. Tien Fu wished she could be in the room to see what was going on. After about twenty minutes, there were footsteps walking out of the parlor. Tien Fu crouched behind a side table. Miss Cameron walked the doctor to the front door and they whispered their words.

"I'm sorry to say the cancer has progressed," the doctor said. "She only has days now."

Miss Cameron released a breath and touched a handkerchief to her eyes. "I wish there was something we could do."

"I'm afraid not." The doctor's voice sounded sad.

Tien Fu wondered if he was always sad; doctors seemed to always be giving bad news.

After the doctor left, Tien Fu stayed hidden until Miss Cameron went up the stairs and disappeared into her bedroom. Only then did Tien Fu creep to the parlor entrance and glance in.

Wrapped in a shawl, Yuen Qui sat in a chair and gazed at Hong Leen, who was sleeping on the couch. Tien Fu felt sorry that Yuen Qui had to sit there all night. She thought of offering to keep watch, but she shouldn't be awake right now. Maybe in the morning she could volunteer to play with Jiao and Kang and read them storybooks.

Tien Fu moved away, up the stairs, not making a sound. She knew where to step to avoid any creaky parts of the wood floor. Once she made it to her bedroom undetected, she climbed beneath her covers and closed her eyes in the dark room, thinking about her own mother and the last time she had seen her. She hadn't known it would be the last time. Was her mother alive and well right now? Tien Fu didn't want to be an orphan like Jiao and Kang, but then she realized that even if her parents weren't dead, in a way, she had already become an orphan. In a way, Tien Fu shared the same fate as Jiao and Kang.

She would help take care of them. She knew what their sadness would be like and how lonely they would feel. After all, she felt that way every single day.

Chapter Twelve

A NEW ROOMMATE

SAN FRANCISCO, 1897

New bedroom arrangements were made whenever new girls arrived at the mission home or when they married or found jobs. Some of the older girls moved away for school when they received sponsorships. Younger girls coveted the empty beds they left behind, but not Tien Fu. She didn't fight to have one of those beds. Her dream wasn't to get someone else's old bed. She wanted more. She wanted to have a sponsor so she could go to college.

As soon as Tien Fu's twenty-something roommate got married, Jiao asked to be her new roommate. It had been a little more than two years since her mother, Hong Leen, brought her and her brother to the mission home. She'd been sharing a bed with her brother since. "I'm seven now and old enough to have my own bed!"

As much as Tien Fu liked Jiao, she had to turn her down. Jiao knew the consequence of not sharing a bedroom with her brother, Kang. "There's not enough space in the mission home for Kang to have his own room," she reminded Jiao. "If you don't share a room with him, he'll be sent to an orphanage for boys. Think about that."

As soon as Jiao stomped out of Tien Fu's room, Dong Ho strutted in and asked, "Which bed is mine?"

Tien Fu couldn't tell if Dong Ho was slow in the head or if she was just not paying attention. There were two beds in the room. Tien Fu was sitting on hers. So what was Dong Ho's question again?

Dong Ho was two years older than Tien Fu, but there had been times when Tien Fu was asked to help her with her homework. School wasn't for her—Dong Ho had said it many times. She would much rather work in the kitchen. Recently, she and her roommate, Lonnie, had been having some disagreements, and they'd been eager to get out of their roommate relationship. If Tien Fu had any deciding power, she would have picked Lonnie over Dong Ho to share a room.

"How about the empty one?" Tien Fu pointed to the bed opposite of hers. Dong Ho gave a sigh of relief and slumped onto the mattress. "At least it's the same size as yours."

All the beds in the mission home were the same size, but Tien Fu didn't need to remind her of that. If Dong Ho didn't remember to come back to this room every night, Tien Fu wouldn't be sad. It would make it easier for her to sneak out of the room at night.

Tien Fu usually waited until her roommate fell asleep to sneak out to check the house, making sure the doors were all locked. She didn't feel safe unless she fulfilled her self-imposed night guard duty.

The night when Dong Ho moved in, Tien Fu kept her eyes closed and her breathing even for so long, she almost accidentally fell asleep. She was waiting for Dong Ho to snore, but this new roommate only tossed and turned. Tien Fu was getting impatient.

Suddenly, in the dark, Dong Ho whispered, "Psst—are you awake?"

Tien Fu didn't answer at first because she was still pretending. But then she got too curious. "Yes," she whispered back.

"Do you like apples?" Dong Ho asked.

This was what she wanted to know in the middle of the night? But then this was also the girl who enjoyed working in the kitchen, so maybe the question wasn't too random after all.

"Of course," Tien Fu whispered.

"Someone brought us a case of apples today, a gift to the home." Dong Ho had kitchen work this week, so she knew all the food that had been coming in. "Miss Culbertson said we have to wait until the weekend to eat them. She wants the apples softer . . . we are going to make apple tarts, I think, but they look so good. I can smell them now just thinking about them. Mmm . . . so good!"

Tien Fu hadn't been hungry for apples, but strangely, she was now. She imagined sinking her teeth into a juicy, sweet apple, and her mouth began to water.

Dong Ho turned on her side. "Tien Fu, you are so good at sneaking around the house."

Tien Fu stiffened. How did she know that? Did others know it too?

"Sneak down to the kitchen and bring the case up here," Dong Ho said, her voice full of excitement. "We'll keep the apples under your bed, and we can share them. No one will know!"

"No," Tien Fu said with a firm voice; she didn't even whisper now. "If I get caught—"

"Shhh—lower your voice!" Dong Ho said. "You won't get caught. I was the one who carried the box to the kitchen, so no one knows how many apples are in the box. You can leave just a couple of them there."

Oooh—now Tien Fu was tempted, but she didn't like it when others told her what to do. "Go get the case yourself," she said.

"What? Are you a gutless ghost?" Dong Ho snorted. "Pfft! I thought you were tough."

Tien Fu scowled. She didn't need to do this to prove she was tough. In fact, she didn't need to prove anything to anyone. "This has nothing to do with how tough I am," she shot back. "I'm not going to steal—"

"Who said anything about *stealing*?" Dong Ho said. "I asked you to *move* the case from the kitchen to our room. It's *moving*, get it? Pfft! I thought you were smart!"

Now Tien Fu was impressed. Dong Ho's logic actually made sense.

"I guess you like squishy apples," Dong Ho continued. "Those apples will just sit there and rot."

"If you want to *move* them so badly, why don't you do it yourself?"

Dong Ho propped up on her elbow. "You don't think I want to? If I could do it myself, would I ask you to do it and then be forced to share the apples with you? The problem is that I don't know how to sneak around the house without anyone hearing me. You do."

That was a compliment. Tien Fu was proud.

"Those apples are a gift to the people who live in the home," Dong Ho said. "That means *you* and *me*. The gift is to *us*! We're moving our gift to our room—what's wrong with that?"

Dong Ho was a genius in disguise. No more argument was needed for Tien Fu to cave. "Fine, I'll *move* the box. But if I get caught—"

"Oh please." Dong Ho slapped herself on the forehead. "You won't get caught. You're quieter than a mouse in this house! And if you do get caught, I'll tell Miss Culbertson I told you to do it."

Tien Fu knew it was now or never. She climbed out of her bed and put on her robe. Dong Ho climbed out of bed too and tiptoed to the door. She opened it quietly, but before she drew it too wide, Tien Fu held up her hand. "Stop! It will creak if you open it farther."

"Ah, see?" Dong Ho whispered. "You know how to do this better than me."

"Stop feeding me that sweet medicine!" Tien Fu hissed. "If I get caught—"

"But you won't! Why are you thinking about something that won't happen before you even do the thing that *should* happen? Just do it!"

Tien Fu slipped into the hallway. The moon was out tonight, bright against the black sky. Its brilliant light shone through the window at the end of the hallway and cast a silvery patch on the floor.

Tien Fu crept quietly, letting the edge of her fingers trail along the wall to keep her balance. When she reached the stairs, she paused for a long moment, listening. All was quiet. She tiptoed down the stairs. She paused more than once, her heartbeat thudding in her ears. Once she reached the bottom of the stairs, she let out a careful breath. Now the hard part: get the box in the kitchen and make it back to her bedroom without waking anyone.

She glanced toward the double front doors of the mission home. The pale yellow of the streetlamp came through the mottled glass on the top half. Down the hallway, the kitchen was pitch black. She would have to feel her way around the corners and table and chairs.

She crept forward, moving her hands in front of her until she found something to touch. Her eyes slowly adjusted, but all she could see were shapes, the outlines of things. Once she reached the pantry, she felt all the baskets and boxes. Then she leaned close and smelled.

Dong Ho had been right. The apples did smell good. Just to be sure, Tien Fu lifted the lid and reached inside. Cold, round, smooth fruit. She'd found the apples. She took out four and placed them in a basket with bananas. Then she lifted the box of remaining apples and backed out of the pantry slowly, each step calculated and mapped out in her mind. Turning, she kept her eyes wide as she navigated her way around the table.

Her smallest toe struck a chair leg and pain burst through her foot. She inhaled sharply, swallowing back a cry. She stood still, waiting for the pain to go away and listening for sounds from others. Luckily, there were only the humming and creaking noises of the house. Tien Fu couldn't stand here all night. Her arms were getting tired. The box hadn't been heavy at first, but now it felt like an elephant. She took cautious steps out of the kitchen. Once in the foyer, she paused again, looking up the staircase leading to the next landing. The same patches of light painted the wood stairs. Tien Fu took a deep breath, then started up, keeping her footsteps light and quick.

By the time she reached the landing, she was out of breath. But she didn't dare stop. She continued toward her bedroom. Dong Ho was still standing there, a triumphant smile on her face. Tien Fu set the box on top of her bed, then rubbed at her aching arms. Dong Ho shut the door and started giggling.

"Hush!" Tien Fu said, but she was equally triumphant. She had done it! Each of them picked out an apple, then slid the box under Tien Fu's bed, pushing it toward the farthest corner. They would have to find a place to hide the apple cores in the morning, but for now Tien Fu was proud to reward herself with the treat.

The next morning when Tien Fu woke up, Dong Ho had already left. Tien Fu instantly knelt and checked under her bed and was relieved to see that the apple box was still there.

Dong Ho had left her apple core on the small table between their beds, so Tien Fu picked it up. She would get rid of both of theirs. As she headed out of the bedroom, she smelled a change in the air. Breakfast was being cooked. Tien Fu hoped she wasn't late for the daytime activities. She didn't want anyone to ask her questions. The thought of anyone questioning her made her feel sick, even if the subject had nothing to do with the moved apples.

As she headed down to the kitchen, a small prick of guilt entered her heart, but she ignored it. The apples were donated. Tien Fu was showing her gratitude for the donor's kindness by doing the right thing—she didn't let them go to waste.

In the first class of the day, Mrs. Cooper was teaching English. She had complimented Tien Fu more than once that her handwriting was neat. Tien Fu sat at her desk, focusing on writing a list of spelling words, when Miss Cameron came to the classroom door and asked to have a word with the class.

Tien Fu snapped her head up. Miss Cameron wasn't looking directly at her, but Tien Fu felt like she was. In fact, she felt as if everyone was staring at her, as if they all *knew* what she'd done.

Miss Cameron's face was flushed and her lips were pressed together. Her green eyes scanned everyone, lingering on Lonnie, Dong Ho, and then finally Tien Fu. Miss Cameron crossed the room to the windows and adjusted the curtains as if clearing her thoughts to find the right words to say. The other girls nervously looked at one another, but Tien Fu kept her gaze straight forward.

"Someone has stolen a box of apples," Miss Cameron said.

Stolen. Tien Fu's face burned hot.

Miss Cameron moved down one of the aisles until she reached Mrs. Cooper's desk. She turned, her dark skirts making a soft swishing noise. "Who took the apples?"

Tien Fu blinked but didn't shift her gaze. From her peripheral vision, she could see that the other girls either shook their heads or looked down at their desks. No one spoke. Tien Fu couldn't believe that Dong Ho was staying quiet. Whatever happened to "If you get caught, I'll tell Miss Culbertson I told you to do it"?

"Apples are a rare treat, you all know that," Miss Cameron continued in a steady voice. She didn't sound upset, but Tien Fu knew that she was. "Stealing them and keeping them for yourself is both wrong and selfish. We all make mistakes, but what we do afterward is important. Not admitting making a mistake is not telling the truth."

Those words hit Tien Fu hard. Her father had taught her to always tell the truth. Ironically, he didn't practice what he preached. Tien Fu's mother hated his hypocrisy. She hated that he had lied about his addictions to gambling and opium smoking. Tien Fu's cheeks burned and her eyes got teary. Had her mother been here, Tien Fu wouldn't have been able to look at her with a clear conscience. Abruptly, she shot up from her seat. All eyes turned to her. "I took them—I stole the apples," Tien Fu said. "I'm sorry."

Slowly Miss Cameron looked over at her. Her eyes were filled with acknowledgment.

"I'm sorry." Tien Fu apologized again. Emotions crashed through her. She'd done the right thing by confessing, she knew it. Even though she hadn't seen her mother for five years, Tien Fu felt like she could feel her mother's pride stretch across the ocean and through the streets of Chinatown, reaching her. Had her mother been here, she would have nodded her approval, just like Miss Cameron was doing now.

"Thank you for telling us, Tien Fu," Miss Cameron said. "Telling the truth and apologizing for your mistake can be hard, but I'm proud that you chose to be brave and humble."

Instead of punishing her, Miss Cameron simply asked Tien Fu to return the apples to the kitchen. If there was a moment when Tien Fu felt that she had been wrong to dislike Miss Cameron, this was it. Her understanding made Tien Fu feel like she had been given a clean slate to start over, to try to be better. With a renewed appreciation for Miss Cameron's kindness, Tien Fu decided to forgive Dong Ho too. After all, everyone could use a second chance once in a while.

Chapter Thirteen

ONE FOOT FORWARD

SAN FRANCISCO, JULY 1897

Dolly wasn't sure if the coughing fit she could hear was part of her dream or coming from one of the bedrooms. When she opened her eyes in the early gray light, she still heard the coughing. Was it Miss Culbertson again?

The poor woman had been quite ill this week, and not much had eased her coughing. She'd asked Dolly to fill in at the board meeting today and give the mission home report to the board members. Dolly lifted the covers and climbed out of bed. As she pulled on a robe and slippers, she wondered how things would go with Tien Fu today. After she'd stolen the apples, then confessed, it seemed they were on better terms. It was hard to tell with Tien Fu though. She could act quite peaceful sometimes, but other times she became defensive or aggressive. Tien Fu was nearly twelve now, her legs and arms had lengthened, and her thin face had become more rounded.

The coughing erupted again, and Dolly hurried out of her bedroom, twisting her hair into a braid as she walked along the corridor. Most of the bedrooms she passed had closed doors, a few had opened doors, and night-lights made patterns on the wooden floor. Many of the girls refused to sleep in complete darkness, and Dolly didn't blame them.

When she approached Miss Culbertson's bedroom, Dolly was surprised to see Tien Fu step out of it. Instead of avoiding her gaze, Tien Fu looked up and said, "Yuen Qui told me to fetch some hot water from the kitchen. I will make some special tea."

"For Miss Culbertson?" Dolly asked.

When Tien Fu nodded, Dolly was impressed. Yuen Qui did have a way with the girl, and it seemed that Tien Fu cared enough to help out their director.

"Very good." Dolly watched as Tien Fu scurried down the hall, light on her feet as always, not making a sound.

Entering the bedroom, Dolly found Yuen Qui sitting by Miss Culbertson's bed. Violet shadows curved beneath Yuen Qui's eyes, and Miss Culbertson's complexion was pale like a gray dove.

Miss Culbertson didn't open her eyes but stayed turned on her side, clutching a handkerchief in one hand.

"I will sit with her so you can get some rest," Dolly whispered to Yuen Qui. "Tien Fu is making tea for her now."

Yuen Qui didn't even argue. She smoothed back the hair from Miss Culbertson's forehead, then rose to her feet. "Thank you." She was gone before Dolly could sit in the vacated chair.

Miss Culbertson's eyes fluttered open and focused on Dolly. "I've decided to retire," she said in a raspy voice. "It's not because of this dreadful cough either. I've been considering it for some time. I'll move back east to be with my siblings and their families."

Dolly's heart thumped with the news. She didn't know how to respond. Miss Culbertson retiring? For good? Who would take over the director position? "Does the board know?"

Miss Culbertson rested her frail hand on Dolly's wrist. "I sent them word yesterday." She pushed up on an elbow with effort. "Miss Cameron, you've been fearless in the rescues, and the

Chinese women look up to you. I want you to be the next director."

Dolly stared into Miss Culbertson's determined brown eyes. Dolly had been teaching for two years at the mission home. But to be in charge? That was a lot different than being a helper. She'd have to oversee all the needs of the residents, the classes, donations, legal matters, hosting visitors, and writing reports for the board.

But how could she tell a woman like Miss Culbertson—who had devoted her life to rescuing hundreds of enslaved women and children—that she wasn't ready? Committing to this position meant giving up other chances she might encounter in her life.

Even as Dolly thought of leaving the mission home someday, she knew she'd miss the girls dearly—Dong Ho's colorful personality and those dimples on her rosy cheeks, Jiao's shy smile, Lonnie's willingness to help everyone, no matter what . . . Dolly would even miss Tien Fu's dark eyes flashing with annoyance.

Dolly's teacher's salary of twenty-five dollars a month would certainly increase, yet . . .

"Miss Cameron," Miss Culbertson said, her voice stronger now. "You have been well prepared. The women and children trust you. They respect and love you." She brought a handkerchief to her mouth and coughed. Her eyes squeezed shut, then she whispered, "You are needed. Desperately."

Dolly's throat was too tight to speak and she blinked back the tears that threatened to give away the depths of her heart. She nodded because she didn't want to disappoint Miss Culbertson. But when Tien Fu brought in the hot water, it was a welcome distraction.

Two hours later, when Dolly was seated in front of the members of the board in the chapel, her stomach felt like it had been turned upside down.

She'd worn her best outfit, but now the full voile skirt in

black over an orange-brown petticoat, along with a purple shirtwaist and leg-of-mutton sleeves, was much too hot. At least she'd pinned her hair up and off her neck into her usual pompadour.

The president of the board, Mrs. Mary Ann Browne, greeted Dolly warmly, then called the meeting to order.

"Miss Culbertson can no longer continue in her role and will retire," Mrs. Browne announced to everyone. "She has devoted many years to this work, but now it is time to assign a new director." Her gaze landed on Dolly now. "Miss Cameron, the board would like you to take the position."

Dolly's neck prickled beneath her high collar. She wanted to say yes, but she knew she could not. "I am only twenty-seven," she said through her parched throat. "I don't feel confident taking on such a role. I belong teaching the girls and caring for their needs."

The silence in the room only made Dolly feel worse.

Mrs. Browne's mouth straightened into a tight line. "Very well. We have prepared for this possibility and have researched a second candidate." She looked at the other women in the room. "I propose we offer Mrs. Mary H. Field the position."

Dolly sat in silence as the board voted unanimously to hire Mrs. Field. Dolly should have felt elated, but she only worried about who this Mrs. Field was.

When Dolly returned to Miss Culbertson's room later that day, the older woman had already heard the news. Instead of looking upset, Miss Culbertson motioned for Dolly to sit near her bedside.

"Mrs. Field will be a fine director," Miss Culbertson said in a gentle tone. "And you may continue where you feel comfortable."

Dolly released a soft sigh. "I am sorry to disappoint you."

Miss Culbertson's mouth lifted into a faint smile. Gratefully, her cough had subsided. "There is nothing to apologize for. You're young, and you have your entire life before you."

Dolly nodded, but still, her heart was heavy with the feeling that she'd disappointed Miss Culbertson.

The sounds of nightly preparations from the women and girls echoed through the hallways outside the bedroom door.

"I heard Dong Ho call you Mama," Miss Culbertson said.

Unable to hold back her smile, Dolly said, "Yes. A few of the younger girls do. Even Jiao, although she still misses her mother very much."

Miss Culbertson reached over and patted Dolly's arm. "For many of them, you are the only mother they'll know. Even Tien Fu."

Dolly exhaled at this. "Do you think Tien Fu will ever stop resenting me?"

"I heard about the apples," Miss Culbertson said. "I think you're going in the right direction with her. Be patient. These girls have lost so much, and they know you understand what it's like to lose a mother at a young age."

Nothing could replace a mother's love, that Dolly well knew. And no, she had not borne a child from her body, but the girls she served day and night felt as if they had become her own flesh and blood.

"I'll never forget the day Dong Ho showed up on our doorstep," Dolly said, "holding a tiny bundle of her earthly possessions gripped in her skinny arms."

Miss Culbertson chuckled softy. "I believe she could have fought off two dragons if needed. She didn't want anyone to touch her things."

Dolly nodded at the fond memory. "Ah Cheng and I helped her into the bath, and still, she kept an eagle eye on that bundle."

"It took a week before she allowed you to peek inside."

"Yes," Dolly said. "Imagine having your most prized possessions be two chopsticks, a broken comb, and a couple of soiled garments."

"Garbage to some people," Miss Culbertson mused.

"Yet priceless as pearls to Dong Ho." Dolly leaned back in the chair and smiled over at Miss Culbertson. "They will miss you."

Tears gleamed in Miss Culbertson's eyes. "I could not leave these girls to anyone else but you. Director or not, you will be their mama, and that is all that matters."

Dolly blinked rapidly. She didn't know if she could claim such an elevated title, but she loved the girls all the same.

Mrs. Field arrived at the mission home the day after Miss Culbertson's departure, so it was up to Dolly to show the woman around. The woman's severe bun pulled at the sides of her face and she wore all black. Dolly guessed her to be in her early forties.

"This place is so dark," Mrs. Field said right away as Dolly led her through the foyer. "Why are the windows so high up?"

Dolly clasped her hands behind her back. "The dark paneling creates a soothing atmosphere, and the high windows make the mission home more secure."

Mrs. Field's brows pulled together, deepening the lines on her forehead. When Dolly brought a few of the younger girls to sing a hymn for Mrs. Field, the woman didn't even smile.

"And this is the director's office," Dolly said, stepping into the place where she'd had many discussions with Miss Culbertson.

Mrs. Field glanced about the room, then set her satchel onto the desk with a *thump*. "This will do. I'd like to be left alone now." She promptly shut the office door.

Dolly stared at the door for a moment, wondering if Mrs. Field was just nervous.

Shaking her head, Dolly headed to the parlor. She stopped in the middle of the beautiful room and gazed at the sun's rays sparkling against the furniture and rug.

A chair shifted, and Dolly spun to see Tien Fu. She'd been hiding behind the chair.

"I don't like her," Tien Fu announced.

Dolly exhaled. She quite agreed with Tien Fu but couldn't admit it. "We need to help the new director all we can. She's new here and has a lot of responsibility."

Tien Fu's mouth flattened and her eyes narrowed. "She doesn't like Chinese girls."

"Heavens, what makes you say that?" Dolly asked, but she knew why Tien Fu thought that. Mrs. Field hadn't enjoyed anything about the tour or introductions.

"And the Chinese don't like Mrs. Field."

Tien Fu had never spoken with so much of her own initiative to Dolly, but this was out of line. "Remember, we need to speak the truth, Tien Fu. We can't say we don't like someone just because they're new and we don't know them."

Tien Fu edged around the chair, her fingers trailing the backrest. "I heard Yuen Qui say that the tong is *glad* Miss Culbertson left."

This told Dolly that Tien Fu was doing what she did best—eavesdrop. "Tien—" Dolly began to say, but someone knocked on the front door with a loud *thump, thump*.

Tien Fu flinched like a scared rabbit. Then she gripped the back of the chair until her knuckles went white.

Was Tien Fu afraid of people knocking on the door?

"I'll answer it." Dolly headed out of the parlor. She unlocked the door and drew it open. She recognized the errand boy who frequently delivered telegrams. He held out an envelope to Dolly. "Thank you." She gave him a small tip and he scampered off.

Dolly shut the door and was about to take the telegram to the new director, but then she read the names on the envelope.

FROM: ANNA CULBERTSON
TO: DONALDINA CAMERON

Tien Fu emerged from the doorway of the parlor. "Is it a rescue note?"

"It's from Anna Culbertson," Dolly said. "Maybe they've already arrived at their new home." She opened the telegram and began to read. Then she brought a hand to her mouth.

MISS CULBERTSON BECAME VERY
ILL ON OUR TRAVELS. SHE DIED
BEFORE REACHING HER FAMILY.

No, this couldn't be true. But it was. The words were plain. Dolly's eyes burned. She remained in the foyer, not moving.

"Miss Cameron," someone said, but it sounded very far away. "Miss Cameron, what's happened?"

Dolly blinked and looked over to see Ah Cheng. Tien Fu must have fetched her. Next, Yuen Qui arrived. Dolly showed them the telegram, and the three women embraced each other.

"We must tell the girls and the director," Ah Cheng said after drawing away from their tight circle.

Dolly nodded. "Tien Fu knows . . . Oh, where has she gone? I need to find her." She felt numb from her head to her toes, but she hurried up the stairs. She found the girl in her bedroom, sitting on the corner of her bed and staring out the window.

Everything about the tenseness of Tien Fu's body told Dolly not to touch her. So Dolly remained in the doorway. "Miss Culbertson is no longer in pain, Tien Fu. She'll be happy in heaven. From there, she can watch over all of us."

Tien Fu didn't respond or move.

"She loved you and trusted you, Tien Fu," Dolly continued softly. "I know that if she could tell you one more thing, it would be to help the younger girls. They look up to you as someone wiser, and you understand what they are feeling."

Tien Fu's narrow shoulders sagged.

"We'll be gathering downstairs to tell everyone." Dolly waited another moment for a response. Tien Fu remained quiet, so Dolly finally left the forlorn girl whose life had changed yet again today.

As Dolly began the slow walk back to the parlor, she knew the girls would depend on her more than ever. It was up to her to be the comforter at this time since Mrs. Field had stayed in her office most of the day.

After the staff delivered the news of Miss Culbertson's passing, quiet settled over the mission home. Dolly canceled classes. Most of them had called Miss Culbertson their "mama," and this loss was deeply felt.

A few days later, Yuen Qui returned from the marketplace with purchases for dinner. She found Dolly teaching Bible study. One look at Yuen Qui's pretty face clouded with worry told Dolly that she needed to excuse herself from class. She asked Lonnie to be in charge in her absence, then followed Yuen Qui.

Tien Fu came after them, her chin lifted stubbornly, always Yuen Qui's little shadow.

"There are rumors going around Chinatown that need to be addressed," Yuen Qui said once they were in the hallway.

"Should we report to Mrs. Field, then?" Dolly asked.

"No, this is about *you*, Miss Cameron," Yuen Qui said in a fearful tone. "The tong wants to stop you at all costs. They've hired lawyers to issue arrest warrants for our girls. The tong will accuse the girls of stealing, and the police will have to return the girls to their owners."

The news rocked through Dolly, although she shouldn't be surprised. "We will find a way," she said. "If Miss Culbertson overcame threats every day, then so will we. As she did, we will continue to put our faith in the Lord."

Dolly stepped past Tien Fu and Yuen Qui and reentered the classroom to resume the Bible study. One day at a time, she would move forward. Threats wouldn't stop her. The words of Officer Cook came to her mind. This was truly a war against slavery.

Dolly stood in front of the classroom and clapped her hands for full attention. "We will memorize the words of the Apostle

Paul. Repeat after me: I can do all things through Christ which strengtheneth me."

The dark-eyed girls clasped hands. They repeated the phrase back to Dolly: "I can do all things through Christ which strengtheneth me."

Dolly nodded, tears gathering in the corners of her eyes. "Again," she said. As the girls repeated the holy words, she drew strength from their sweet voices.

Tien Fu joined the back row and repeated each word along with the others, her eyes fierce and intent on Dolly. Was Tien Fu slowly becoming her ally?

Soon after dinner, Dolly received a note delivered anonymously to the mission home. The address was in the heart of Chinatown. She showed Mrs. Field the note, but the woman said, "Go do your rescues. I'll not walk through dirty Chinatown."

So Dolly sent word to Officer Cook. Ah Cheng came too and they met two officers at the bottom of the Sacramento Street hill just as the sky grew inky black.

"Did you hear about the tong's threats?" Officer Cook asked Dolly as they walked along the dark street.

"Yes," Dolly said. "They will be after *me* now."

"And you're still coming on rescues?"

Dolly cast him a sideways glance. "What do *you* think I should do, Officer Cook?"

"I think you should carry on, Miss Cameron," he said.

A smile curved her mouth. "I intend to." She wasn't looking at him, but she could feel his approval. Threats or no threats, she would keep putting one foot in front of the other.

They reached the building Dolly remembered from another rescue. The place seemed quiet. Had the slave owners been warned of the raid?

"Let's go." Dolly headed inside and up the steps. She stopped before a numbered door with faded Chinese inscriptions. Dolly knocked, but there was no answer. Then she tried the doorknob. It opened.

With this rescue, Cook and Riordan didn't have to use their sledgehammers to break down doors or smash windows.

"I'll go in first," Cook said. "Stay back."

He moved in front of Dolly, but she quickly followed, looking for any hidden girl.

There was no one in the room—at least no living person.

Hanging from the ceiling was an effigy of a human form. The long skirt, the bronze wig, and the green-painted eyes left little doubt of whom the hanging effigy was supposed to look like. Even though the swaying body was fake, the dagger plunged into the center of the chest was real.

The message was clear. The tong wanted Dolly dead.

This was no game or joke.

Dolly drew in a shaky breath.

"Miss Cameron," Cook said in a quiet voice. "Let's go."

She paused one moment longer, staring at the hanging form. Seeing this image only made her want to keep working. She would put her future into the Lord's hands, and she wouldn't be afraid.

When she returned to the mission home that night, she hugged every girl, including Tien Fu.

Chapter Fourteen
A BIRTHDAY CAKE

SAN FRANCISCO, 1897

"Happy birthday, Jiao," Yuen Qui said, smiling as she set a cake in front of the girl.

Jiao beamed proudly. Her little brother pressed against her side, eager to taste the cake. With Yuen Qui's help, Tien Fu had made the cake. She had tasted a small edge before she frosted it with pink icing. Everyone had gathered in the dining room to sing "Happy Birthday" to Jiao—everyone except for the new director, Mrs. Field. Tien Fu was glad though. Whenever the director was in the room, everyone had to be more serious. Even Miss Cameron was grumpy when the director was around.

"Can I cut the cake?" Jiao asked in a high-pitched voice.

"No," Yuen Qui said with a chuckle. "One of the older girls can do it."

"I will," Tien Fu said at the same time that Dong Ho raised her hand and shouted, "Pick me!"

"All right, Dong Ho," Yuen Qui said. "You may cut the cake."

Tien Fu shrugged. She did get to make the cake. As much as she would like it, it wouldn't be fair for her to be in charge of everything. She moved toward Kang and sat down with him on her lap. Spending time with him made her wonder about her own brother. He would be about fifteen by now and would have changed so much. If they saw each other again, would they even recognize each other?

Everyone bustled around, eating, chatting, and laughing. Tien Fu tried to smile, to be cheerful for Jiao, but she couldn't. She caught Miss Cameron glancing at her a few times. She didn't want undue attention, but she didn't even know how to explain to herself why she was sad all of a sudden. *Nothing was wrong—and everything was wrong.* That about summed up Tien Fu's feelings at this moment.

Here they all were, stuffed in this house, strangers living together because their parents had sold them, or abandoned them, or lost them. How could that ever be made right?

She set Kang down on the chair and pulled another plate of cake toward him. With that distraction, she slipped away into the empty foyer. Just before she was about to head up the stairs, Mrs. Field came out of her office. As usual, she was wearing dark colors, and her brown hair was pulled back from her face, twisted into a tight bun that never seemed to move.

"Where are you going?" Mrs. Field said.

Tien Fu winced. "Upstairs. I forgot something in my room." It was true. She'd forgotten to *stay* in her room.

"You're on kitchen duty this week. You need to stay down here and clean up."

Tien Fu would help clean up, just not right now. "I'll be back down soon."

"No." Mrs. Field grabbed Tien Fu's arm. "You will stay down here. I don't like you sneaking around the house and listening to things that you shouldn't be."

This woman made absolutely no sense. Tien Fu could hardly stand it. What did Tien Fu's listening to things have to do with her kitchen duty? She shook her head and pulled back her arm, but Mrs. Field's grip was firm.

"You need to learn to be obedient," Mrs. Field continued, her hand slowly twisting. "When I ask you to do something, you do it. No questions and no excuses."

Tien Fu's arm burned. Mrs. Field had given her plenty of reprimands, but she'd never grabbed Tien Fu's arm this way. It felt like she intended to break it. Tien Fu tugged away with force, finally breaking the director's grasp.

"Go to the kitchen now!" Mrs. Field pointed toward the kitchen. "I'll not allow disobedient girls to live here. We're a house of order—do you understand?"

Oh, yes, Tien Fu understood clearly. "There's no difference between you and my last owner who gave me scars and bruises," Tien Fu yelled, shaking in rage. "It's *you* who shouldn't be allowed to live here. A poisonous heart like yours can't be here. This is a house of love—understand?"

The director's mouth fell open and her eyes rounded. Tien Fu didn't care if she had gone too far. She stormed into the kitchen and quietly bent over the sink to wash the baking pans and bowls. She scrubbed and scrubbed until all the dishes were clean. Then she wiped down the counters, the icebox, and the stove. Next she swept the floor. That's when Ah Cheng came in. "What are you doing?" she asked. "The party is still going on."

Tien Fu shrugged. "I'm cleaning up."

"I can see that." Ah Cheng leaned against the counter. "I've never seen the kitchen so spotless." She paused. "When I'm upset, I clean too."

Tien Fu noticed a stain on the floor. She grabbed a rag and knelt to scrub it out. Ah Cheng only watched. Laughter and chatter came from the other room. Someone started singing and others joined in.

Ah Cheng knelt next to Tien Fu and set a hand on her back. "What's happened?"

Tien Fu met Ah Cheng's gaze. Over the years, Ah Cheng

had gotten some wrinkles about her eyes that only made her look kinder. But her kindness wasn't enough to convince Tien Fu to tell her what had happened. Then Ah Cheng saw the bruise on her arm.

"Did you get into a fight?" Ah Cheng's expression hardened.

There was no point in pretending nothing had happened, so Tien Fu told Ah Cheng about her interaction with Mrs. Fields. The cruel truth tasted bitter on her tongue.

Ah Cheng's gaze flitted to Tien Fu's bruised arm again. "I'll speak with Miss Cameron."

"No," Tien Fu said immediately. "Don't tell anyone! I don't want Mrs. Field to hurt more girls in the house."

"What?" Ah Cheng looked confused. She sat back on her heels.

Tien Fu shook her head. "She just—she doesn't like us Chinese."

Ah Cheng fell quiet for a long time, then she said, "Remember the saying from our ancestors, 'The mouth that eats other people's food is softened; the hand that takes other people's possessions is shortened'? In San Francisco, many people look down on us Chinese. If it's not Mrs. Field, it'll be someone else. If you don't want others to look down on you, you've got to be strong, capable, independent."

Tien Fu nodded. She wanted to be all those things, but it was difficult. Sometimes she was tired, frustrated, and discouraged. No matter how hard she tried, it didn't seem that she had much of a chance to succeed. After all, she was just a former slave girl who continued to live on others' charity.

Yuen Qui came into the kitchen and scanned the room. In a cheerful voice, she said, "Wow, you cleaned this place beautifully!"

Ah Cheng rose to her feet. "Tien Fu did it all by herself. I think she deserves an extra piece of cake."

Tien Fu slowly stood and draped the rag over the edge of the kitchen sink. "I'm not hungry."

"Are you sure?" Yuen Qui asked, her forehead wrinkling.

Tien Fu appreciated Ah Cheng's and Yuen Qui's kindness, but now she just wanted to be alone. "I'm exhausted"—she moved past them—"I'll see you in the morning."

Before either woman could reply or ask her to stay, Tien Fu left the kitchen. Thankfully, Mrs. Field wasn't in the foyer. Tien Fu scurried up the stairs and down the hallway to her bedroom. Once inside, she huddled on her bed, pulling her legs up, nestling her chin against her knees, and closing her eyes.

Her hands ached from scrubbing so hard, and the pain took her thoughts back to when she was six—right after her father had let their maids go—and Tien Fu had to learn to clean the house with her mother. Her hands had ached like they did now, and her mother would massage them with herbal oils. Tien Fu wondered if her mother was working around the house all day alone or if her family finances had eventually improved and she could hire help now.

Did her mother still make her own tea? Did she dry the leaves, crush them, blend them?

Tien Fu didn't know if she would ever meet a mother figure who would love her despite her flaws, weaknesses, and shortcomings. Definitely not Mrs. Field.

Just then, Mrs. Field's voice came from the hallway. "This has gone on too long."

"They're celebrating a birthday," Miss Cameron's voice responded. "We need good things to celebrate and look forward to."

Tien Fu slid off her bed and crept to her door, hoping to hear better.

"There are one or two birthdays per week!" Mrs. Field raised her voice. "Every other night there's a party. There's a cake. The girls think life is all a party. But look at them. They struggle to learn English, they make sloppy stitches in sewing, and the staff has taken over most of the cooking. Half of them were sleepy today during Bible study because they were up late celebrating another birthday last night."

Tien Fu cracked open the door ever so slowly.

Miss Cameron's reply was clear. "They're *children*, Mrs. Field. They have lost everything. *Everything*. They need joy in their lives, plain and simple. We can teach them the Bible scriptures about the plan of happiness, but we also need to *show* them."

"Through birthday parties?"

"Through enjoying each other's company, through celebrating the good things in life, through showing our love for them."

Mrs. Field didn't reply. In a moment, footsteps walked away.

Tien Fu waited several heartbeats, then opened the door wider and looked out. Miss Cameron was only a dozen steps away, leaning against the wall, her head bowed.

Sometimes Tien Fu felt sorry for Miss Cameron. While taking care of the girls in the mission home, she could be bossy and strict, but Tien Fu's own mother had acted that way too. Perhaps that was what a mother did to show her love. And now Mrs. Field was bossy toward Miss Cameron. Could that be a sign of Mrs. Field's maternal passion? No. Tien Fu wasn't ready to think of Mrs. Field as that kind of female leader yet. In Bible study, Tien Fu had learned that the greatest commandment was to love God, and the second was to love one's neighbor as oneself. Between Mrs. Field and Miss Cameron, it was clear which woman was trying to live those commandments.

Miss Cameron wiped at her cheeks, then straightened from the wall. She walked slowly to the stairs and headed toward the birthday celebration downstairs. As Tien Fu watched her from behind, a lump grew in her throat. She didn't know why.

Chapter Fifteen

OVER THE ROOFTOPS

SAN FRANCISCO, 1899

"Good morning," Dolly greeted Ah Cheng and Yuen Qui as she walked into the kitchen after breakfast had been served and cleaned up. It was almost time for their staff meeting, but Tien Fu lingered, drying a glass. Dolly was certain the now thirteen-year-old teenager wouldn't go too far since she still made it a habit to eavesdrop. Dolly didn't exactly mind though. She wouldn't say that Tien Fu had fully warmed up to her, but the trust between them had grown the past two years.

Dolly fixed herself a cup of orange blossom herbal tea from a blend created by Tien Fu, and as it steeped, she settled at the dining table. Then Mrs. Field walked in. The director wore her usual dark colors—a navy blouse and navy skirt—and her hair was pulled into a severe bun.

"You're excused, Tien Fu," Mrs. Field said in a sharp voice.

Tien Fu flinched, and Dolly pressed her lips together. Mrs. Field didn't need to be so stern with the girls all the time.

Tien Fu set the dried glass on the shelf, then scurried out of the kitchen.

Mrs. Field didn't even notice Tien Fu's downcast expression. Instead Mrs. Field smiled a rare smile as she took a seat at the head of the table. "Hello, everyone." Her pale blue eyes surveyed the staff. "I've brought Kipling's new poem to share in place of a scripture. I think you'll find that it applies to our work at the mission home. Even the title 'The White Man's Burden' reflects our work with the Chinese girls."

Dolly wrapped her hands around her warm teacup. What did the director mean? Helping to rescue Chinese slaves was not a burden.

"Listen carefully." Mrs. Field cleared her throat. "'To wait in heavy harness / On fluttered folk and wild— / Your new-caught, sullen peoples, / Half devil and half child.'" She lifted her gaze and stared straight at Dolly as if in challenge.

Dolly hated to think of what Ah Cheng or Yuen Qui thought.

Mrs. Field smiled again and set the poem down, then folded her hands atop the table. "I haven't been here as long as all of you, but these rescued girls have vulgar habits. The question becomes, despite all our efforts, can those habits truly be changed?"

Dolly's neck prickled with angry heat. She was about to answer when Mrs. Field continued.

"The women from the brothels have no integrity." Mrs. Field's gaze cut to Ah Cheng and Yuen Qui. "This might be difficult to hear. But even when we do our best to act as true disciples of Christ, some souls are too depraved to be saved."

Dolly gripped the edges of the table. Mrs. Field was so wrong. Dead wrong.

"The women at the mission home are low-grade Mongolians. They are a bad influence on the younger, more innocent girls." Mrs. Field tapped the poem on the table. "Allowing them to live among the more innocent girls is lowering everyone's morale and decency."

Ah Cheng and Yuen Qui both kept their gazes on the table. The complaints from some of the girls, including Tien Fu, now made sense. Dolly had brushed them off or tried to make peace between everyone. But if Mrs. Field believed the abused women they rescued were beyond saving, then why was she allowed to be the director? Did the board know about Mrs. Field's convictions?

"I disagree, Mrs. Field." Dolly clasped her trembling hands on her lap. "The work we do at the mission home is *not* a 'white man's burden.' Each woman we help is capable of living a full and joyful life. We are here to offer light to *all* the souls who come to us for rescue, no matter their race or background. The women are like a crop of wildflowers, and they will develop with our sunshine and water."

Mrs. Field pursed her lips. "Well, *Miss Cameron*," she said in a rude tone. "We all know *your* opinion. You never stop giving it. The staff might be devoted to *you*, but you are not the director or on the board. Your opinion is simply your opinion, not a fact."

Dolly exhaled slowly, and although she wanted to yell at this woman, she kept her voice calm. "Many of the rescued women leave our mission home and find employment. Or they marry and raise families. Some are sponsored and attend college on the East Coast. *That* is a fact."

"Do we truly know what happens when they leave?" Mrs. Field said, arching her neck. "Or is someone telling us what we want to hear? You coddle the girls at the mission home too much. You've allowed them to stay in their beds when suffering from melancholy. You even let pregnant women stay here."

Dolly was stunned at the terrible words from Mrs. Field. What in the world were Ah Cheng and Yuen Qui thinking?

Beyond the kitchen, Dolly heard a tumble of footsteps. Someone was coming. Tien Fu appeared in the dining room and produced a note. Had the teenager heard Mrs. Field's hateful words?

Mrs. Field snatched the note from Tien Fu. "I'll take this."

Tien Fu was a stubborn girl, and she stood next to the table as Mrs. Field read the note.

Mrs. Field's brows pulled together tight as she scanned the words. Then she snapped her gaze to Dolly. "You've been sent for once again, Miss Cameron, to go *save the world.*"

Dolly's face burned hot, but she rose from her chair and took the note. She read through the lines quickly. The immigration office wanted her to come to the immigration station. She'd leave right away. Anything to get out from under the disapproving eye of Mrs. Field.

Dolly wished she could take both interpreters with her, but she didn't want to leave the girls abandoned to Mrs. Field.

"Yuen Qui, will you come with me?"

The young woman nodded and stood.

When Dolly returned, she'd speak to Ah Cheng about what Mrs. Field had said. Dolly hoped the interpreters knew that she didn't share the same feelings.

Tien Fu followed Dolly and Yuen Qui to the front door. Dolly turned to Tien Fu. "Stay out of Mrs. Field's way while we're gone. Help Ah Cheng if needed."

Tien Fu nodded like an obedient child.

Dolly and Yuen Qui stepped outside. The fall day was cool, but the sun felt lovely on Dolly's face. As they walked to the corner, she said, "I'm sorry about what Mrs. Field said."

"I know who you are, Miss Cameron," Yuen Qui said in her accented English. "You are *not* Mrs. Field."

"Thank you," Dolly whispered.

They hailed a buggy, and when they arrived at the harbor, Dolly was already feeling better. She breathed in slowly and exhaled slowly.

Moments later, she and Yuen Qui stepped into the immigration office.

The immigration officer looked up and adjusted his spectacles. "Thank you for coming." He nodded to Yuen Qui. "We have a fifteen-year-old girl in custody. When I asked her where she's from, she started crying. Maybe it will help her to speak to a woman. Find out if she's speaking the truth."

Dolly didn't hesitate. "Show us to the girl."

The immigration officer led Dolly and Yuen Qui past two doors, then stopped at the third. Dolly entered the room to find a Chinese girl sitting alone on a bench. Her hair was parted in the middle, and she had two braids curving over her shoulders. She clutched a small satchel against her.

Dolly sat next to her and smiled. "Hello, I'm Donaldina Cameron. I'm from the mission home in San Francisco. What's your name?"

The girl's gaze darted to Yuen Qui as she interpreted Dolly's words. Then the girl looked back at Dolly.

"Donaldina Cameron," Dolly said again, then she pointed at the girl's chest. "What's your name?"

"Jean Ying," the girl whispered.

"And where are you from, Jean Ying?" Dolly asked.

Another darted glance at Yuen Qui as she interpreted.

"I am from Canton."

Dolly nodded. "Wonderful. Are you here with your family?"

"They are waiting for me," Jean Ying said in a halting tone. "My uncle has a job for me at his restaurant. They are waiting for me."

No matter the questions that Dolly asked, Jean Ying kept giving the same answers.

Finally, Dolly nodded. "We wish you all the best in San Francisco, Jean Ying. But if you ever need help, please send word to 920 Sacramento Street."

Jean Ying lifted her chin, although her dark brown eyes were wary.

Dolly sensed that the immigration officer was right. Something wasn't right. Jean Ying was holding back information, but there was nothing else Dolly could do.

After Dolly and Yuen Qui left the office, they returned to the mission home. The closer they got, the more Dolly thought about Mrs. Field's cruel words. Just before they reached the front steps leading to the porch, Dolly stopped Yuen Qui. "Your people are *not* a burden," Dolly said quietly. "All humans need a helping hand now and then on this earth. Right now is the time that your people are in need. The Lord has given me the chance to help."

Yuen Qui clasped Dolly's hand. "Thank you, Miss Cameron. You are good to us."

"Now, let's go speak to Ah Cheng and Tien Fu so they understand how important they are to me too."

During the next few weeks, Dolly avoided Mrs. Field as much as possible. She wanted to report to the board about what Mrs. Field said at the staff meeting.

One night, after everyone in the house had gone to bed, Dolly sat in the dining room alone as the sun set. If she had known all that she did now about Mrs. Field, would that have changed her mind about becoming the director? Dolly sighed. It was impossible to change the past. She just had to continue forward, one step at a time.

"Miss Cameron, there you are." Ah Cheng came into the room. "There is a man here to see you at the front door."

"Oh." Dolly had been so lost in her thoughts, she hadn't heard anyone knock. It was completely dark now, and she knew that no good news came at night.

The Chinese man at the door held out a red handkerchief. His hair was cut short, jagged against his forehead. His deep brown eyes were desperate, and he kept glancing toward the street. Was he afraid that someone would see him at 920?

"Can you help?" the man asked in Chinese, and Ah Cheng interpreted. "A girl was sold to a very bad house. She says that you will come get her. But the tong are watching for you. Now they have their own lawyers."

Dolly didn't have any idea who the girl was, but it didn't matter. She took the handkerchief from the man.

"We will come," she said. "Tonight."

After Ah Cheng interpreted the English to Chinese, the man bowed deeply. "Thank you. Thank you." He bowed again. "I did not know what to expect. The highbinders call you Fahn Quai."

"What does he mean?" Dolly asked Ah Cheng after she'd interpreted.

"Fahn Quai means *foreign ghost*."

The man continued. "They tell the paper daughters on the ships that you will capture them. You will force them to eat poison. They make the girls afraid of you before they arrive in San Francisco. They tell them to run and hide if they see you coming with the policemen."

Dolly's breath stilled. "What do *you* think, sir? Am I Fahn Quai?"

A shout came from somewhere outside the building. The man flinched and looked toward the door. When he met Dolly's gaze again, he said, "I think you are an avenging angel. You are the light in the darkness of Chinatown." He bowed. "I am honored to meet you."

Another shout sounded outside.

His face paled. "I must leave. Please, I was never here, and I never spoke to you." He opened the door and disappeared into the black night, leaving Dolly to stare after him.

Ah Cheng didn't say anything as she shut the door and bolted it.

More shouts came from the street. Dolly moved to the high window and peered out. In the darkness, a group of dim figures confronted the man who had just left the mission home. In a flash, a fight broke out.

A gunshot stopped all the commotion.

The men scattered like litter tumbling with the wind. Where

they'd just been standing, a man was lying upon the ground. Crumpled and abandoned.

"Oh no." Dolly pressed a hand to her stomach. The man had just sacrificed his life to deliver his message. "Call the Chinatown Squad," she told Ah Cheng in a strained voice. "There has been a murder on our street. We will also need help for our rescue."

"Should we go out tonight?" Ah Cheng asked.

Dolly still held the red handkerchief. The delivery had cost a man's life tonight—a man who had put his trust in her. She faced Ah Cheng. "We must go out tonight. The tong will not stop at any cost. Neither will we. Tell Officer Cook we'll need as many men as he can spare. And we'll need a search warrant if the tong now have their own lawyers."

Ah Cheng drew in a shaky breath. "I will make the call."

After Ah Cheng left the entryway, a small sound from the landing caught Dolly's attention. She saw a flash of white clothing disappear into the corridor. Tien Fu.

Dolly hurried up the stairs and went directly to the girl's bedroom. The door was locked.

"Tien Fu," Dolly called softly through the door. "Ah Cheng and I are going on a rescue. You will be safe here, I promise."

The door cracked open, and Dolly gazed down at Tien Fu's tearstained face. Beyond her was her sleeping roommate, already in bed.

"I heard the gunfire," Tien Fu whispered.

Dolly's throat tightened. "A man sacrificed his life tonight to help us save another girl. He has brought the mission home honor."

Tien Fu sniffled and wiped at her face.

Dolly put her hand on her shoulder. "Do you want to stay with Yuen Qui?"

Tien Fu nodded and she walked with Dolly to Yuen Qui's bedroom. After explaining the circumstances, Dolly was able to leave the two of them together. Her heart hurt for Tien Fu, but Dolly was also grateful for the girl's growing trust in her.

An hour later, Dolly and Ah Cheng left the mission home. The moon above made the streets a dull silver, like ribbons of paper. As they walked past the location of the murder, Dolly blinked back hot tears.

Three officers waited at the bottom of the hill: Cook, Riordan, and James Farrell.

Officer Cook's expression was grim. "Are you sure you want to go on this rescue, Miss Cameron? One man has already died tonight."

Dolly took a deep breath. "Do you have the search warrant?"

"Yes. But we might meet resistance anyway."

Dolly eyed the officers. Farrell carried an axe, and Riordan and Cook held sledgehammers. "If you're willing to come, then I don't want to back out."

All three officers nodded. "Let's go," Cook said.

It was nearly midnight by the time they reached the narrow three-story house in Chinatown. Lights glowed from inside. Someone was waiting for them.

"We should divide up," Cook said. "I'll knock on the front door. The rest of you find the back entrance. Wait for my signal."

Dolly and Ah Cheng slipped around the back of the house with Farrell and Riordan.

No lights glowed from the back of the house. They waited in the inky darkness for Cook's whistle, but no signal came.

After several moments, Dolly whispered, "We need to go inside the back way. It's been too long."

"I'll try the door," Farrell said, but it was locked. "Stand back." He swung his axe against the door latch until it broke.

It was now completely dark inside, though moonlight glimmered enough to see the back stairs. Dolly rushed into the house.

Above, sounds of scuffling feet and muffled voices reached them. They hurried up the stairs.

"They're going to hide her," Dolly whispered. "Hurry." She started opening doors as they moved down the hall, but all the rooms were empty.

She stepped into the last room, and Farrell's flashlight revealed a long crack in the far wall. Dolly pressed on the crack, and it turned out to be a secret panel that opened. "There's a ladder here to the roof."

With one hand grasping her skirts, she started up the ladder.

The two officers and Ah Cheng followed, but Dolly was the first to the rooftop. Two buildings over, three dark forms crouched on the roof. Knotting her skirt in her hand, Dolly made a running leap toward the next rooftop.

The officers followed. The moonlight was her only guide, and she leapt to the next roof. Now the three people ahead of her stood up and ran.

Then they stopped. Two of the people tried to push the third person off the roof. The girl screamed and wrenched away from her captors.

"Stop!" Dolly ran straight at them. "Let her go!" She lunged and grabbed the girl's arm.

Farrell caught up, yelling, "Everyone stop! I have a warrant!"

Dolly held on to the trembling, crying girl, who opened her fist and revealed the other half of the handkerchief.

Her captors backed away from Farrell. They were two women, and one of them spat on the roof. "You are dead to all Chinese if you go with Fahn Quai."

If these slave owners considered *her* a foreign ghost for demanding freedom, then she'd gladly accept whatever name they called her, as long as the enslaved women were freed. Dolly tightened her grip around the girl's thin shoulders.

"Come with us," Ah Cheng said from the other roof. "You will be safe."

Once they reached the street level and rejoined Officer Cook, Dolly realized this girl was Jean Ying. The same fifteen-year-old from the immigration office. Another paper daughter.

At the mission home, Dolly and Ah Cheng helped Jean Ying bathe and dress. The abuse marks on the girl's skin were hard to look at. Dolly felt like another crack had been added to her heart. When they brought Jean Ying to the kitchen, Tien Fu was waiting with a plate of food for the trembling girl.

"You will be safe here," Tien Fu told the girl in soft Chinese.

Dolly's eyes pricked with tears to see Tien Fu speaking to Jean Ying in such a gentle way.

Jean Ying ate everything they placed before her at the table, and all the while Tien Fu sat next to her.

"I am sorry I lied to you," Jean Ying said in a faint voice when she at last looked up.

Jean Ying's entire story came out through Ah Cheng's interpreting. Her father was a wealthy manufacturer in Canton, and she was kidnapped one day when walking to meet some friends.

"I am from Zhejiang," Tien Fu said. "My Lao Ye sold me to pay his gambling debt."

Jean Ying blinked. "I am sorry for you too."

Tien Fu only nodded.

It was the first time Dolly had heard Tien Fu speak of what had happened to her so long ago. Dolly looked from Tien Fu to Jean Ying. They were the same ages, yet Tien Fu was healthy, educated, fearless. Jean Ying was malnourished and frightened. But oh, so very brave.

"The kidnappers took me to Hong Kong," Jean Ying said, her voice just above a whisper. "They sold me for one hundred seventy-five Hong Kong dollars to an agent. On the boat to Gold Mountain, the agent told me to memorize a new family name."

Tien Fu patted the girl's arm. "We all have new names."

Jean Ying's tears started then. "I don't want a new name, and I don't want to be in America. I want to go back to my family."

Dolly reached for Jean Ying's hand. "We will write to your family and tell them you are here."

Jean Ying nodded, then she lowered her head. Her shoulders shook with sobs.

Tien Fu and Ah Cheng both wiped at the tears on their faces.

When Jean Ying finally lifted her head, she said, "What if they don't want me back? I am a soiled dove now."

Dolly tightened her hold on the girl's hand. "You have done nothing wrong, dearest Jean Ying. Your family will be overjoyed to know you are still alive. That is all that matters."

Chapter Sixteen

SOUND OF THE GONG

SAN FRANCISCO, MARCH 1900

Tien Fu was reading a storybook to Kang one night when the gong sounded throughout the house. When someone came to the mission home with a warrant to arrest a former slave girl, Miss Cameron rang the gong to signal the undocumented girls to hide.

"Stay here," Tien Fu told Kang. She knew he wouldn't be in danger, but the newly arrived girls might be. Miss Cameron was still waiting for guardianship papers on them. But even if those papers were secured, sometimes the arrest warrant meant the girl would still be taken into custody. Of course those girls hadn't stolen from their owners. The warrant for them was merely a way their owners used to take them back.

The mission home had prepared the rescued slave girls for situations like this. They had practiced the drill regularly and knew how to respond to the gong signal. Those who had been in the mission home for at least a few months or longer, like Tien Fu, met in the hallway and together filed down the stairs in an orderly manner and stood in the parlor to be inspected. Their hope was to curb any searches throughout the house.

The new girls would hide somewhere else. This included seventeen-year-old Chan Juan, who had been forced to work in a brothel—a place where men paid money to visit girls who were trapped in a bad life. Chan Juan had arrived at the mission home only three days earlier.

On her way down to the parlor, Tien Fu found Chan Juan at the landing, gripping the banister as the other girls moved past her. Panic and terror filled her eyes.

Tien Fu understood the fear and the confusion. She wished none of this was real either—being sold into slavery, being abused by her owner, being robbed of dignity. Even though Tien Fu didn't know Chan Juan well, they were bound by a shared experience that only those who had survived slavery truly understood.

Chan Juan was so new to the place, Tien Fu was certain one of the late-night visitors was her owner. If anyone really needed to hide tonight, it would be Chan Juan.

Miss Cameron was speaking through the closed door to their visitors. It would only be a matter of minutes before she would have to unbolt the door and let the men inside.

Tien Fu wasn't going to let Chan Juan's former slave owner take her away. Having lived her life both in and out of the mission home, Tien Fu knew the day-and-night difference. She wouldn't want to go back to being owned by any human being. She was not a thing. She was not property. No one was. The haunted look in Chan Juan's eyes spurred Tien Fu into action. Reaching for Chan Juan's hand, Tien Fu spoke softly, "Don't be afraid. I'll help you hide so you don't have to go back to slavery."

Chan Juan turned her fearful gaze on Tien Fu. "Where do I hide? They will find me!"

"No, they won't find you if you come with me"—Tien Fu squeezed Chan Juan's hand—"Do you trust me?"

Their gazes connected.

Below, all the girls had already assembled in the parlor.

Miss Cameron said to the people outside, "You must have a warrant, or I won't open the door."

"Now," Tien Fu said. "We must go *now*."

Chan Juan took a shaky breath and nodded.

"Hold my hand and don't let go." Tien Fu led her down the stairs. She could see the shadowy forms of the visitors through the upper glass of the double doors. Terror lanced through her, but she pushed it back.

As Miss Cameron pulled the first bolt, Tien Fu led Chan Juan past the parlor where the other girls had gathered in silent fear. Tien Fu didn't stop, neither did she let go of her friend. "We need to hide in the basement."

"The basement?" Chan Juan tugged on Tien Fu's hand, stalling them. "I can't go down there!"

Tien Fu understood her fear of the underground. When she was little, her parents had warned her about going into a basement. Chinese feng shui theory taught that yang energy is positive, bright, and lively. Like heat, it naturally flowed upward. But yin energy was negative, dark, and cold, so it naturally flowed downward. That's why people buried the dead underground—because life, light, and energy had gone out of the body. Some Chinese people believed that ghosts lived in underground spaces, such as a basement, lurking and haunting the living.

"Your owner won't dare go down there, so it's the best place to hide," Tien Fu assured Chan Juan. "Don't worry. I'll stay with you."

Chan Juan bit her lip.

The second door bolt sounded. Chan Juan must have heard it too. Without another moment of hesitation, she nodded to Tien Fu and followed her through the basement door. Once it shut, they were both plunged into darkness. But Tien Fu knew the way.

"Step down," she whispered. "Step down again."

They bumped into each other a couple of times until they reached the open area underneath the house.

"Keep walking," Tien Fu said as she felt along the wall and

guided Chan Juan to one of the far corners. "We'll sit here and wait."

In the dark, cold, dank basement, they huddled together and listened for movement above. The men were definitely inside the house now, their thudding footsteps audible. Chan Juan shivered. Tien Fu put her arm around her new friend, pulling her close. It didn't matter that Tien Fu was three years younger—right now, she was the protector.

It sounded like the men were banging through cupboards in the kitchen, knocking over stuff in the pantry, checking behind folding doors and slamming them. Then the footsteps faded, but Tien Fu wasn't fooled. The men were likely searching upstairs.

She imagined they had a police officer with them—ironically someone from the Chinatown Squad too. They had to serve the search warrant though. Yuen Qui had told Tien Fu that the police officers weren't ever happy about it when they had to work with the slave owners.

"Are they gone?" Chan Juan whispered in a trembling voice. Her body was shaking, so Tien Fu rubbed her shoulder.

"They're searching upstairs. Too bad they won't find you there."

It was meant to be a joke, but Chan Juan only started crying.

"Shhh—" Tien Fu hushed. "We need to stay as quiet as possible."

Chan Juan sniffled, then drew in a deep breath. "All right."

The minutes dragged on, and the air around them turned colder and colder.

Tien Fu's ears were attuned to every sound in the house. The men hadn't returned to the main floor yet. Were they looking in every drawer and closet in every bedroom?

Quietly Tien Fu hummed one of the hymns she'd learned in Bible class. She couldn't remember all the words—something about Jesus. After she got through the first verse, Chan Juan asked, "What's that song called?"

"I can't remember," Tien Fu said. "But it makes me feel peaceful."

"Me too," Chan Juan said.

So Tien Fu hummed through another verse, then abruptly stopped when she heard footsteps again. The men were on the main level. Would they come to the basement next? It wasn't unheard of. There was a tunnel only about ten feet away that Tien Fu would take Chan Juan in if the basement door opened. She held her breath, listening to every footstep, every murmur of sound, but the basement door didn't open.

When they heard the thud of the front door shutting, relief flowed through Tien Fu. Still, she waited, listening for the lighter footsteps of one of the staff members. Finally, they came.

The basement door opened, and someone came down the stairs, holding a gas lamp. The orange glow bounced against the walls as they neared.

"Chan Juan?" Miss Cameron called out. "They're gone now. You're safe."

Chan Juan moved to her feet, and Tien Fu rose beside her.

"Tien Fu? You're down here too?"

Tien Fu nodded.

"I was afraid to come down alone," Chan Juan said.

Chan Juan was still shaking, so Tien Fu kept ahold of her hand.

"I'm so glad you're safe," Miss Cameron said in a gentle tone. "Thank you for helping her, Tien Fu. You saved her from being taken away by a cruel man."

Tien Fu nodded. Her memories were still vivid of having been passed on from one owner to another, finding hope and joy with the Roos family briefly and then being passed on again and again to abusive owners. She wouldn't want Chan Juan to have the same experience, being robbed of the hope and joy she'd found in the mission home.

Miss Cameron took Chan Juan's other hand and together they walked out of the basement.

Some of the other girls were still in the parlor. They gathered around Chan Juan, hugging her and patting her on the back.

"I'll get her some tea," Tien Fu said, then slipped into the kitchen.

As she worked, she felt something swell inside of her. Tonight she had not thought twice about helping another person—someone she didn't even know. She had shown care, kindness, and love. As Tien Fu measured tea leaves into a teapot, a renewed realization came to her: Even though she had been a victim, she was also a survivor. And tonight she had chosen to create a new identity for herself.

This night, she was a rescuer.

Chapter Seventeen

SAFE AND SOUND

SAN FRANCISCO, MARCH 1900

Dolly double-checked the bolts on the front doors of the mission home again. She had locked them, but it gave her peace of mind to check one more time. An hour had passed since Chan Juan's former owner and the policemen had left. All the girls had returned to their rooms. Tien Fu had made Chan Juan mint tea and then helped her get settled into bed. The angst of the evening was over—until the next raid came for another girl. Another night, another search . . . it would all happen again.

Tien Fu had become more responsible over the past months. Dolly wouldn't say they were close though. Tien Fu still had some trust issues. But Dolly was impressed with Tien Fu. Undeniably, the fourteen-year-old girl had taken on the role of a protector tonight. She might have been scared of doing some things, but venturing into the basement wasn't one of them. It was no small feat to convince Chan Juan to hide in the basement when it was clear that, like most of the girls in the mission home, she had been petrified of entering that space, believing that evil spirits lived underground. Dolly was proud of Chan Juan for her bravery.

Dolly exhaled as she headed toward the kitchen. Everything in there had been cleaned up, although the teakettle still contained just enough hot water for a cup for Dolly. She reached for a teacup and filled it halfway with the hot water, then she chose her favorite tea mix of orange blossom herbs from Tien Fu's blend. Before she could take the first sip, Mrs. Field walked into the kitchen. She wore her dark-colored dressing gown, making the edges of her face sharper. She had stayed in her room the entire day. This was the first time Miss Cameron had seen her.

"We need to have a serious talk, Miss Cameron," the director said. "We can't have this kind of trouble in the mission home, men coming in and out at all hours, searching the place, upsetting our schedule . . . It needs to stop."

"I agree," Dolly said.

Mrs. Field narrowed her eyes and set her hands on her hips. "Then what are you going to do about it? I have suggestions, but please tell me your ideas."

Those words were like barbed wire slicing across Dolly's skin.

"I can speak to the police about only allowing warrants to be served in the afternoons so they won't disrupt sleep or the morning classes."

Mrs. Field let out a dry laugh. "Do you think the police will listen to *you*? If you have so much influence in Chinatown, perhaps you should just stand on the street corner and tell people to stop buying and selling girls."

Dolly's head hurt. Her chest ached. Her eyes burned. She was so tired. Mostly, she couldn't stand talking about this with such an insulting person.

But Mrs. Field wasn't finished. "We need to draw the line at harboring criminals. They might bring harm to the other girls."

Dolly couldn't be silent now. "They're *not* criminals, Mrs. Field! Each girl is valuable here. As long as I work at the mission home, every single girl will be protected to the best of my ability."

Mrs. Field scoffed. "In the next raid, there'll be no hiding in the basement. We might as well give up the girl and save everyone the trouble of being searched and kept up at all hours of the night."

Dolly bit the inside of her cheek to calm down her emotions. Then in an even voice, she said, "I'll not allow that to happen, Mrs. Field. Being the director doesn't mean you get to choose who lives here and who doesn't."

Mrs. Field's eyes narrowed. "I'll be submitting a complaint to the board about this, Miss Cameron. Be ready to face the consequences."

Dolly smiled, although her heart was pounding. "I look forward to it."

Mrs. Field swept out of the room. Dolly was glad to see her go.

As soon as the director retired for the night, Dolly sat at the typewriter and wrote her *own* report. She'd mail it to the board, and—come what may—Dolly would either sink or swim with the consequences.

She closed her eyes and released a long breath, then she said a quick prayer. She hoped that their attorney, Henry E. Monroe, would be able to get the guardianship papers tomorrow for Chan Juan. It had to happen. They couldn't lose the young woman. *Please, Lord.*

"Miss Cameron?" Ah Cheng said from the doorway.

Dolly opened her eyes. Ah Cheng's frown told Dolly this wasn't good news.

Ah Cheng walked into the kitchen and handed Dolly a rumpled piece of paper. "This message just came."

Dolly was so tired, she didn't even know if she could read anything right now. "Can it wait until morning?"

Ah Cheng shook her head. "No, it can't wait. I am sorry."

With strength she didn't know she had left, Dolly took the note. The message said that someone would be waiting at the bottom of the hill to lead the way to a girl who needed help.

Dolly met Ah Cheng's gaze. "We cannot call the Chinatown Squad—they were just here with the search warrant."

"I know," Ah Cheng said. "We still need to go."

"Then I will be ready in a few minutes."

When the two women left the mission home, the sky was black and stars glittered overhead. Dolly would have enjoyed a beautiful spring night like this if she wasn't going on a rescue, likely to a terrible place keeping slave girls.

The Chinese man at the bottom of the hill waited alone. He was dressed in dark clothing with a long queue down his back. The man greeted Ah Cheng in Chinese. He nodded to Dolly but said nothing more to her. He motioned for them to follow. He walked briskly, and Dolly kept up easily with his long strides.

They walked several streets, cut into the narrow Baker Alley, and as they passed a few people on the sidewalk, Dolly felt their eyes on her. Her height, pale skin, and auburn hair made her stand out. She and Ah Cheng walked closer together as if they could protect each other better. The buildings on both sides of the alley rose up two or three levels. Someone was crying. In another building, two men were arguing.

The cold air prickled Dolly's skin, and she wished she had more protection tonight. Her nose wrinkled when the scent of opium drifted through an open window. The scent singed her throat and her eyes watered.

It wasn't too late to turn back. Maybe she and Ah Cheng could come the following night. Dolly stole a glance at the interpreter. Her expression was set with determination. If Ah Cheng could walk this alley, so could Dolly.

Their steps continued forward, one after the other, keeping up with their guide. The man slowed as they approached a building that Dolly knew was a gambling den. From the outside, all seemed quiet, but once the man opened the door, music and laughter spilled out.

"Come," the man said in Chinese.

Dolly stepped forward with Ah Cheng. But the man pointed to Ah Cheng and shook his head.

"You must go without me," Ah Cheng whispered to Dolly. "I won't be welcome."

Dolly looked about the dark street. Other men loitered about. The opium scent was strong. "I don't want to leave you here alone."

Ah Cheng lifted her chin. "Then hurry."

Dolly had no choice. She walked into the gambling den behind their guide. The thick smoke of both opium and tobacco burned her throat and chest. Men sat at the gambling tables that dotted the room. Behind some of the men stood young women dressed in fine silk clothing, their eyes outlined with colored makeup and their cheeks rosy.

"Fahn Quai," someone hissed. Dolly stiffened at the nickname. Someone laughed and pointed at her. Everyone was looking at her now.

Where had her guide gone? Dolly scanned the faces of the men at the tables as they tapped their fists on their gambling tables. *Thump. Thump. Thump.*

Dolly's heart raced. What did this all mean? Where was the guide? Where was the girl she was supposed to rescue? Had she been led into a trap?

With foreboding, Dolly realized that some of these men were members of the tong. Their modern American clothing of stylish suits and hats gave them away. And now she was in the middle of them with no policemen.

Dolly took a step back, then another. Nothing was good about this situation. Then she spotted the guide against the far wall. He grasped the arm of one of the girls who looked about eighteen years old. She was staring at Dolly with eyes that were decorated with thick makeup but filled with deep fear. She wore a lovely silk dress, but on her thin wrist was a frayed and knotted bracelet made of silk.

The thumping on the tables continued. Now the men chanted "Fahn Quai," and it sent a shiver through Dolly. She had to act now!

She weaved through the tables until she reached the girl's side. "Do you know who I am?" Dolly said in memorized Chinese.

The girl nodded.

"What's your name?" Dolly continued.

"Kum Quai."

"Kum Quai," Dolly repeated. "I'll take you to safety if you allow me."

The girl nodded once again. She grasped Dolly's hand.

The thumping and chanting had stopped. All eyes turned on them. Dolly knew that whoever this girl's owner was, he was not here. They had to escape fast before someone alerted him.

"Come." Dolly led the girl out, past the tables, past the heckling men.

One man grabbed Kum Quai's silk dress. She cried out and gripped Dolly's hand harder. The other girls laughed as if it were a game. But Dolly knew this was no game. She didn't know where the guide had gone, but she had no time to look for him. She pushed through the door once she reached it. Outside, Dolly drew in a deep breath of clean night air.

Ah Cheng immediately grasped Kum Quai's other hand.

By now, a crowd had gathered at the end of the alley. Dolly's heart raced. Would someone try to stop them? Thankfully, Kum Quai walked quickly alongside them. It felt like the longest walk of Dolly's life.

On the way out of Chinatown, Kum Quai hardly spoke, even when Ah Cheng asked questions. As soon as they reached the mission home, Dolly bolted the doors while Ah Cheng told the girl they were going to give her a bath and some food.

Kum Quai nodded, looking dazed.

As they headed up the stairs, Ah Cheng told Dolly, "The people on the streets said that Kum Quai's owner is away in San Jose. He is a powerful man."

Dread rippled through Dolly. The man certainly wouldn't let his beautiful slave girl be taken from him. Tomorrow Dolly would need Attorney Monroe to file for guardianship of both Chan Juan and Kum Quai.

Once the bath was ready, Kum Quai stepped in and, shockingly, started to pull at her hair. She yanked and yanked until she was crying.

"No, no, Kum Quai," Dolly cried. "Don't hurt yourself!" She reached for the girl's slippery arms, but she only turned away.

"What's she doing?" Dolly asked Ah Cheng, who talked with Kum Quai in a gentle voice.

Ah Cheng looked over at Dolly. "She says she doesn't want to be beautiful anymore. If she pulls out her hair, her slave owner won't want her back."

The breath left Dolly and she tried to come up with an answer. "Tell her we can cut it short."

This seemed to calm Kum Quai so that they could finish bathing her. Once she was wrapped in a clean robe, they led her to the kitchen.

There, Tien Fu was making hot tea. It had become her self-appointed habit for the late-night rescues.

As Dolly and Ah Cheng walked into the kitchen with Kum Quai, Tien Fu turned to look at the new girl. The teacup dropped from her hands and hit the counter.

"Tien Fu, are you all right?" Dolly asked.

Tien Fu's mouth opened. Kum Quai had halted and was staring at Tien Fu.

"Tai Choi?" Kum Quai whispered.

"Kum Quai?" Tien Fu said.

"Yes," Kum Quai said, nodding and laughing. "Yes!"

Tien Fu rushed to the girl and they embraced.

Dolly stared at the pair in wonder. "How do they know each other?" she asked Ah Cheng.

"I don't know," Ah Cheng said.

When the girls drew apart, they spoke so rapidly that there was no way for Dolly to follow. Dolly had never seen Tien Fu smile so much, and that alone filled her heart.

Slowly, the story came out as Ah Cheng interpreted for Dolly. The two girls had met in Shanghai, after Tien Fu had been sold to a woman there named Yi. Kum Quai was living in a neighboring house with the Rooses, a rich family that had taken her in, along with other orphans. Two years ago, in 1898, a man named Little Pete had recruited Kum Quai in Shanghai to participate in the Trans-Mississippi International Exposition. She was scheduled to return to China when the exhibit ended, but Little Pete forced her to work in San Francisco as a mui-tsai.

Tien Fu was furious at what had happened to Kum Quai, but she was overjoyed to have been reunited with her.

"How are your feet?" Kum Quai asked Tien Fu.

Tien Fu pulled up her pant legs and lifted her bare feet.

Kum Quai smiled. "So much better, my friend." She held up her wrist, displaying the frayed silk bracelet that looked like it was barely staying on.

Tien Fu's mouth fell open. "You still have it?"

Kum Quai laughed. "Yes!"

Then, from the secret pocket of her shirt, Tien Fu drew out a hairpin that Dolly had never seen before.

Kum Quai gasped, laughed again, then hugged Tien Fu.

"Do you want it back?" Tien Fu asked, new tears on her face.

"Oh no," Kum Quai said, putting her hand over Tien Fu's. "I am cutting all of my hair off tonight."

Tien Fu blinked in surprise, but Kum Quai was determined. So Ah Cheng found scissors and asked Kum Quai to sit in a chair.

Tien Fu sat next to Kum Quai and held her hand as Ah Cheng cut off her long silky black hair. Kum Quai looked content with her decision, shown by the bright spark of joy in her eyes.

After Kum Quai had eaten two almond cookies and finished her tea, Dolly showed her where she'd be sleeping. Dolly knew she should retire to bed herself, but she headed to the office where she recorded Kum Quai's rescue. Tonight's rescue had been so fearful, and there was guardianship paperwork to do tomorrow, but Dolly knew the Lord's hand was in every step. This was the work He had called her to do, and He would help her do it.

When Dolly went up the stairs to her bedroom, she found Tien Fu sleeping outside Kum Quai's bedroom door. Dolly hesitated. Should she leave her be? Finally, she walked away, leaving Tien Fu to remain close to her friend.

The following week, soon after breakfast had been cleared and the girls had gone to class, someone knocked at the double front doors. Dolly had ordered that only she be allowed to answer the door that week. Through the upper glass, Dolly could see it was an official visit. She didn't recognize the constable or the Chinese man who stood on the front step. Dolly rang the warning gong. Since it was daytime, everyone would be alerted to stop lessons and assemble in the parlor. There was no time to hide in the basement.

Dolly was relieved that she had secured guardianship papers for both Chan Juan and Kum Quai. She pulled the bolts, then cracked open the door. "Yes?"

The constable's brown eyes assessed her. "We have a warrant issued by the San Jose court of law for Kum Quai's arrest."

Dolly felt like the air around her had whooshed out of the house. She kept her chin lifted, although she wanted to shut the door on the men and lock them out forever, but she couldn't do that. Reluctantly, she opened the door a bit wider to take the warrant. The man on the doorstep named Chung Bow had charged Kum Quai with grand larceny.

Even if she contacted their lawyer right now, Kum Quai would have to appear before a San Jose judge. Not even guardianship papers could protect the girl from a court date. Still, Dolly had to try. "There has been a mistake. This girl is not here."

"What's this?" Mrs. Field said, striding into the foyer.

Dolly grimaced and handed over the warrant.

Mrs. Field read it, then said, "They have a legal right to come in." She eyed the constable. "There's no need to search the house. All the girls have gathered in the parlor."

Dolly had no choice but to stand aside.

The constable and Chung Bow followed the sounds of the gathered girls.

Dolly felt helpless as she watched the constable and Chung Bow stand before the girls and women in the parlor. Kum Quai, with her shorn hair, stood next to Tien Fu. Dolly could only pray that the guardianship papers would make her safe.

Chung Bow snatched the warrant and held it in front of Kum Quai. He barked short words at her in Cantonese.

"Is this her?" the constable asked.

Chung Bow nodded.

"Wait!" Dolly said. "We have official guardianship papers for the girl. I will bring her on the court date to face—"

"We will take her now." The constable grasped Kum Quai's arm and tugged her toward the entryway.

A couple of the younger girls burst out crying. Dolly's stomach flipped, and it felt like her heart had plunged to her feet. Kum Quai hadn't made a sound, but her expression was terror-stricken. Tien Fu stood with her hands clenched into fists, silent tears in her eyes.

Mrs. Field stood to the side of the room, her arms folded, her lips pursed.

Dolly's gaze connected with Ah Cheng, then with Yuen Qui. None of them could do anything. Dolly couldn't bear this. She hurried after the trio. Before the door shut, she grasped the edge. "I'm going with her," she called back to the mission home staff. "Someone send a message to Attorney Monroe. Tell him I'm going to need help in San Jose."

"Miss Cameron." Ah Cheng rushed into the hallway. "You will be—"

But Dolly didn't wait. She ran toward the buggy where the men had loaded Kum Quai. "I'm coming too," she said in a single breath. "I am the girl's guardian."

"That's unnecessary," the constable said.

Before he could stop her, Dolly climbed into the buggy and sat next to Kum Quai. Dolly grasped her hand, and the girl buried her face against Dolly's shoulder.

The buggy started forward, and Dolly's heart drummed with fear of the unknown. The drive to San Jose was fifty miles. This would take the rest of the day and most of the night. Dolly wished she'd brought a shawl or something warm to drape over Kum Quai.

The buggy stopped in Palo Alto to change horses. While there, the constable announced that a judge had agreed to hear the case. So Dolly and Kum Quai entered the cold courthouse with the constable and Chung Bow.

A judge with graying hair and thick eyebrows met them. He folded his arms as the constable explained the charges. "We will need to assemble a jury and witnesses," the judge said, glancing over at Dolly and Kum Quai.

Dolly stepped forward. "I am witness enough. We can hold a trial right now."

The judge shook his head. "If we can assemble a jury

tomorrow, we'll hold the trial here. But the girl will have to spend the night in jail."

Dolly couldn't leave the poor frightened Kum Quai, who couldn't understand the words of the judge. "I will stay with her, then."

The judge raised a single brow. "As you wish."

With that, Dolly was on her way to jail.

Chapter Eighteen

A NIGHT IN JAIL

PALO ALTO, 1900

The hardpacked dirt of the Palo Alto jail would be their bed for the night.

Dolly looked around the locked cell inside a small shack behind the court building. There was no latrine. A few boxes were stacked in the corner, and bits of lumber were scattered about. There was a bucket with stagnant water. Dolly sniffed it, then tasted the water. It was stale, but not bitter.

"Here, drink some." Dolly held the bucket to Kum Quai.

After Dolly drank some of the water too, she crossed to the boxes in the corner. A folded blanket sat on top of a box. It smelled musty and there were mice holes chewed in it.

But the blanket would be better than nothing. Dolly flattened the cardboard boxes and arranged them upon the ground. "Lie down here, Kum Quai." She knew that the girl wouldn't understand her English, so Dolly motioned with her hands.

Kum Quai stepped forward, her arms wrapped around her torso. She was trembling either from cold or fear or both.

Dolly rubbed a hand over the girl's back. "We'll be all right, Kum Quai. We need sleep. Tomorrow everything will look better."

Kum Quai might not understand Dolly's English, but she nodded and knelt on the boxes. Then she lay on her side and closed her eyes. Dolly draped the threadbare blanket over her.

Dolly sat on the dirt floor, her back to the wooden wall. She drew her knees up and once again wished she'd brought warmer clothing for the both of them. Resting her chin on her knees, she closed her eyes. She wouldn't sleep, she was sure of that, but it was good to hear Kum Quai's breathing relax and soften.

Dolly had never been in a jail cell, and while this was not a regular cell, she felt confined all the same. Locked in. Trapped.

It only made her feel more protective of Kum Quai. What would have happened if Dolly hadn't come along? Her heart ached as she watched Kum Quai sleep. Was this how a mother felt? Protective? Desperate? Hopeful?

Blood-related or not, Kum Quai deserved a mother's protection.

Dolly closed her eyes again. This time she silently prayed for rest and for safety.

She was so tired, so exhausted, so cold. She just wanted this night to be over with. When footsteps sounded outside the jail cell, Dolly lifted her head.

"Who is it?" she called out.

Kum Quai stirred on her cardboard bed.

"Someone is here to pay bail for the Chinese girl," the jailer said.

Dolly recognized the man's raspy tone. All thoughts of sleep and exhaustion left. She scrambled to her feet. "Who?"

"He said he's a friend of Kum Quai," the jailer said.

The breath left Dolly, replaced by dread. She moved to the door. "She has no friends who are men. We will wait here for tomorrow's trial."

But the jailer had other ideas.

Dolly heard the key turning in the lock. "Help me!" she whispered to Kum Quai, who was now sitting up.

Dolly grabbed one of the lumber scraps and propped it against the door. Kum Quai joined her and together they added more lumber pieces to brace against the door.

"Don't come in," Dolly called out in a trembling voice.

The door rattled as the jailer pushed against it. Dolly and Kum Quai shoved the opposite way.

"We reject the bail money," Dolly added.

The jailer left in a huff, and Dolly sagged against the door.

She met Kum Quai's gaze. Dolly reached for the girl's hand. "We will stay here, Kum Quai. We will be safe."

Kum Quai gripped her hand, then whispered, "Lo Mo."

"Yes, I will be your Lo Mo." Tears filled Dolly's eyes. Those two small words said everything that Kum Quai couldn't express. Lo Mo meant *old mother*, but it was an affectionate title.

Then a massive shudder ripped through the door.

Kum Quai screamed.

The jailer had an axe.

Dolly pulled Kum Quai away from the door. They huddled in the corner as the jailer broke a hole through the door. He reached through and pushed aside the lumber.

There was nowhere for the women to go. They were trapped.

"She's coming with me," the jailer growled. "Bail's been paid." He was tall, strong, and Dolly was no match for the bearded man.

He strode forward and wrenched Kum Quai from Dolly's grasp.

Kum Quai burst into tears.

"Don't you touch her!" Dolly yelled, lunging after them.

"Stay out of this!" the jailer barked.

Dolly ran after them, grabbing for Kum Quai. But the jailer seemed to have the power of an ox. He half carried, half dragged

Kum Quai across the dirt yard beneath the moonlit night to where a buggy waited.

Dolly had no idea who was in the buggy. "You are not authorized to do this," Dolly shouted. "She's going to trial tomorrow."

The jailer ignored Dolly and loaded the crying Kum Quai into the buggy.

Dolly grabbed the edges of the buggy door and climbed in too.

Two men were inside, and one of them was restraining Kum Quai as she cried "Lo Mo" over and over.

"Let her go!" Dolly reached for Kum Quai, but the second man shoved Dolly, hard. She grappled for something to hold on to. But the buggy lurched forward, and she tumbled out. She fell onto the road, scraping her arms and bruising her hip.

"Stop now!" Dolly scrambled to her feet, ignoring the aching and throbbing.

The buggy was already moving fast, the horses being whipped into galloping.

Even if Dolly ran, there was no way she could catch up.

She stared after the buggy that carried the crying Kum Quai. How had this happened? How had Dolly lost her?

Slowly she spun, looking for anything or anyone to help her. The jailer had disappeared. She began to walk toward the town lights, limping with pain. Dolly didn't care about her injuries; she only cared about finding someone to track down a kidnapped girl.

Dolly's limping turned to a loping run as she picked up her skirts and headed for a druggist's shop up ahead. The windows were all dark, but maybe someone lived on the second floor. She pounded on the door, then the windows. "Help me!" she cried. "Someone, please help!"

It was the middle of the night, but Dolly didn't care.

Finally, the front door opened a crack. "What's all this about?" an older man said.

"They've taken her." Dolly choked back the threatening sob. "They've kidnapped her."

The man stepped out, rubbing at his face with one hand, spectacles in another. "*Who* was kidnapped?"

Dolly took a gulping breath. "Kum Quai. She's a Chinese girl, and I'm her guardian." She explained the events at the mission home, the charges and the impending trial, how they'd been in the jail cell just down the road. "Can you help me, sir?"

"I'm Dr. Hall," he said. "Let's get you to the hotel down the road. I'll call the sheriff of San Jose and alert him about the traveling group."

They hurried along the silent dark streets to the Larkin Hotel. Dolly's head ached, her throat throbbed, and her body felt weak.

Once they reached the hotel, the proprietor offered her a hotel room.

"I won't be sleeping," Dolly said. "I need to know what's going on the moment it happens."

The proprietor nodded. "I'll fetch you a blanket, then. You can wait on the sofa in the lobby."

Dolly clutched the blanket to her as she listened to Dr. Hall telephoning the sheriff's office. When the call finished, Dr. Hall turned toward her. "The San Jose sheriff is sending a search party to recover your ward."

Dolly's knees nearly buckled. "Thank you. Thank you very much."

"You should rest now, Miss Cameron," Dr. Hall said. "Hopefully, we'll have news by the time the sun is up."

Dolly waited on the sofa, curled up with the blanket. She hated to think of what Kum Quai was experiencing at this very moment. The hours passed, and finally, the shadows of the lobby lifted as the night softened to gray. When the sun rose, Dolly was fully awake again. How had Kum Quai fared? Where was she now?

Dolly stood and paced the lobby. Where was Dr. Hall, and when would she hear something? The sky was orange with dawn by the time Dr. Hall arrived at the hotel.

Next to him walked a police officer.

Neither man looked happy, and Dolly feared the worst. "What is it?" she rasped. "Where is Kum Quai?"

Dr. Hall stopped before her, then took off his spectacles and rubbed his forehead. "Her group was stopped last night by the Palo Alto justice of the peace. And the Chinese men demanded a trial on the roadside."

Dolly blinked. "W-what?"

"The trial was granted by the justice of the peace, but Kum Quai waived the right to a trial and counsel." Dr. Hall cleared his throat. "I'm sorry to say that she pleaded guilty. She was fined five dollars, which was paid by one of her escorts."

Dolly's legs wobbled and she reached for the wall. But it was too far away.

Dr. Hall grasped her upper arm. "Are you all right, ma'am?"

"She doesn't even speak English," Dolly whispered.

"It seems that one of the men with her interpreted."

Dolly didn't know whether to laugh or cry. "Of course he did." She pulled her arm away and walked to the sofa, then turned. Anger pulsed through her. "The girl's *kidnapper* was granted a trial at two thirty in the morning. And now where is she? Abducted again!"

"We do not know where she is, ma'am," the police officer said. "I work here in Palo Alto, and we are trying to find her before . . . "

The expression on Dolly's face told him to stop speaking. Slave girls had been killed for deserting their owners.

"How can we help you, Miss Cameron?" Dr. Hall asked in a

gentle, respectful tone. "Do you need to telephone anyone? Do you need a meal? Do you need an attorney?"

"I have an attorney," Dolly murmured. Was she in a nightmare? How could this be happening? She looked directly at the policeman. "I want to know who is behind all this. We need to find out who filed the charges on behalf of the Chinese owner."

The two men before her promised they would do everything they could to help. Dolly had no choice but to believe them.

Now she did have someone to call. The mission home. She had to tell Mrs. Field what had happened. Dolly hated to think of what Ah Cheng and Yuen Qui would think. And what about Tien Fu? The poor girl—to have been reunited with her friend only to have this terrible abduction happen.

Dolly was so very tired and hungry. She couldn't remember the last time she'd eaten, but she asked to use the hotel phone. The phone rang three times. Four. Five. Why wasn't anyone answering?

Then finally, it was answered.

"Occidental Mission Home, may I help you?"

"Tien Fu?" Dolly said. "Why are you answering the phone? Where is Mrs. Field?"

"Miss Cameron?" Tien Fu said in a rush. "What's happened? Where are you?"

Dolly closed her eyes and exhaled. "I'm in Palo Alto . . . but I need to speak with Mrs. Field. Please call her to the phone."

"She has one of her migraines," Tien Fu said. "Ah Cheng is shopping. Yuen Qui is making tea for Mrs. Field."

Well, Tien Fu would find out soon enough, but Dolly still hesitated. "Can you write down this message? It needs to be very exact. I don't want you to forget anything." It was a silly thing to say to Tien Fu. She'd remember.

"Attorney Monroe needs to call me at the Larkin Hotel."

She continued to tell Tien Fu a short version of Kum Quai being snatched out of jail, then going through a trial on the road.

Tien Fu was very quiet, and Dolly was surprised she didn't ask questions as she spoke.

"Do you understand what I'm telling you, Tien Fu?"

"Yes," Tien Fu whispered.

Was she crying? Dolly wondered. She wanted to cry herself.

"We will find her," Dolly said. "Please believe that. The police here are helping, and Monroe will help too."

"I want to help," Tien Fu said in a strained voice. "Tell me what to do."

Dolly had no answer. "I don't know, dear Tien Fu, I don't know. Right now I think the only thing we can do is pray."

When Dolly hung up with Tien Fu, she felt lighter. She'd delivered the hard news. Finally, she took the hotel proprietor up on the offer of a hotel room to sleep. When she awoke, it was past sundown. She washed up and redid her hair. Then she hurried down to the hotel lobby.

There she discovered that the newspapers had found out about the kidnapping. She sat down in the lobby to read them. One article said that a group of students at the nearby Stanford University were posting handbills announcing a protest:

ON TO PALO ALTO!
OUR REPUTATION IS AT STAKE.
BRING OWN ROPE.
NO. 3 HALL. 8:00 TONIGHT.

Dolly was stunned. Another newspaper article named the city officials involved in the Kum Quai situation. The judge who had ordered Kum Quai to be thrown in jail was named. The jailer was listed, as well as the justice of the peace officer, the San Jose sheriff, and even the lawyer who had filed the charges in the first place.

All the names had been exposed.

"Miss Cameron?" a man said.

Dolly looked up from her chair.

The man standing before her was middle-aged, wearing a gray suit, and smelled of pipe smoke.

"I'm Attorney Weigle." He extended his hand. "I've been on the telephone with Monroe, and I'd like to represent you in this case."

Dolly stood and shook Weigle's hand. "Monroe sent you?"

"Yes, may I sit?" He pointed to the chair opposite her.

"Of course."

They both sat down, and Weigle adjusted his cuffs. "You need to write an official statement about what happened. The sooner you write the events down, the more accurate they will be. Tomorrow we will—"

Shouts came from outside the hotel.

Dolly turned toward the window. A large group of college students was marching down the street.

Dolly rose to her feet along with Weigle. "What's going on?"

"It's the protest against how your Chinese ward was treated. I didn't know it would be this large." He moved toward the front door.

Dolly followed and stepped out of the hotel. Hundreds of college students were marching together. "Oh my goodness," she murmured.

The students carried flashlights, torches, and lanterns. Their shouts echoed along the streets:

"To the jail!"

"Burn it up!"

"Tear it down!"

Their voices and energy crackled like an approaching

thunderstorm. In the middle of the crowd of students, a couple of men were carrying an effigy of a man.

"What's that?" she said.

"It represents the justice of the peace," Weigle said. "The one who let your ward be abducted again."

Dolly watched with mixed fascination and horror as the mob turned down the side streets leading to the jail. She didn't even know she was crying until she felt hot tears running down her cheeks.

"You should go back inside." Weigle turned to her. "I don't know what will happen."

"No," Dolly said in a clear voice. She inhaled the cool evening air. The sight of hundreds of students supporting Kum Quai made Dolly proud. "I want to watch."

She walked along the street, a good distance behind the mob. Weigle kept pace with her. When they arrived at the jail site, the students removed everything from inside the jail cell—the filthy blanket, the boxes, and the wooden boards. They carried the items back to the street, where they lit them on fire, along with the effigy of the justice of the peace.

As the orange flames reached toward the dark sky, the mob started chanting again. Demanding justice. Demanding reform. Promising change.

Dolly couldn't agree more.

Chapter Nineteen
CALL TO ACTION

SAN FRANCISCO, 1900

In the deep of the night, Tien Fu sat on the landing of the stairs, her knees to her chest as she kept watch on the house. Mrs. Field had never come out of her room that day, even when Tien Fu told Ah Cheng and Yuen Qui everything that Miss Cameron had said.

How could Miss Cameron and Kum Quai have gone to jail? They had been nothing but good; they didn't belong in jail. They should be in the mission home, warm, safe, and far away from the awful slave owners.

Tien Fu rocked back and forth, worrying about her newly reunited friend and angry for what was happening to her. Tien Fu had been a witness to the girls coming into the mission home from brothels, gambling dens, cribs, and courtesan houses. These girls were all survivors of the same human trafficking network run by highbinders, brothel owners, tong members, corrupt lawyers, and government officials who took bribes and looked the other way when crimes were committed.

Why? Tien Fu wanted to know. Why did these men and women continue to persecute innocent girls and women? Why did the slave owners pollute Chinatown with corruption, evil, and greed? Didn't they know that the Chinese girls and women deserved happiness too? They never asked to live like rats in dark corners, hunted and sold as if their lives were of little value. Why weren't they granted the same rights as men in Chinatown, to choose the life they wanted for themselves?

The more she thought of Kum Quai and the thousands of others who had been kidnapped or sold into slavery, the more outraged Tien Fu felt. She wanted to help other mui-tsai get out of the miseries forced on them. She wanted to fight against the system. But she was only fourteen and couldn't do some of the things that Miss Cameron could—yet. What could she do now? How could she help? What would free Kum Quai?

Tien Fu closed her eyes and said a quiet, simple prayer. She prayed that Kum Quai would be found. She prayed that Miss Cameron would return to the mission home safely. She prayed that they could find a way to help not only Kum Quai but many others.

When Tien Fu finished her prayer, nothing changed in circumstance, but she felt more calm. She had appealed to the highest power; now she would do her part. She knew what that was now. She would organize the girls in the house into groups with chore assignments, so when Miss Cameron returned, she would have more time to focus on getting Kum Quai back.

The following morning Tien Fu was up before dawn. She'd slept little, but there was a lightness to her step, and she hummed as she prepared breakfast. When the girls and the staff members trickled into the kitchen, Tien Fu beamed. "Eat up, everyone. We have a busy day ahead of us."

She handed a filled plate to Ah Cheng. "Could you please take this to Mrs. Field? Tell her not to worry about getting out of bed today. She can rest all she needs to."

Ah Cheng's brows shot up so high that Tien Fu almost laughed at her comical expression.

"How nice of you," Yuen Qui said. "But what do you mean by having *a busy day*?"

Seeing that she had everyone's attention, Tien Fu shared the conversation she'd had with Miss Cameron the day before and updates on Kum Quai's situation. "Let's pray for their safe return. In the meantime, let's ease Miss Cameron's burden as much as we can. Today we clean. When Miss Cameron returns, we'll ask her what else we can do to help."

Surprisingly, not a single girl complained or looked annoyed, even though cleaning wasn't everyone's favorite task. So Tien Fu divided them into groups and assigned different areas of the house to clean: wiping down the kitchen counters, sweeping the kitchen floor, cleaning the bathrooms, dusting the bookshelves, washing the windows, polishing the staircase banister, and mopping the hallway floors. By the afternoon, the mission home was spotless.

When Miss Cameron arrived, Tien Fu was excited to greet her.

"The house looks wonderful!" Miss Cameron said.

She looked different than the last time Tien Fu had seen her. Thinner—even though that was unlikely. But her eyes were shadowed, her skin more pale than usual.

"We cleaned for you, Miss Cameron," Tien Fu said. "And we're ready to help in more ways too."

The girls came out of different rooms and swarmed to the door to hug Miss Cameron. A toddler clung to Miss Cameron's leg and reached up with open arms. Miss Cameron picked her up and rubbed noses with her, making her giggle.

"I polished the banisters," Jiao reported to Miss Cameron.

"Oh, thank you, Jiao." Miss Cameron looked exhausted, but a kind smile never left her face. She swept her gaze across everyone. "Thank you for all of your help."

"Miss Cameron, I'm so happy you're back!" Lonnie said.

All the others nodded.

Tien Fu was happy too. She'd never thought she would feel this way toward Miss Cameron. Gone were the ill wishes in her heart, leaving only love and respect. It was almost like a gift Tien Fu gave to herself too.

"Where's Kum Quai?" Jiao asked.

Miss Cameron lowered her head and sighed. She motioned the girls to follow her to the parlor. She sat in one of the chairs. Some crowded around. Some sat on the floor. Others stood in the back. Even though Miss Cameron's report wasn't news to Tien Fu, she still listened intently as Miss Cameron shared updates.

The girls gasped at the danger Miss Cameron had faced. They cheered when Miss Cameron told them about the college students from Stanford.

"You see, the world is taking notice of how Kum Quai was treated," Miss Cameron said, triumph in her voice.

Tien Fu didn't miss the worry in Miss Cameron's green eyes though. Until Kum Quai was safely back in the mission home, Tien Fu would continue to worry too.

"Where's Kum Quai now? In jail again?" Lonnie asked, her forehead creased with concern.

"No," Miss Cameron said. "She's with the slave owner who took her away from us. At least, that's my best guess."

"He's a bad man," Dong Ho said, an edge to her voice.

Tien Fu agreed. Kum Quai was alone, and she didn't speak English. How would she survive this? What if someone knew something about Kum Quai's kidnapper but didn't know who to tell?

Tien Fu had had seen posters on the exterior walls of tall buildings before. The mental image of those announcements sparked an idea in her.

"What if we make posters about Kum Quai and put them all

over Chinatown?" Tien Fu suggested. "We'll get the word out. Maybe someone can help us find her."

"Oh, I want to make a poster. Can I?" Jiao asked.

"Me too!" several girls called out.

Miss Cameron smiled at Tien Fu. "Excellent! Let's turn this into a reward. I'll donate the money. People respond better if there's a reward."

Tien Fu's chest warmed. She was ecstatic that her idea was well received and supported. As the girls hurried to the classrooms to collect paper for the posters, Miss Cameron crossed to Tien Fu and set a hand on her shoulder. "Thank you!"

Tien Fu didn't pull away like she used to. She stood tall and said, "I'll do everything to help Kum Quai. She shouldn't be treated like this. None of us should be."

Miss Cameron's eyes were misty as she nodded. "You're right."

Tien Fu swallowed against the new lump in her throat. "I'll take the office typewriter to the dining table." Then she hurried away, eager to embrace this project with a profound purpose.

A few weeks later a trial date was set. Miss Cameron traveled to the courthouse once again to testify against Chung Bow and Wong Fong—the two men behind the kidnapping of Kum Quai—and face their corrupt attorney, Herrington. But a terrible blow was delivered. Herrington announced that Kum Quai had willingly married Chung Bow.

Frustrated, Miss Cameron returned to the mission home and spent hours in her room. When she finally came out, it was obvious that she had been crying. Tien Fu rose from the end of the hallway where she'd been waiting. "What can I do, Miss Cameron?"

Miss Cameron shook her head and said in a near whisper, "I don't know. The marriage license is legal, and there was no objection to it, of course." Her voice was bitter. "No one knows where they are right now."

"Should we make more posters?" Tien Fu asked.

"Not right now." Miss Cameron released a sigh. "I'm putting out word to all of my contacts in Chinatown though. I hope at least one person will come forward with information."

The ensuing days at the mission home were bleak. Tien Fu heard more than one argument between Miss Cameron and Mrs. Field, who thought everyone needed to forget about Kum Quai and her fate. Miss Cameron disagreed, and Tien Fu agreed with Miss Cameron.

One morning, when Tien Fu was cleaning up the kitchen, she overheard Ah Cheng and Miss Cameron talking about a man.

"Jun Ling is keeping his ears open. He'll report to us if he hears anything," Ah Cheng said.

"He's a good man and a good friend to the mission home," Miss Cameron said, then paused. "What is it, Ah Cheng? You are blushing! Do you think of Jun Ling as more than a friend?"

Tien Fu stilled, listening carefully.

"He's asked me to marry him," Ah Cheng said.

Dolly yelped. "Oh my goodness. How wonderful!"

"I know," Ah Cheng whispered. "I never thought I'd . . . find so much happiness."

Even though Tien Fu liked Ah Cheng, she was grateful that it was her and not Yuen Qui who would be getting married and moving away.

A few days later, Miss Cameron received a tip that Wong Fong would be arriving in San Francisco on a train. She rounded up Officer Cook to help apprehend the man.

That day, Tien Fu waited in the foyer for Miss Cameron to return, even though Mrs. Field threatened more chores if Tien Fu didn't return to class. The moment Miss Cameron walked in, Tien Fu jumped up from her chair and burst out, "What happened?"

volunteered. Dr. Gardner asked Kum Quai if she had a *chuck-jee*. I thought it was probably some form of document—"

"It's a legal registration card," Ah Cheng chimed in.

"Yes, thank you!" Miss Cameron said. "Of course, Kum Quai didn't have it because she wasn't supposed to stay in the country after the Trans-Mississippi International Exposition, so she was placed under arrest."

The girls gasped, and Tien Fu stared. Kum Quai had been arrested? Again?

"Don't worry," Miss Cameron continued. "It's good news. It means that Kum Quai had to be taken into custody and protected until another trial." She raised a hand to stop the questions. "But Herrington said that Kum Quai and his sister needed to wait in his buggy during the rest of the proceedings. Wouldn't you know it, but Herrington tried to flee with them, driving the buggy wildly away from the courthouse."

Miss Cameron grinned, and Kum Quai laughed.

"The courtroom went into chaos. Everyone ran outside. Men untied their horses and pursued the buggy. Herrington took a detour but was blocked by a padlocked gate. Both Attorney Herrington and his sister were arrested, and the judge placed Kum Quai in my custody under a federal mandate."

Everyone in the room cheered.

Tien Fu clapped her hands together, then stood to hug Kum Quai. Her friend would have to go to court again. But right now she was home, she was safe. And Tien Fu couldn't have asked for a better blessing.

"We caught Wong Fong at the train station," M
said. "He's in custody and a trial will be set."

"What about Kum Quai?" Tien Fu asked in a bre

"She wasn't with him, but I'm not giving up."

Tien Fu didn't know how she could stand all the
agony, and the uncertainty anymore. But she had no
went through the motions of daily tasks and classes, bu
thoughts, and prayers were continually with Kum Qua

When Miss Cameron went to Wong Fong's tria
once again paced the foyer, hour after hour. She co
sleep, or focus on anything. Twice, Yuen Qui brought h
both times the tea went untouched and turned cold.

Night had fallen by the time Tien Fu heard the ap
carriage. Her heartbeats thumped in her ears as she unl
door and swung it open before Miss Cameron could kno

There, on the front step, were two figures. Miss C
taller silhouette and . . .

"Kum Quai!" Tien Fu shrieked. She stared in disbe
knees wobbled, and she covered her face with her hand
rippled through her. She felt Kum Quai's arms around her.

Other girls came down the stairs, asking questions, cryi
laughing. Everyone was talking at once. Then they followe
Cameron and Kum Quai into the parlor where they sat
sofa. Tien Fu knelt next to them, her hand gripping her fri
She didn't know if she could ever let go. "You're here! I can
lieve it!" Tien Fu must have said it a hundred times.

When everyone had settled down, Miss Cameron expla
"If I hadn't been a witness to the events, I wouldn't have beli
it myself." Her cheeks glowed pink, her eyes bright. She sm
at Kum Quai, who smiled back. "Kum Quai was accompar
by Attorney Herrington's sister to testify in Wong Fong's tr
She was veiled, but I knew it was her. The court requested
interpreter, so Dr. Gardner, an official government interpret

Chapter Twenty

A PLAGUE

SAN FRANCISCO, 1901

Dolly set a newspaper that she'd just read on the table. The staff had gathered for a meeting, and she had something very serious to discuss. She took her seat, looked at Mrs. Field, then to the other staff members.

"The rumors are true," Dolly said. "The bubonic plague has spread and taken root in Chinatown."

Yuen Qui gasped. "Oh no. What will happen?"

"We will stay away from Chinatown," Mrs. Field said. "That's what will happen."

Ah Cheng stood. She walked to the kitchen window and gazed outside, her hands set firmly on her hips. The interpreter would never argue with Mrs. Field directly, but Dolly knew that Ah Cheng wasn't happy about this situation.

None of them were. "Chinatown will go into full quarantine," Dolly said.

Mrs. Field gave a stiff nod. "I agree with the mandate. This will stop the spread of the disease."

Dolly couldn't say if that was true.

Ah Cheng turned from the window. "They quarantined in Hawaii, but it did no good."

"They even burned homes and shops." Dolly folded her arms against the uncomfortable prickle of her skin. "Yet the plague still spread to San Francisco."

Mrs. Field settled her gaze on Dolly. "We will stay out of Chinatown completely, then. Even if someone asks for a rescue. You don't want to put the rest of us at risk, do you?"

"Of course not," Dolly said. But it wasn't that simple—none of this was simple.

"It's decided, then," Mrs. Field added. She stood and walked out of the room, putting an end to the meeting.

Dolly watched the director walk out. The mission home had already stopped the visits from sponsors and donors. These visits allowed the girls to show off their talents, such as singing and recitations. After their performances, the visitors would donate money, and now their funds were lower than ever.

"She might be right," Yuen Qui said in a tentative voice.

Ah Cheng folded her arms. "Should we turn down pleas for help?"

They all knew Mrs. Field's opinion. But now the interpreters were looking at Dolly for answers.

Dolly already knew her answer. "We will go on rescues if we are called. We will find our way around any obstacles. I will not ask this of anyone. Only come if you are comfortable." She didn't want either woman to do something she was afraid of.

"I will go," someone spoke from the kitchen doorway.

Dolly turned to see Tien Fu. The girl had the curves of a young woman of fifteen. She was taller, her scars faded, her intellect sharp and fast. Even though Tien Fu was capable of interpreting—and she had no fear of helping the slaves who were brought to the mission home—Dolly couldn't allow her to go on rescues yet. Tien Fu would draw the attention of the tong in the wrong way. What if she were kidnapped?

Even though it had been a year since Kum Quai's return to

the mission home and the court battle that had allowed her to stay in the country, Dolly wasn't taking any chances with any of her girls.

Yuen Qui smiled sweetly at Tien Fu. "Thank you for the offer, dear Tien Fu. Right now we are being extra careful. We don't know how the plague will affect us all."

Tien Fu's face flushed pink. Dolly worried that Tien Fu's feelings had been hurt.

"If we need you," Yuen Qui continued, "we'd be happy for your help."

Tien Fu nodded, then left the doorway. As silent as a cat, as always.

Dolly exhaled. "It seems that not everyone at the mission home is afraid of the plague."

Both Yuen Qui and Ah Cheng smiled, but there was worry in their eyes.

Dolly's own words haunted her a few days later when a young girl arrived crying on their doorstep. Dolly guessed her to be about nine years old.

"Come inside, child," Dolly said in Chinese. She drew the crying girl into the house and shut the door. Ah Cheng appeared almost immediately.

Ah Cheng crouched in front of the girl and placed her hands on her shoulders. "You need to take deep breaths. Tell us your name."

"Leung Kum Ching," the girl managed to say between broken sobs.

"Hello, Leung Kum Ching," Dolly said, crouching too.

"What's happened?" Ah Cheng asked the girl.

"My sister is dying," Leung Kum said on another sob. "Our owners left her on the street to die. They say she has the plague." She shook her head rapidly. "But she doesn't have the plague."

Dolly glanced at Ah Cheng. Could this girl know the difference? "Ask her how long her sister has been sick."

Ah Cheng asked the question in Chinese, and Leung Kum held up two fingers. "Two days." She wiped at the tears on her cheeks. "She will die if you do not come. The Chinese doctor won't open his door."

Dolly straightened with a sigh. Full quarantine of Chinatown had been in effect for days now. How could anyone leave a young girl outside to die though?

Fear, that's how.

Immunizations had been sent from the US surgeon general in Washington, DC, to San Francisco. But superstitions stopped some people from getting the immunization.

Now even Ah Cheng hesitated.

"I can go," Dolly said in a quiet voice, even though they wouldn't be able to call upon the police for help. "It doesn't sound like the plague."

Ah Cheng looked from the crying girl to Dolly. "I will come with you."

Dolly's heart warmed. What would she do without Ah Cheng always at her side? Dolly reached for the young girl's hand. "Ask which street we'll find her sister on."

Yuen Qui and Tien Fu agreed to feed Leung Kum in the kitchen while Dolly went to find the girl's sister.

She headed out of the mission home in the late afternoon light with Ah Cheng. They didn't want to wait until dark. It might be too late. Even though Dolly was dressed in dark colors and brought a cotton umbrella to conceal her identity, she was still at risk of being noticed as not belonging in Chinatown.

Ah Cheng led Dolly down Sacramento Street and turned onto Sutter. The orange light of the afternoon sun scaled the buildings on both sides. It wasn't long before they saw the barriers in front of the first street of Chinatown.

And there were guards.

Dolly stopped at the corner. "What should we do?" she asked Ah Cheng. "We don't have clearance from the board of health to bring a girl outside the barriers."

"The herbalist's shop has a skylight."

Dolly's heart thumped hard. "Yes, you're right. Let's go."

They hurried in the opposite direction, parallel to the barriers. Dolly kept her gaze lowered, not meeting anyone's eyes.

When they reached the herbal shop, Ah Cheng knocked quickly. The man's wife used to live at the mission home and he'd courted her, then they'd married.

When the herbalist opened his door, Ah Cheng said, "We need help. Can we come in?"

The herbalist ushered them inside.

Once Ah Cheng explained, the herbalist nodded. "You can go through the skylight. The roofs are close together."

The herbalist brought over a stool. Ah Cheng boosted Dolly and she climbed through. Once on the roof, she helped Ah Cheng up.

Dolly straightened and scanned the rooftops of Chinatown. "This way," she told Ah Cheng.

Together they scurried along the rooftops and leapt from one building to another. The jumps weren't too far, though Dolly wished she wasn't wearing a skirt.

Once they reached the street that Leung Kum had told them about, Dolly knelt at the edge of the roof, looking for a way down.

"There." Ah Cheng pointed. "We can climb down into that alley."

Ah Cheng was right. The alley walls were made of protruding bricks. How would they return this way with a sick little girl though?

"Wait," Ah Cheng said. "Here's a skylight opening."

They both knelt and peered through, but the glass was too grimy to see anything.

Ah Cheng wrenched it open, then said, "I think the shop is abandoned."

Dolly descended first. The shop looked like a former bakery, but the ovens were stripped out, and broken furniture was stacked in one corner.

Ah Cheng sneezed at the dust.

They crept through the empty shop and exited into the alley. Twilight shadows only made the alley seem darker. Dolly ignored the prickle of fear climbing up her neck.

Together they headed to Commercial Street. People milled about, and Dolly used her cotton umbrella to keep her face hidden from anyone who might report her to the guards.

They slowed down when they reached the tenant building. "There she is," Ah Cheng whispered.

A young girl lay across three wooden chairs, curled up like a rag doll.

They rushed to her side. Dolly knelt and scanned the girl for signs of the bubonic plague. She didn't see any blackened skin on her fingers, and there wasn't any bleeding around her mouth or nose. Dolly guessed her to be older than her sister by a couple of years. She touched the girl's shoulder. "She's warm and still breathing."

"We are here to help you," Ah Cheng said softly.

The girl didn't open her eyes or respond.

"Let's take her to the mission home," Dolly said. "From there we can call the board of health." She looked to Ah Cheng for confirmation, and the interpreter nodded.

So Dolly scooped the little girl into her arms. They returned to the alley and entered the abandoned shop. With both Ah Cheng and Dolly working together, they were able to lift the girl through the skylight. The roofs were harder to leap from one to another while carrying the girl. But it had to be done. Dolly refused to trip or let go. Once they reached the herbalist's shop, dark had fallen over Chinatown, pierced with glowing lights.

They'd made it this far. They would make it the rest of the way.

Tien Fu was waiting with Leung Kum when they arrived at the mission home with her sister.

"You found her," Leung Kum cried.

"No one can touch her until we find out what's wrong," Dolly said.

Tien Fu interpreted, keeping her arm about the younger sister.

Dolly settled the sick girl onto the sofa in the parlor. Dolly didn't want to take her up to the floor with the bedrooms in case she was contagious. Ah Cheng went to fetch a blanket.

"I will keep everyone away," Tien Fu said. "Oh, and Mrs. Field wants to see you."

Dolly looked over at Tien Fu and saw the frustration in her gaze.

Ah Cheng walked in just then with a blanket. Dolly took it and laid it over the sleeping girl.

"No one touches her but me," Dolly told Ah Cheng. "Tien Fu is making sure no one comes into the room. I'll be back in a moment. I'm going to call the board of health."

Ah Cheng nodded. Dolly washed up in the kitchen, then hurried to Mrs. Field's office, dreading seeing her.

Mrs. Field walked out of the office just as Dolly arrived.

"How could you bring a sick girl here?" Mrs. Field's eyes seemed to be on fire. "You've just given the entire mission home a death sentence."

Dolly clasped her hands tightly in front of her. "I am calling the board of health right now, and I will follow their advice. No one needs to touch her except me."

"If the girl has the plague," Mrs. Field hissed, "I will see to it that you're dismissed." The director turned on her heel and strode down the hallway, her shoes tapping on the hardwood floor.

Dolly telephoned the board of health. The doctor who answered the phone said, "I'll send an ambulance to 920. You can come with the little girl. We'll do our best to help her."

Dolly thanked him. When she hung up, she took a steadying breath. The doctor had been kind. Not everyone was angry like Mrs. Field.

Dolly headed to the parlor to tell Ah Cheng the good news.

Leung Kum pleaded to come.

"You cannot go right now," Tien Fu told the girl. "Miss Cameron will take good care of your sister."

Leung Kum nodded and grasped Tien Fu's hand.

It was all Dolly could ask for.

When the ambulance showed up, Dolly bundled the sick little girl into it. The ride to the building on Jackson Street in the dark was so very slow. When they finally arrived, the same doctor whom she'd spoken to on the phone came out and ushered them into an exam room.

Dolly sat stiffly in a chair, silently praying. She hoped the little girl would recover. The doctor checked the girl's body for signs of bubonic plague. When he pressed on the right side of her stomach, the girl's eyes flew open and she cried out.

The doctor looked at Dolly. "She has acute appendicitis."

Oh no, Dolly thought. Her mother had died from appendicitis. Perhaps medical science had advanced enough to treat this little girl? "Is it too late for surgery?"

The doctor hesitated. "Yes, I'm afraid so."

Dolly buried her face in her hands. She didn't want to cry, not here, not when she had to be the strong one for the two Chinese sisters. But the tears came anyway.

"I'm very sorry," the doctor said softly. "We will move her to a comfortable bed. I'm sorry to say she won't last more than a day or two."

Dolly wiped at her cheeks and drew in a deep breath. "Can I bring her sister to say goodbye?"

"Of course." The doctor patted her shoulder. "Again, I'm very sorry."

Dolly felt numb, but she couldn't sit here and cry. Leung Kum was waiting to hear the news. Dolly rose to her feet and bent over the little girl. Resting a gentle hand on her forehead, she whispered, "I'm very sorry, sweet child. I'll bring your sister as soon as I can."

Only the soft breathing of the little girl filled the room.

Dolly let herself cry during the ride back to the mission home. When she reached it, she wanted to be strong and supportive to Leung Kum. But when Ah Cheng turned all the bolts to let Dolly inside, her heart broke again.

Leung Kum stood in the entryway, waiting, her face tearstained. Behind her, Tien Fu stood.

"Did the doctor see her?" Leung Kum asked through Ah Cheng's translation.

Dolly knelt in front of her and took the young girl's hand. "Your sister is very, very sick."

Ah Cheng interpreted.

"Will she die?" Leung Kum asked, her chin trembling.

Dolly's throat squeezed tight, but she managed to whisper, "Yes. I am very sorry, my dear."

New tears filled the girl's eyes.

The lump in Dolly's throat turned painful. "You have time to tell her goodbye."

"I don't want to say goodbye."

"I know." Dolly pulled the little girl close, and Leung Kum moved into her arms. Dolly rested her chin atop the girl's newly shampooed hair, which was still damp. "When I was a young girl of five years old, my mother got very sick. She had the same disease as your sister."

After Ah Cheng interpreted, Leung Kum lifted her face, her eyes wide. "Did she die too?"

"She did." Dolly's voice hitched. "But my mother is in a very lovely place now called heaven. She will never be sick again, and she's always happy."

"Oh." Leung Kum blinked slowly. "My sister will like heaven. Are there flowers there? My sister loves flowers."

Dolly smoothed back the girl's damp hair. "Yes, dear. I believe there are flowers in heaven. Your sister will be very happy. She will miss you, but she won't be sick anymore."

Leung Kum bit her trembling lip and nodded slowly.

Behind her, Tien Fu sniffled. The girl slipped away and headed up the stairs. Dolly would need to check on her later to see if she was all right.

Leung Kum's next words touched Dolly's heart.

"I will tell my sister where she's going," Leung Kum said. "I will tell her how beautiful heaven is."

"Do you want me to come with you to say goodbye to your sister?"

Leung Kum nodded emphatically.

"Then I will come," Dolly said.

Ah Cheng reached for Leung Kum's hand. "I will come too."

Chapter Twenty-One

THE BRIDAL BOUQUET

SAN FRANCISCO, 1901

Tien Fu knocked on Kum Quai's bedroom door, but there was no answer. Tien Fu had searched for her everywhere else, and she highly doubted Kum Quai would be in the basement, so she knocked again. "Kum Quai, it's me, Tien Fu. We're going to the flower market. Yuen Qui wants to know if you'll come with us."

There was a shuffling inside and then the door cracked open. Kum Quai's face appeared. Her hair hung lank about her face, and her eyes were swollen from crying.

"Are you sick?" Tien Fu asked.

"Yes," Kum Quai said in a raspy tone. "I'm sick of everyone being happy. I'm sick of everyone pretending that Ah Cheng getting married is the best thing in the world."

Tien Fu felt like she'd been slapped, although she knew Kum Quai wasn't mad at her. How in the world would Ah Cheng's wedding make Kum Quai angry?

Tien Fu looked up to Ah Cheng. She was loyal, clever, and helped Miss Cameron in many things. She stood for what she thought was right against Mrs. Field. Now that she was getting married and leaving, Tien Fu was sad. Maybe this was why Kum Quai couldn't be happy.

Ah Cheng would have the love of her new husband. She would have a home. She would have things that Tien Fu didn't. If there was one thing Tien Fu truly wanted, it would be to belong to a real family, with grandparents, parents, siblings, aunts, uncles, and cousins—like what she used to have, but what was now lost to her.

Kum Quai wiped her nose against her sleeve. "I'm not going to the flower market. No one really cares if I go or not. I'm not needed."

"Then I won't go either," Tien Fu rushed to say. "I'll stay with you. I can bring you tea or something to eat. Are you hungry?"

Kum Quai rested her head against the doorframe and closed her eyes. Tien Fu didn't move, determined to be there for her.

Since Kum Quai's brutal abduction, prison stay, forced marriage, and finally the rescue that brought her back to the mission home the second time, she had changed. When Tien Fu met her in Shanghai years earlier, she had been sweet, courageous, and friendly. But over the past few months, her bright smile had faded, her kind words disappeared, and she hardly left her room. She never attended classes and refused to learn English.

Kum Quai was Tien Fu's first true friend since she left her family, the big sister she never had. It made Tien Fu sad to see her friend hurt so deeply. She wished she knew how to cheer her up.

"You go with the others," Kum Quai whispered, her eyes still closed. "You shouldn't have to babysit me. I was forced to be a prostitute, then kidnapped, then forced to marry my slave owner. I can't ever change that . . . I've seen things and been places that most girls wouldn't ever be able to recover from." Her eyes opened. "You still have a chance for a happy life. You're so smart, so fierce, and so loyal!"

It wasn't fair that Ah Cheng was marrying for love, and Kum Quai had been forced to marry a horrible man she didn't love.

Maybe if Tien Fu talked to Ah Cheng about how much pain Kum Quai was in, she would agree to take her happiness elsewhere.

"I'll tell Ah Cheng to get married somewhere else," Tien Fu said. "This house should be a safe place for everyone. I don't want you to feel bad."

Kum Quai's smile was faint. "I have no doubt you'd tell Ah Cheng that, but it's not fair to her. This is my problem. I know that. But I still can't stop my emotions." She sniffled.

"I can stop the wedding," Tien Fu said in a determined tone, "then you won't be sad."

"That's impossible," Kum Quai said. "I'll always be sad."

Tien Fu understood how hard it was to let go of one's own pain to be happy for someone else. Every time a girl was adopted by a family or a young woman married, Tien Fu felt the sting of loneliness. She remained at the mission home year after year, unnoticed, unwanted, unloved.

Knowing there was nothing she could do to cheer up Kum Quai, Tien Fu slowly walked away. Everywhere else in the mission home, everyone was fully absorbed in the wedding preparation: shopping, cleaning, decorating, cooking.

Had Tien Fu's father not sold her, he would probably have arranged for her to marry a strange man by now. She was fifteen, marriageable age. For once Tien Fu was glad that her father was out of her life so he wouldn't be able to force her to marry. She only knew a few nice men—Attorney Monroe, the doctor, the policemen on the Chinatown Squad, and her sponsor, Mr. Horace C. Coleman, who promised to pay for college if she wanted to go.

When Tien Fu reached the landing, Yuen Qui was walking up the stairs. "Are you coming, Tien Fu? What about Kum Quai?"

"Kum Quai is having a hard day," Tien Fu said in a stiff tone. "Not everyone is happy about a wedding, you know."

Yuen Qui didn't look offended by Tien Fu's sharpness. "I understand. I'll talk with her."

"I don't think she wants to be bothered anymore."

Yuen Qui looked surprised at this. "Well, thank you for speaking to her, then. You've been a good friend to her." She paused. "We are leaving in a few minutes—"

But Tien Fu shook her head. "I changed my mind. I'm not going either."

Was the wedding all anyone could think about? How could they be so insensitive and not care that the celebration was hurting someone else's feelings? Happy chatter and delighted laughter had been ringing in every corner of the building for the past few days, but now Tien Fu found it almost intolerable.

She headed to Ah Cheng's room. The door was ajar. Tien Fu stepped quietly closer and peered in. Miss Cameron and the bride were sitting next to each other on the bed—their backs to Tien Fu—and chatting away. Ah Cheng was in her white wedding dress. Even from behind, the dress looked beautiful.

Tien Fu thought of Kum Quai—surely she hadn't worn a beautiful wedding dress for her forced marriage. Would Tien Fu ever have the same experience as Ah Cheng, wearing a gorgeous wedding dress and being a beautiful bride? Probably not. Tien Fu didn't think she would ever be a bride. She would never be adored like Ah Cheng. Never be as pretty as Yuen Qui. Never be as important as Miss Cameron. Envy shot through Tien Fu, hot and fast.

She hurried down the hallway and turned the corner. Everything was quiet here and allowed her time to think. Ah Cheng's wedding felt like a betrayal. She was leaving her dear sisters in the mission home to be with a husband. Then and there, Tien Fu decided she would skip the wedding. If Kum Quai wasn't going, then Tien Fu didn't want to either. She would support the one person who had been a true friend to her.

Voices sounded around the corner. Ah Cheng and Miss Cameron had left the bedroom together. Jealousy grew in Tien

Fu's heart and the thought of revenge struck her. She hurried to Ah Cheng's bedroom, tiptoed toward her dresser, and snatched the bridal bouquet. Then she backed out of the room quietly. Without the bouquet, the ceremony couldn't start. Ah Cheng couldn't marry. And Kum Quai wouldn't be sad and hurt.

Tien Fu sped silently to her bedroom and locked herself in. If her roommate tried to come in, Tien Fu would say she was sick and tell her to stay out. Guilt was filling her chest, but she ignored it. She felt justified.

Just then, an unexpected knock on the door startled her. She almost fell off her mattress. Tien Fu shoved the bouquet under her bed in a panic and pretended to be asleep.

"Tien Fu?" Miss Cameron's voice came through the door. "Can I speak to you for a moment? It's important."

Tien Fu didn't respond. But Miss Cameron knocked again with more intensity. Finally, Tien Fu opened the door a couple of inches. "I'm sick, Miss Cameron." She pretended to sound tired.

"I'm sorry to hear that," Miss Cameron said. "What's wrong?"

"My head and my stomach hurt." Tien Fu hoped Miss Cameron wouldn't insist on taking her temperature. "I think I just need to rest today."

"Oh, that's bad news." Miss Cameron's brows creased. "I was hoping you could be in charge of having the guests write their names in the ledger. Not all of them will sign because they might not know how to write. You can ask for their names, then sign for them."

Tien Fu stared at Miss Cameron, thinking she must be out of her mind. Of all the wedding-related jobs, this one was definitely not for her. Now she didn't even need to pretend to be sick. She had another excuse to turn down the task. "No, I can't do that. I mean—what if I misspell their names?"

"I'll go over the names with you afterward to see if there should be any corrections," Miss Cameron said, looking directly into Tien Fu's eyes. "You're the best speller at the mission home and the only one I can trust with this task."

Her compliment should have made Tien Fu feel good, but instead guilt scalded her chest. It was unbearable to hear Miss Cameron use the word "trust" after what Tien Fu had done to Ah Cheng. But she could feel Miss Cameron's sincerity. If Miss Cameron trusted her, it meant that she thought Tien Fu was important. It meant that she had worth. In a way, that meant she was worthy of love too. There were over fifty girls and many staff members in the home, and Miss Cameron came to *her*. Didn't that mean something? Tien Fu simply couldn't say no. But to be completely trustworthy, she needed to be honest. Like she had confessed about taking the apples a couple of years ago, she needed to confess to taking the bridal bouquet now. She looked at the floor, drawing in a deep breath for added courage.

"When you feel better, I'll see you downstairs," Miss Cameron said. She stepped back from the door, then headed down the hall.

Tien Fu stared after her. She hadn't had a chance to confess!

Just then, Miss Cameron turned around and said, "Oh, and if you've seen Ah Cheng's bouquet, can you make sure it gets back to her room right away? We start in less than an hour."

Tien Fu's heart rattled. Miss Cameron *knew*. How she knew, Tien Fu wasn't sure. But she knew and had chosen not to embarrass her. Without another word, Miss Cameron disappeared around the corner, leaving Tien Fu to think about her choice and the consequence.

The sounds of wedding guests starting to arrive reached Tien Fu. Right now she had an important decision to make. Just as the guests were coming to celebrate Ah Cheng with gifts for her and her groom, Miss Cameron had come to Tien Fu, offering a chance of repentance. Tien Fu decided to receive the gift with humility and gratitude.

She retrieved the bridal bouquet from under the bed. She

would return it to Ah Cheng and apologize, then she would sit in the foyer and help the guests sign their names in the ledger.

Tien Fu always wanted to feel needed. She felt that way today. Now she could see how much Miss Cameron, Ah Cheng, and Yuen Qui had relied on her for help. She wanted to be reliable. She wanted to be trusted. When the wedding was over, Tien Fu would find a way to help Kum Quai too.

Chapter Twenty-Two

A NEW DIRECTOR

SAN FRANCISCO, 1901

The morning after Ah Cheng's wedding, breakfast and the staff meeting were delayed an hour so everyone could get extra rest. Dolly was a few minutes late when she walked into the dining room. Since Mrs. Field hadn't arrived yet and Ah Cheng was gone, it felt strange. Before they could talk about the wedding festivities, Mrs. Field entered. But instead of taking her usual seat, she stood at the head of the table.

"I am finished," Mrs. Field said in a stiff tone.

"Finished with what?" Dolly asked, wondering which task the director was speaking of.

Mrs. Field looked steadily at Dolly. "This place. This job. *Everyone* here. I am turning in my resignation." She promptly stepped out of the room.

Dolly stared after her. None one else spoke. After a few moments, Yuen Qui said, "What happened?"

Dolly met her deep brown eyes. "I have no idea. Should I go after her? Perhaps the wedding made her tired? She must not be thinking clearly."

But Yuen Qui disagreed. "I think it's time, Miss Cameron," she said with a soft smile.

Dolly's pulse jumped. "Time for what?"

Yuen Qui looked over at the other staff members. They all nodded. Then Yuen Qui folded her hands atop the table. "Miss Culbertson wanted you to be the director here. You weren't ready, so we have all been patient under Mrs. Field for the past three years." She paused. "Are *you* ready now, Miss Cameron, to be the director?"

Dolly opened her mouth, but no words came. *Was* she ready to be the director? Would the board agree? She looked from Yuen Qui to the other staff members she'd served with. She loved every woman in this room like a sister, and she loved the girls in the mission home like her daughters—Lonnie, Dong Ho, Kum Quai, Jiao, Leung Kum, Tien Fu.

Dolly drew in a breath as her heart fluttered. "Are you sure?" she asked, her voice cracking.

Yuen Qui reached for her hand and squeezed. "We are sure."

"All right. I'll speak to the board."

Dolly could hardly believe she had agreed to be the director. She had been working at the mission home almost six years. Since that foggy morning in 1895 when she'd arrived at 920 Sacramento Street, her life had drastically changed. She'd been challenged. She'd been tested. And she'd been blessed.

A half laugh escaped Yuen Qui. She stood and pulled Dolly into a hug. Then everyone else hugged Dolly too.

"I am sure the board will approve." Yuen Qui wiped the tears from her face, then clapped her hands together. "Come, let's tell the girls in the kitchen. They'll be overjoyed!"

"Wait," Dolly said. "I should speak to the board first before we tell the girls. But let's skip classes today. I'd love to take a few of the girls on an outing. The weather is beautiful."

Yuen Qui smiled. "Which girls?"

"Whoever is on cleanup duty today." Dolly knew that would include Tien Fu.

When they entered the kitchen, several girls were cleaning up after breakfast, but Tien Fu was nowhere to be found. Yuen Qui clapped her hands together. "Miss Cameron has an announcement, everyone."

Dolly met the girls' gazes. "Who would like to go on an excursion with me today? Perhaps a ride on the ferry to Oakland?"

Every hand shot up, and a couple of the girls giggled.

Lonnie set down the dish she was drying and rushed to Dolly. She wrapped her arms about her waist. "Thank you, Mama."

Dolly squeezed her back. "You're welcome, dear." Lonnie was a teenager now but was still as petite as a nine-year-old.

Lonnie, Leung Kum, Jiao, and Dong Ho left the mission home with Dolly. Lonnie insisted on holding Dolly's hand. As they walked toward the ferry dock, Dolly breathed in the crisp air. Wispy white clouds painted the sky in a wide arc. The sun's rays were neither too hot nor too weak. By the time they loaded onto the ferry, most of the seats were taken. Dolly steered the girls to the railing. Lonnie stayed close, still clasping Dolly's hand. As the ferry pulled away from the city, the sounds of the dockworkers, tourists, horses, and buggies faded, replaced by the rumble of ships and the screech of seagulls. The salty breeze was a welcome change from the streets of San Francisco. Dolly and the girls watched a brave seagull land a couple of feet away. It pecked at a few things, then took off. The girls giggled as it flew past.

For Dolly, the sea air and the giggling girls were both invigorating. The intimidation of becoming the director of the mission home began to fade away. Two things turned in her mind. Miss Culbertson's belief in her before she died, and the warm conviction that played in her thoughts: *you are prepared.* She was more prepared than Mrs. Field had ever been.

The staff and interpreters were some of the best women Dolly knew. With them, she wouldn't—or couldn't—fail. She could only do her best. And if the Lord wanted her to be an instrument in this work, then He would make up for her weaknesses.

"Mama." Lonnie tugged at Dolly's arm. "What would the mission home do without me?"

Dolly held back a laugh as she looked at Lonnie. "I don't know what the mission home would do"—she pulled Lonnie close—"but I know *I* couldn't do without you."

"It's my turn to stand by Mama," Jiao said.

Lonnie reluctantly moved over, and Dolly nodded in approval. Jiao hadn't forgotten her mother, Hong Leen. But like many of the girls, Jiao called Dolly "Mama." Dolly wrapped an arm about Jiao's narrow shoulders, and the girl leaned her sun-warmed head against Dolly's hip.

"How long until we get there, Mama?" Lonnie asked.

Dolly pointed to the coast of Oakland. "It won't take long. See those green hills? That's where we're going."

Dolly felt the gazes of the other passengers watching her and the girls. She knew they might be curious about why a group of Chinese girls called a white woman "Mama."

As they neared Oakland, Lonnie crowded next to Dolly and pointed to the harbor. "I see the harbor!"

Beyond, trees interspersed with buildings and homes followed the curve of the hills. Some of the passengers rose and crossed to the railing.

"Excuse me, ma'am," a middle-aged woman said. Her clothing was cut in the latest fashion, and she wore a wide lavender hat. Dolly guessed her to be a tourist from the East Coast.

The woman's blue eyes met Dolly's. "Are all these little girls yours?"

Other passengers were close enough to hear Dolly's answer. "Yes, they are."

The woman's eyes widened and she touched her throat. "*All* of them?"

"All of them." Dolly reached for Jiao's hand and shared a smile with Lonnie.

The woman's brows rose. "You . . . are such a young woman though . . ."

Dolly tilted her head, waiting for what the woman might say next.

The woman swallowed. Without saying anything else, she flashed an uncertain smile at Dolly, then returned to her seat.

Dolly brushed off the comments and turned toward the sea again, leaning against the rail. Her Chinese daughters surrounded her on both sides. It didn't matter to Dolly that she didn't share blood with these girls or that her skin was a different color. They were her daughters, and she was their mother. Her heart soared at the realization. Today would be a day of gratitude, she decided. A day of joy. And tomorrow Dolly's life would change for the better.

By the time they returned to the mission home, Dolly felt renewed. She'd put smiles and laughter into the girls and that was all she'd wanted. Her only regret was that Tien Fu hadn't joined them.

That night, sleep was difficult. She couldn't stop thinking about what the board would say and who would take her old position in the mission home.

Maybe Frances P. Thompson, who volunteered at the mission home once a week. The girls were fond of her. By the time the sun rose and the birds chirped, Dolly was already dressed. She wrote a note to Frances and then headed out of her bedroom. There, on the floor in front of her door, was Lonnie. She was sound asleep. How long had she been there? All night?

Dolly crouched and tapped the girl's arm. "Lonnie," she whispered. "What are you doing on the floor?"

Lonnie blinked open her eyes. "I wanted to tell you something."

Dolly held back a smile. "It's so early. Didn't you want to wait until the sun was up?"

Lonnie yawned. At this, Dolly did smile.

Lonnie moved to her feet, then nestled against Dolly. "We need to call you something in Chinese."

"Oh?" Dolly wrapped her arms about Lonnie.

"We'll call you Lo Mo."

Dolly tightened her hold. Kum Quai had once called her Lo Mo, and now with Lonnie saying it too, Dolly felt honored.

"Whatever you wish, Yoke Lon," Dolly said in a tremulous voice, using the girl's Chinese name.

Lonnie's smile was huge.

"Now let's get you back to bed," Dolly said. "Today is an important day, and you need your rest."

"Why is it important?" Lonnie asked.

Dolly ran her hand along Lonnie's braid. "You'll find out this afternoon."

The day sped by with Dolly feeling more and more nervous about the board meeting. Frances's written reply came an hour before the board arrived. She agreed to take Dolly's position.

When Dolly entered the chapel, the board members were quietly chatting to one another. Many of them had been part of the mission home since it was first created. They'd volunteered countless hours raising funds, petitioning lawmakers, sharing messages of tolerance, and providing educations. Dolly had been nervous all day, but now peace and confidence enveloped her. When she walked to the front of the room and turned to face everyone, the board members fell silent, all eyes on Dolly.

She drew in a breath. "You might have already guessed what I'm about to say"—she clasped her hands together—"I want you to know that I haven't made this decision because Mrs. Field resigned. I've been thinking about this for many years."

The women in the room smiled at her. Several ladies nodded

for her to continue. The love and support in their gazes felt overwhelming.

"I'd like to accept the position of the director of the mission home if you all agree. But if you've already found someone else for the position, I'll be happy to continue on as an assistant—"

"There's no other," the president said immediately. "I move that we vote now. All in favor?"

"Aye," one woman said. Her vote was followed by a chorus of voices saying, "Aye."

Dolly couldn't stop smiling as her entire body filled with warmth and light. The women on the board all trusted that she was the best candidate for the job.

Outside the chapel doors of the mission home lived fifty girls and women—most of them were Chinese, but they'd had Japanese girls come to live there as well. Dolly loved each of them like her own family. Even though some days were hard and some nights were difficult, Dolly didn't want to be anywhere else.

After the unanimous votes of support had been officially recorded, the president stood at the front of the room. "We have more people than ever who want to visit the mission home. It's become a part of the Chinatown tour. This will be wonderful for collecting donations. We need to come up with ways to welcome visitors but also keep the girls protected."

Dolly wanted to protect the girls who struggled to socialize with others, but she also wanted to give the girls who were eager to interact the chance to connect with some of the visitors. The board members discussed various plans throughout the day. By the time Dolly went to bed that night, her mind was crowded with new ideas.

Chapter Twenty-Three

LO MO

SAN FRANCISCO, 1901

Dolly thought she was dreaming when she heard the knock on the door, but the knocking continued, and finally she realized it was real. *It has to be close to midnight*, she thought as she climbed out of bed and drew on a shawl. *It must be a rescue call.* When she opened her bedroom door, Frances was standing in the hallway, holding a gas lamp, her eyes wide.

"What is it?" Dolly asked.

"A note has been delivered."

"I'll get dressed, then."

Dolly was about to turn, but Frances said, "A distinguished guest from the White House is on his way."

Dolly paused. "Who?"

Frances held out the note. "This came from a messenger waiting on the porch."

Dolly took the note and read it silently in the light of the gas lamp. Her mouth dropped open. "We need to wake everyone and give President William McKinley the warmest welcome possible."

By the time Dolly made it downstairs, the rest of the staff were busy gathering the girls into the chapel to wait for President

McKinley and his wife. Most of the girls were clearly sleepy, but others were bright-eyed, eager to meet someone so important.

When the presidential entourage walked into the mission home, the First Lady grasped Dolly's hand in a warm handshake. Ida McKinley's hair was tightly curled and she wore an elegant dress. Her eyes were soft and warm. "Thank you for having us. I know it's very late, but we saw lights on."

Dolly didn't tell Mrs. McKinley that many of the girls in the mission home were afraid of the dark, so night-lights were common in the bedrooms.

"Welcome," Dolly said as the President and his wife walked through the main floor.

Dolly had read enough about the McKinley family to know that they had lost two children. Also that the First Lady suffered from a nervous condition.

"My wife dearly wanted to visit with the children before we leave early in the morning," the President said. Even though he was an austere-looking man, with a square jaw and a commanding presence, his smile was genuine and his manner friendly. He walked into the chapel and shook everyone's hands. All the girls and women beamed at him. They'd even brought down their babies—who, of course, would never remember this moment, but their young mothers would.

Then the President turned to his wife and led her to a comfortable chair. "Let's get you settled, Ida."

She gratefully took her seat, her face glowing as she gazed at the younger girls. "Come sit by me if you'd like."

The younger girls knew enough English to understand, and soon a half dozen had gathered close. Dolly smiled, feeling her heart expand at the sight.

When the President finished greeting everyone personally, he turned to Dolly, his hands behind his back. "Miss Cameron, I've heard of the remarkable work you've done for the people of San Francisco. I would like to commend you for it."

Dolly couldn't imagine how he'd heard about *her*. "Thank you, Mr. President. It's an honor to have you in our home." Her gaze slid past him to the chapel in general and the rooms beyond. Thankfully, the girls had kept up on chores and the place was tidy. Dolly wished they had fresh flowers on the side tables, but that couldn't be helped now. If they had received the notice of the President's visit earlier, Frances would have had the girls baking sweets all day.

Frances seemed nervous—as they all were—but she stepped up and said, "The girls would like to sing for you, Mr. and Mrs. President, if that's all right."

"Of course," the President said.

"We'd love that." Ida clapped her hands together as her smile widened.

Dolly sat in her own chair and listened to the girls sing in their sweet voices. Next they offered recitations of poetry and scriptures. Tien Fu stood in the very back of the crowd with an interested expression on her face. Next to her stood Kum Quai—she'd been doing very well in class lately and seemed to thrive on learning. Lonnie, Leung Kum, Jiao, Dong Ho, and all the girls performed to the best of their ability. Dolly was proud to see that even though some of the youngest ones yawned occasionally, they gave it their all.

At the end of each performance, the First Lady clapped in appreciation. The President joined in, which only made the girls giggle and flush pink.

"How do you like living in the mission home?" Mrs. McKinley asked the girls.

Lonnie threw her hands into the air. "I love it!"

Mrs. McKinley laughed. Then she turned to Dolly. "They're in school, yes? Right here?"

"That's right," Dolly said. "We teach them English, and they learn to read and write in their native language as well. We teach sewing skills, including darning socks and piecing quilts. The girls earn money by making buttonhole strips. We also sew our own clothing, comforters, and bed linens. With thirty-five to fifty girls in the house at any given time, we're making about one hundred and forty garments every four or five months."

"Goodness," Mrs. McKinley said. "There *is* a lot going on here. Do you make time for anything fun?"

Dolly smiled. "Of course. We take field trips to places like the Golden Gate Park. We ride the ferry on nice days. We love feeding the ducks."

Mrs. McKinley settled back in her chair, seemingly pleased at Dolly's answer.

"Well, I'd love to hear another song," President McKinley said.

The children were only too happy to sing again.

After the McKinleys left, Dolly and the staff ushered the younger children back to bed. With the house now quiet, Dolly had time to review the evening in her mind. That was when she realized that Yuen Qui hadn't come down to the chapel. Perhaps she was too tired. She had been coughing for a couple of days, but she was still working as usual.

A week earlier, Dolly and Yuen Qui had gone on a rescue trip to Los Angeles. On their return with the rescued girl, around midnight, the train pulled into a deserted small-town station. A constable boarded the train, woke them from their sleep, then flashed a warrant for the rescued girl. Without mercy, he pulled the three ladies off the train, leaving them to shiver in the chill of the dark night. Since that night, Yuen Qui had been constantly tired. She had also developed this persistent cough.

Dolly headed toward Yeun Qui's bedroom to check on her.

She knocked softly on the door, then turned the knob. "May I come in?"

Yuen Qui answered with a quiet moan.

Dolly stepped into the room. In the dimness, she could see the outline of Yuen Qui in her bed. Her shoulders were hunched, and she held a handkerchief to her mouth. She coughed deeply, and it sounded worse than Dolly remembered.

Dolly turned on a lamp. "Are you all right?" What she saw in the light sent panic through her. Yuen Qui's complexion was dreadfully pale and her face was sweaty.

"Oh my goodness!" Dolly rushed to Yuen Qui's side and placed a hand on her forehead. Her skin was too warm. Then Dolly noticed the dark red stain on the handkerchief Yuen Qui held to her mouth. She had coughed up blood.

Dolly struggled to remain calm. "I—I'll call a doctor."

Yuen Qui grasped Dolly's arm. "Don't call the doctor," she whispered, her eyes rounding with fear. Some people preferred traditional Chinese medicine. They didn't trust doctors who practiced Western medicine and only prescribed drugs to temporarily mask the symptoms of illnesses and diseases instead of curing their root causes. But Dolly felt that Yuen Qui needed more than an apothecary who examined a patient's tongue and took her pulse, then prescribed a medicinal or herbal remedy.

"I only need more tea," Yuen Qui said, her tone pleading. She released Dolly's arm and brought the handkerchief to her mouth, then she coughed again, harsh and deep. More blood appeared on the handkerchief.

Dolly winced at the painful sound. She hated to see her friend in such distress. She was torn between the choices of calling a doctor or honoring Yuen Qui's wishes. "I'll fetch you some tea," she said when Yuen Qui's coughing faded. "Lie down and try to rest while I'm gone."

Dolly left the bedroom, her heart racing as she hurried down the hallway. She came to a stop when she saw a figure at the end of the hallway. Tien Fu straightened from where she leaned against a wall. Before Dolly could say anything, Tien Fu disappeared around the corner to her own bedroom.

Even from two floors below, in the kitchen, Dolly could hear Yuen Qui's coughing fit. Dolly wished she could call for a doctor to make it all better. Instead she made herbal tea in the quiet stillness and hoped this was truly the help Yuen Qui needed.

By the time Dolly returned to Yuen Qui's bedroom, the cough had subsided. Dolly handed over the tea. Thankfully, it brought enough relief that Yuen Qui fell fast asleep and stayed rested without being interrupted by her coughs.

Still, Dolly sat in the bedroom for another hour. The minutes ticked by as she listened for any change in Yuen Qui's breathing, any struggle or worsening of symptoms. Finally, when Dolly could hardly keep her eyes open, she returned to her own bedroom. Somehow she slept a few hours, but the moment her room lightened with the approaching dawn, she woke with one thought: *Yuen Qui*.

How was she? Had she slept the rest of the night? Was she any better?

Dolly drew on her robe, ignored everything about her hair, and hurried to Yuen Qui's room. When she cracked open her door, she was relieved to see that Yuen Qui was still sleeping peacefully. However, she also discovered a surprise: someone else was asleep on Yuen Qui's bedroom floor. Tien Fu was curled up on the rug, huddled beneath a blanket.

Quietly Dolly crossed to the bed and found another handkerchief with bloodstains. Yuen Qui's complexion was even paler than the night before. Dolly looked from Yuen Qui to Tien Fu and knew she couldn't delay any longer. She dashed downstairs to her office and telephoned the doctor, asking him to come immediately.

Two hours passed before the doctor arrived. By that time, the rest of the household had finished morning chores, eaten breakfast, attended devotion, and started their classes and activities.

While the doctor examined Yuen Qui, Dolly sat in a bedside chair, waiting anxiously. Tien Fu hovered at the bedroom doorway. Dolly knew that Tien Fu idolized Yuen Qui, and in this delicate moment Dolly simply didn't have the heart to send Tien Fu back to her class.

Yuen Qui's eyes fluttered opened and closed as if she was trying to wake up. The doctor straightened and turned toward Dolly, his expression grave. "Yuen Qui has an advanced case of tuberculosis."

This was the last thing Dolly wanted to hear. She wished the doctor had declared that Yuen Qui was suffering from a severe case of a common cold and that she would get better in a week, although that would be a horrible lie to tell herself. No one with a common cold coughed up blood. But instead the doctor had just announced Yuen Qui's death sentence. There was no cure for tuberculosis. No procedure or medicine—Chinese or Western—that could help.

Dolly rose to her feet, wringing her hands together. "Are you sure?"

"I'm sure, Miss Cameron." The doctor slowly packed up his medical bag, then turned to look her square in the eyes. "And I am very sorry."

Dolly's eyes burned with tears. How could this be happening? Yuen Qui was young, intelligent, vibrant, and so kind.

The doctor paused for a moment. "I'll come back in a couple of days to check on her again."

Dolly nodded, her throat thick. She couldn't believe there was a time when she would actually ask this question. "How long does Yuen Qui have?"

A movement at the doorway caught both of their attention.

Tien Fu had disappeared. The doctor looked back at Dolly. "Not long. Maybe two weeks."

Dolly felt like the ground was shaking beneath her. She reached for the back of the chair to steady herself. "Have there been any recent medical developments to treat tuberculosis?" she asked against all hope.

Sorrow filled the doctor's eyes. "Nothing. I'm so sorry, Miss Cameron." He squeezed her shoulder. "I'll inform Miss Thompson, then show myself out."

Dolly felt numb. She looked over at Yuen Qui, who appeared to be resting. Dolly sank back into the chair and watched Yuen Qui as the sounds of the house hummed beyond the bedroom door. The girls went about their day. A door slammed. Voices rose and fell. Someone started singing. Dolly thought of going to Tien Fu. But her legs and arms felt so heavy. And her head ached, throbbing with exhaustion and grief.

Since coming to the mission home, Dolly had experienced so many losses. First Miss Culbertson passed away. Then Hong Leen left behind two little children. The Chinese messenger was shot in the street, giving his life to save another. Leung Kum's sister had died. Ah Cheng got married and moved away. Mrs. Field had quit. Then Mrs. Browne had retired from the board. Now sweet, lovely Yuen Qui was on her deathbed.

There was nothing left for Dolly to do but pray. Pray that she would be able to endure without Yuen Qui's help. Pray that the girls in the mission home would find comfort, peace, and solace for the loss of their beloved friend.

"Please, Lord," Dolly whispered, "give me strength." She knelt and clasped the sleeping woman's hand. Yuen Qui stirred but didn't open her eyes. Her condition would only get worse. Pretty soon, everyone in the mission home would know about her imminent death. Tien Fu especially would suffer deeply, Dolly knew.

Tien Fu had put Yuen Qui on a metaphorical pedestal, seeing her not merely as her role model but also as a near-perfect human being. If anyone had asked Tien Fu what she wanted to be when she grew up, she would have said, "Yuen Qui," as if her name was a profession, a title.

It was time to find Tien Fu. Dolly went to her room. When she arrived, the door was locked.

"Tien Fu?" Dolly said through the door. "It's Miss Cameron. I want to speak to you about what the doctor said."

Tien Fu had to be inside, but there was no answer. Dolly tried again. "Tien Fu, please open the door. I'll do my best to answer any questions you might have."

Dolly thought she heard a quick sniffle, but then all was quiet. She slid to the floor outside the bedroom and leaned against the wall, hoping and praying that Tien Fu would eventually let her in.

Just then, Frances found her. "What's happening? Why are you sitting on the floor?"

Dolly looked up. "Tien Fu heard everything the doctor said, and she refuses to open her door."

Frances set her hands on her hips, then lowered her head. "Perhaps she needs to work out her grief on her own."

Dolly could only hope that was the case. "What if she sees no way out of her grief except following Yuen Qui into the afterlife?"

Frances's head snapped up at this. "That sounds a little too extreme, don't you think? Tien Fu is close to Yuen Qui, but she has other friends too, you know. We'll all rally around her."

Yuen Qui had received a death sentence. Whoever knew and loved her would be affected in a negative way. Dolly hoped that everyone in the mission home would unite together in love to lift up one another during this trying time. If Tien Fu needed more support, then that was what she would get.

Over the next few days, Yuen Qui's body became more frail.

She slept most of the time except when Dolly or Frances woke her to feed her broth. They took turns nursing her through fevers, night sweats, chest pain, and coughing. Dolly stayed up for long hours every night; sometimes she felt like she was halfway between a dream and reality. She couldn't deny that her friend was dying, neither could she imagine what the mission home would be like without her.

Through it all, Tien Fu had isolated herself, speaking to no one, doing chores alone, and skipping all her classes. Every night, when she showed up at Yuen Qui's bedroom with her own blanket, Dolly gave her a nod, a wordless permission, allowing her to curl up on the floor and quietly cry herself to sleep. This was the way Tien Fu had chosen to grieve, and Dolly simply couldn't bear to separate these two close friends, especially in the final days when they had limited time together.

One morning, in the middle of the third week, Dolly walked into Yuen Qui's room and found Tien Fu standing next to the bed, gazing at her friend. Yuen Qui's eyes were closed and she wasn't breathing. The room seemed dim around her, even though sunlight came through the single window. The colors of the room faded to lifeless gray. Dolly could only stare at Yuen Qui's lovely face, so peaceful and still in death.

Even though Yuen Qui's passing was predicted—expected, even—and Dolly had had weeks to prepare herself for this moment, it was still hard to believe Yuen Qui was truly gone.

Dolly's knees felt weak, and she sank onto the floor next to the bed. She grasped the quilt and buried her face in the fabric. Her heart was shattered. Awful pain burned her throat and her stomach, and she burst out sobbing.

Her friend was gone.

Together Dolly and Yuen Qui had traveled the depths of the underworld of San Francisco, leading girls from the darkness into the light. But now . . . that had all ended. Yuen Qui would never open her eyes again. She would never smile again. She would never go on another rescue with Dolly. She would never comfort another frightened slave girl.

"No, no, no," Dolly cried over and over. How could a woman so good, so full of purpose and with so much more to give be taken from the world? Why hadn't her prayers been answered?

Dolly was startled by a light touch on her shoulder. She had somehow forgotten that Tien Fu had remained in the room. Dolly should be comforting her, but she didn't even have the strength to move.

"Lo Mo, don't cry," Tien Fu said. "I'll grow up and help you."

Lo Mo. Lo Mo. Lo Mo. Out of love and respect, the girls in the mission home had been calling Dolly Lo Mo, but not Tien Fu. If this strong-willed fifteen-year-old girl had held off deciding if Dolly deserved that title, then it was now settled.

"This is my promise to you," Tien Fu said in an earnest tone. "*I* will help you with the rescues. I won't be afraid. I'll work hard—harder than anyone. I promise."

Dolly raised her head and drew in a deep breath. She wiped the tears from her cheeks and turned to Tien Fu. Their gazes connected. Tien Fu dropped to her knees next to Dolly, leaned forward, and wrapped her sturdy arms about Dolly's neck.

Dolly drew her in a tight hug. Tien Fu trembled and the two cried in each other's arms, sharing the same anguish, the same grief, the same sorrow. But Dolly felt another shift that was different than her intense pain. She and Tien Fu had connected on a deep level. And the bond between them that had perhaps been there all along strengthened. A mother, Lo Mo, and a daughter, Tien Fu.

Love, understanding, and acceptance sprouted between them like a seed made of the light of Yuen Qui. It would grow, flourish, and thrive. And Yuen Qui's memory would live on inside of them both.

Chapter Twenty-Four

A PROMISE

SAN FRANCISCO, 1904

For the past three years, since Yuen Qui's death, Tien Fu had been making a cup of tea every night and placing it by a portrait of Yuen Qui in her old bedroom, remembering and honoring her beloved friend.

"I made a promise to Miss Cameron. I'll help her like you did," Tien Fu whispered to the picture. "I might not be as good as you, but I am trying." She imagined Yuen Qui smiling back at her and telling her thank you in her soft voice.

Before witnessing Miss Cameron's profound grief over Yuen Qui's death, Tien Fu had struggled to connect with Miss Cameron—a lady from a wealthy and loving Scottish family, a woman never sold into slavery and abused. What did she know about sorrow and pain? Miss Cameron's life was so privileged that Tien Fu had constantly compared her with her own mother, using it as an excuse to despise Miss Cameron.

My Niang could do her own talking in different dialects; she didn't need any interpreters. My Niang alone could prepare a Chinese New Year feast; she didn't need any cooks. My Niang could walk with bound feet into deep mountains, into a rushing river, into town, to gather firewood, to do the family's laundry, to buy rice and tea; she didn't need a coachman to drive her in a carriage.

But the more Tien Fu compared anyone with her mother or herself, the more miserable she became. Comparison was poison. She had learned that from the Bible. Joseph of the Old Testament had been mistreated by his jealous brothers who always compared themselves with him. But when Joseph's brothers sold him into slavery and he was taken to Egypt, he wasn't bitter. Instead, he found ways to bless others—saving Egypt from famine, saving his own father, forgiving his brothers, and helping them build a new home in a foreign country.

Tien Fu's experience wasn't as dramatic as Joseph's, and she would never be as heroic as Joseph, but she understood now that she had been rescued at a young age for a reason. She was in the mission home for a reason. She had a purpose. Over the years, her childhood stubbornness and resentments had changed, blooming into a burning desire to help slave girls get out of bondage. Every girl and boy deserved to live the life of their choosing—to love, to be happy, and to be free.

Like Joseph, Tien Fu might never see her mother again. It had been nine years since she left her family home and become motherless, but Yuen Qui had filled that lonely space. So had Kum Quai and Ah Cheng. And now Miss Cameron.

"Auntie Wu," a small girl's voice said from the doorway, interrupting her thoughts. It was three-year-old Hung Mui, the youngest child at the mission home. She called Tien Fu by the prestigious title of Auntie, even though she was only eighteen years old.

"What is it?" Tien Fu said with a smile.

The little girl hovered in the doorway, her small teeth gnawing at her bottom lip. "Miss Cameron says hurry and come."

Tien Fu's brows darted up. Something didn't seem right. If it was an important, urgent matter, why would the director send a three-year-old?

"Is someone at the door?" Tien Fu asked.

Hung Mui thought about it and then decisively said, "No."

Perhaps that was good news, then. There wasn't a raid or a letter requesting rescue. It had been a long day—Tien Fu was ready to go to bed. She headed to the doorway. "Where's Miss Cameron?"

"In the kitchen." Hung Mui had no problem coming up with the answer. She reached up for Tien Fu's hand. Tien Fu grasped the small, warm hand and headed toward the stairs. The mission home was strangely quiet. It was well after the dinner hour, but still, there was usually talking, singing, and playing this time of the evening.

"Are you sure Miss Cameron is in the kitchen? It looks dark. Maybe she went to her office."

Before Hung Mui could reply, the lights flew on and dozens of girls shouted, "Happy birthday!"

Tien Fu stared at the crowd, speechless. In the middle of the table sat the largest cake she had ever seen, iced with multiple-colored flowers. From Miss Cameron to the staff members to the girls and women, every person in the mission home had gathered around the table and filled up the rest of the room.

"It's your birthday?" Hung Mui asked in a delighted voice. She sounded so innocent, it might be entirely possible that she didn't know Miss Cameron had asked her to be a big part of the surprise party.

Tien Fu laughed, then swung the little girl up on her hip. "It sure is."

Tien Fu had been eight years old when she was rescued from the cruel Mrs. Wang. The day she arrived in the mission home, she declared it was her birthday: a symbol of her rebirth, of her new life as a free person in a new country. That was ten years ago, and Tien Fu had nothing but gratitude for the second chance she had been granted, like Joseph in Egypt, to create her own path.

Hung Mui patted Tien Fu on the arm and asked, "Can I eat the cake now?"

"Of course, let's all eat the cake!" Tien Fu said with a chuckle. "It's so beautiful. Look at all the colors on it."

Miss Cameron smiled at her from the other side of the table. "No one knew what your favorite color was, so we used them all."

Tien Fu laughed. "That's because I don't have a favorite color." And she didn't. "Thank you, everyone. I'm sure the cake is delicious, and I was very, very surprised."

The next hour was lighthearted as bedtimes were delayed so everyone could enjoy the cake and visit. After the dishes were cleaned up, Tien Fu lingered in the kitchen and chatted with Kum Quai.

Miss Cameron allowed socializing between the older girls and Chinese men she approved of in the mission home on Sunday afternoons. Kum Quai had been speaking to one of those Chinese men. Now that she had just turned eighteen, Tien Fu realized that she was eligible for the social hour too. But she was content in her role and responsibilities in the mission home; she didn't want anything to change.

By the way Kum Quai's cheeks pinked when she spoke of her beau, Tien Fu was sure the man would be her fiancé soon. Three years earlier, on Ah Cheng's wedding day, Tien Fu had stolen the bridal bouquet to stop her from getting married, from being happy. She had tried to punish Ah Cheng for having found her true love. Tien Fu had been an immature and selfish teenager then but had since learned to celebrate her sisters' joy. Now it made her happy to see Kum Quai happy.

A knock sounded at the front door, and Miss Cameron swept out of the room. Tien Fu couldn't help but go on alert. "I'll be right back," she told Kum Quai.

She reached the door just as Miss Cameron had unbolted it. It must not be the policemen with a search warrant because she hadn't sounded the gong.

A young Chinese man stood outside. He had a boyish face, but judging from the fine lines around his eyes, Tien Fu guessed he was close to thirty years old.

"Are you Miss Cameron?" he asked in accented English.

"Yes."

The man looked at Tien Fu, then back at Miss Cameron.

"My name is Huan Sun. I sold my shop. All the money is here." He held out a thick envelope to Miss Cameron. "Please—rescue Mei Lien."

Without taking the envelope, Miss Cameron asked, "Who's that?"

"The woman I love," Huan Sun said. "She escaped the brothel Ah-Peen Oie owns. Then people from a different tong caught her. They want money for her, but I'd rather give it to you for her rescue. I don't trust the tong."

Tien Fu knew that Ah-Peen Oie owned a high-end courtesan house. She was a ruthless mistress, and a couple of the girls at the mission home had escaped the woman. Their stories were sad to hear.

"And you trust me?" Miss Cameron asked.

Huan Sun didn't hesitate. "You are the only one who can help."

Miss Cameron and Tien Fu nodded at each other. Then Miss Cameron looked back to Huan Sun. "Can you take us to her? Or do you have an address?"

"I'll show you where she is," Huan Sun said. "We must hurry before the tong moves her again." He handed the envelope to Miss Cameron. "Please take it."

Miss Cameron gently pushed the envelope back and shook

her head. "That won't be necessary. We'll do all we can to help Mei Lien. Her safety is the greatest reward for us."

Huan Sun repeatedly thanked her, his expression a mixture of gratitude and relief.

Miss Cameron reached for the cloak she kept by the door. The January night would be brisk, and who knew how long they would be gone.

"Call the police station," Miss Cameron told Tien Fu. "Ask them to send the Chinatown Squad."

Unfortunately, when Tien Fu called, the policemen were dealing with a restaurant fire in the heart of Chinatown. As she reported this to Miss Cameron, she looked at Huan Sun. "Don't worry. We'll still come."

Tien Fu dashed into the kitchen and picked up a basket of food and drink, then she grabbed a thick blanket from the parlor. "I'm ready," she said when she entered the foyer. "Let's go."

Once they reached the bottom of the street, they hired a buggy and quickly piled into it. Huan Sun told the driver an address just outside of San Francisco and promptly fell silent as they rattled along.

Soon, they neared the location where Mei Lien was being kept. Huan Sun pressed the thick envelope into Miss Cameron's hands again. "Take the money. I must go into hiding. Tell Mei Lien I love her. I only want her safe and happy."

Miss Cameron refused to take it. "You'll need it while you're in hiding."

Huan Sun placed a hand over his heart. When the buggy slowed, he hopped out. Watching him disappear into the shadows of the night, Tien Fu wondered about the person who had sought for her own rescue ten years earlier. Who was it? Who had that much love for her? Who thought her young soul was worth saving? Did that person also vanish into a dark corner after seeing Tien Fu was safe and free? Tien Fu might never know who that nameless hero was. The only way to show her gratitude was to pay it forward, right now, helping Mei Lien.

The building in front of them rose two floors. On the main level, lights shone from the windows. Anticipation climbed up the back of Tien Fu's neck. She had gone on plenty of rescues with Miss Cameron, but they had always had a policeman with them. This time she would have to be extra vigilant. She drew in a deep breath and assured herself that she could do this.

She wondered where Mei Lien had come from. Had she been sold by her family or kidnapped? Did Mei Lien suspect that help was just outside?

They walked right into the front door. A man who looked ancient with drooping wrinkles rose from a table where he'd been reading.

"We're closed for tonight," he said in Chinese.

Miss Cameron said nothing but hurried past him, Tien Fu right behind her.

"Stop!" the man yelled, but he was much too slow to catch up with them. Instead he rang a bell, alerting everyone in the building that something was wrong.

Miss Cameron picked up her skirts and raced down the hall to chase after muffled sounds of cursing, smashing, and banging. Tien Fu followed close on her heels.

"In here," Miss Cameron said, throwing open a door.

They both stopped cold.

A group of Chinese men sat around a table, smoking. Their eyes all locked on Miss Cameron and Tien Fu. None of them spoke, but they examined Miss Cameron in silent scrutiny. Tien Fu suspected that they knew who she was; if not in person, by reputation.

"Where's Mei Lien?" Miss Cameron said in Chinese. Tien Fu didn't need to interpret.

One of the men chuckled. Others sneered. Miss Cameron's

gaze darted about the room, and Tien Fu crouched to look under the table.

"She's not here," one man said in Chinese.

No joke! Tien Fu stifled her scoff. Only a fool would make that statement in this circumstance. It reminded her of the Chinese folktale of a man who feared that someone might steal his three hundred silver dollars, so he buried the money deep in the ground and erected the sign *There are no three hundred silver dollars here!* right on the spot.

Tien Fu heard a thump overhead. Her gaze instantly connected with Miss Cameron's. As if they had the same thought, the two of them dashed out together. This time the men pursued. They weren't old like the doorman, and Miss Cameron and Tien Fu were on their own without police protection. The situation made Tien Fu's heart zoom to her throat.

"Through here," Miss Cameron panted, tugging Tien Fu through a door and locking it. Then they turned to face a flight of stairs. In unified motion, they sprinted up the steps while the men banged on the locked door below, cursing in Chinese. It was unnecessary for Tien Fu to interpret for Miss Cameron at this moment. She alone would take the insult.

The more swear words Tien Fu heard, the more furious she became. Why did these men choose to do this? Why weren't they home with their families or loved ones? Were they proud of what they did, dehumanizing and abusing girls and women?

Reaching the second floor, Miss Cameron opened each of the doors on one side of the hallway and called out Mei Lien's name. Tien Fu did the other side. When they reached the end of the hall, no one had answered.

Miss Cameron walked into the last room and turned a slow circle in the dark. She paused. Then she pointed to a cupboard on the far side of the room and motioned Tien Fu to walk with her. Without making a sound, Miss Cameron knelt and unlatched the cupboard, then drew it open.

Inside the small space, a woman sat with her knees pulled up. Her dark eyes stared out at them.

"Mei Lien?" Miss Cameron said in a soft voice.

"Mei Lien," Tien Fu echoed, then spoke in Chinese. "Huan Sun sent us. We're from the mission home. We've come to take you to safety."

Mei Lien's eyes grew wider, filling with fear. "No, no! Fahn Quai!"

Tien Fu wasn't surprised. "Miss Cameron has been called much worse. My name is Tien Fu Wu, and we're here to rescue you from the men who hold you captive."

Mei Lien only stared.

From below, the men were still banging on the door and cussing. By now, they would have had enough time to get an axe and break through the door to chase after Miss Cameron and Tien Fu. Maybe they were too afraid of the consequences of injuring Miss Cameron, a powerful woman in San Francisco.

"Come with us," Tien Fu said. "We'll give you a safe place to live. You'll have food. We'll teach you to read and write. You'll be free to find your own path—"

"I can't," Mei Lien said, her voice trembling. "They'll make my Niang pay."

This was a common threat. But Mei Lien's owner probably didn't even know where she was from, not to mention how to find her mother.

"They have no power to harm your mother," Tien Fu said. "We'll make sure of it." She held out her hand. "Come, you'll see."

Mei Lien shrank away.

The banging still sounded below. Tears dripped down Mei

Lien's cheeks, and Tien Fu wished she could stop the woman's pain.

"Tell her about Huan Sun," Miss Cameron said.

"Huan Sun sent us," Tien Fu said. "He sold his shop and tried to give us all that money so we could come find you. We told him to keep his money."

Mei Lien slowly blinked.

"We told him that we would find the woman he cares about and that we would take care of her."

"Why?" Mei Lien whispered.

"We'll show you why," Tien Fu said. "But first we must get you to safety."

Mei Lien raised a shaky hand and put it into Miss Cameron's outstretched one. "Huan Sun really sold his shop?"

"Yes," Tien Fu said. "He wanted us to tell you that he loves you and only wants you safe and happy."

Mei Lien's lips quivered. She lowered her head and took a deep breath. "Then I will come with you."

Relief shot through Tien Fu. Mei Lien's body was shaking, so they wrapped each of her arms around their shoulders to support her and help her out of the cupboard. They moved to the window, which Miss Cameron opened wide.

"I knew it," Miss Cameron said. "A fire escape."

From below, the banging on the door turned to chopping. The men had finally found an axe, it seemed. But Miss Cameron, Tien Fu, and Mei Lien were already out the window and heading down the fire escape. The cool night air was a blessed relief. They half ran, half stumbled toward the buggy. Once inside, the driver whipped the horses into action just as two men dashed out of the building.

Tien Fu didn't waste any time in taking out food and drink from the basket she had brought along while Miss Cameron draped a thick blanket over Mei Lien.

After her first bite of a cold wonton, Mei Lien said, "Thank you. It's so kind of you."

Through Tien Fu interpreting, Miss Cameron said, "You'll soon have plenty to eat. We'll take care of you. Huan Sun would like that."

Mei Lien pressed a hand at her chest and nodded slowly.

Tien Fu looked out the back window of the buggy. "We've lost them," she said. She could hardly believe that they had escaped those men in the tong and successfully accomplished the rescue.

Mei Lien's exhaustion led her to sleep part of the way back to San Francisco. When the buggy stopped near 920 Sacramento Street, Tien Fu woke her and said, "We'll have to take a tunnel into the mission home. There might be people watching for you."

Mei Lien's face paled. "A tunnel? Underground?"

"I'll come with you," Tien Fu said, opening the buggy door. They were in a small alley, one with brick buildings on both sides. A sliver of light came from the cloudy night sky above.

Miss Cameron stayed in the buggy, and it took her to the front door of the mission home. If anyone was watching, they would see only Miss Cameron arrive.

Tien Fu led Mei Lien along the alley until they stopped at a board on the ground. It covered a grate, and after Tien Fu lifted both, she said, "Down here. Feel for the ladder."

Mei Lien stared into the blackness. "I can't."

Tien Fu grasped her hand. "You must. I've been through this many times. There are no evil spirits inside."

Still, Mei Lien scanned the dark alley. "Is there no other way in?"

"Huan Sun told us what happened. The tong went to great lengths to recapture you. They'll try to find you again," Tien Fu said in a matter-of-fact voice. "You need to go through this tunnel or I can't protect you."

Mei Lien squeezed her eyes shut. "For everything Huan Sun has done for me, I'll go." She knelt on the ground, then felt for the top of a ladder. Carefully, she turned and descended into the darkness.

Tien Fu came after her and pulled the grate and board back into place, sending the two of them into utter blackness.

"Go slowly and feel your way," Tien Fu said quietly, her voice sounding hollow in the narrow space.

"How far down do we go?" Mei Lien asked.

"We're halfway there," Tien Fu's voice returned. "Keep moving."

The darkness was thick, like a living, breathing thing, but Tien Fu was grateful for the protection the tunnel provided. At the bottom of the ladder, she said, "Now we have to crawl. Hold on to me and let me guide you."

Mei Lien grasped her clothing, then knelt.

Together they crawled, their damp palms slipping against the ground more than once.

"You're doing fine," Tien Fu said, even though the young woman's breathing sounded labored. "Keep moving."

Then the tunnel curved upward, and bits of dirt and rock slid past them.

"We're here." Tien Fu rose to her feet. They'd made it. Her heart soared. She grasped Mei Lien's hand and helped her stand. The area was still underground and the darkness still surrounded them, but at least they could walk now.

"Come." She clasped Mei Lien's arm. "Miss Cameron will be waiting for us."

Tien Fu's legs were shaky, and she was sure that Mei Lien was ready to collapse. But they successfully reached the top of the narrow stairs of creaking wood. Then Tien Fu opened a door and light spilled through.

Miss Cameron stood on the other side of the door with a

burning candle in hand, waiting for them. "You are safe now, Mei Lien."

Mei Lien squeezed Tien Fu's hand and asked, "Am I really free?"

"Yes," Tien Fu replied. "That's your new identity now—a free woman, always and forever."

"Thank you, Tien Fu," Mei Lien whispered.

"It's my honor," Tien Fu whispered back.

On this, her eighteenth birthday, Tien Fu had been granted the privilege of helping an abused paper daughter gain her freedom, her rebirth, her new purpose. What better birthday gift could it be for both Tien Fu and Mei Lien to share a new sisterhood under the same roof?

After a hot meal and a warm bath, Mei Lien rested in her new bed. Tien Fu went into the kitchen. Slowly and methodically she crushed tea leaves, measured, blended, and steeped. When she had her cup of steaming tea of lemon and orange, she walked up the stairs and sat on the top step.

In this peaceful, quiet moment, she looked back on her six-year-old self, being sold to one person after another, lost, hurt, angry, always wondering if she would ever see her family again, always wondering if anyone would ever love her like her mother did. She had since made peace with her destiny. That bitter girl no longer lived inside her. Her heart had become as sweet as her tea.

Tien Fu lived in Zhejiang for the first six years of her life, but she had been living in San Francisco for the last twelve. This was home now. Like Joseph in Egypt, Tien Fu had been led by the hand of God. America was where she was supposed to be. She had been called to this work, rescuing God's children in bondage, and she had chosen to answer the call.

Just then, light footsteps sounded from the hallway, walking toward her. "I thought I might find you here," Miss Cameron said in a quiet voice.

Tien Fu lifted her gaze. She was about to stand, but Miss Cameron said, "No, you're fine. I'll sit with you if you don't mind."

When Miss Cameron settled onto the top step, she said, "You were remarkable tonight, Tien Fu. So calm and helpful."

"I have a good teacher in you, Miss Cameron."

Miss Cameron smiled, then patted Tien Fu's hand. "Remember, on that terrible day when Yuen Qui died, you made me a promise?"

Tien Fu nodded. She would never forget that moment or her promise.

"I remember thinking how I wanted to believe you, but I wasn't sure if you could carry out your promise." Miss Cameron released a sigh. "You were young. You're still young. But you've shown me time and time again that you're extremely loyal and determined."

Tien Fu looked over at Miss Cameron. In the shadowy stairway, her eyes were bright with tears.

"Thank you, Tien Fu. You've been such a tremendous help to me and to everyone." Miss Cameron dabbed at her cheeks.

Warmth expanded inside of Tien Fu, and she was bursting with gratitude for Miss Cameron—her new mother, her Lo Mo—for her endless love, kindness, and sacrifices.

The night crept forward, and somewhere below, a clock chimed the late hour. Neither of them moved. Right now Tien Fu reveled in the fact that all was well within these walls.

If she listened really intently, she could still hear her six-year-old self say to her mother, "Don't cry, Niang. I'll come home soon."

Yes, she had made a promise to her mother.

Yes, she had made another promise to her new mother.

If she listened really intently, she could still hear her fifteen-year-old self say, "Don't cry, Lo Mo. I'll grow up and help you."

Tien Fu Wu, a paper daughter and a slave girl who grew up to become an interpreter and a rescuer, would keep both promises.

READER QUESTIONS & ANSWERS

Note to Teachers: If you'd like more information for your classroom about the topic and history behind the story, please visit the Shadow Mountain Publishing website to download the Teacher's Guide (https://shdwmtn.com/paperdaughters).

Q: Did Tien Fu Wu ever get a chance to go home?

A: Twenty-four years after her father had sold her to pay his gambling debts, Tien Fu Wu kept the promise she'd made to her mother and returned to China in the fall of 1916. Unfortunately, Tien Fu's search for her family in Zhejiang province was unsuccessful. "I never found any of them. I couldn't find the place," she told a historian many years later (Interview with Tien Fu Wu, by Him Mark Lai, 1971).

For over two decades, while she was in America, there had been a political revolution, uprisings, and foreign powers' attacks and colonization in China. It's possible that Tien Fu's family had been forced to leave their war-torn hometown like countless others during those riotous times.

Without any blood ties to her motherland, Tien Fu returned

to San Francisco to the only home she knew and to Miss Cameron, her new mother who had helped raise her.

Q: Why didn't Tien Fu Wu go back to using her birth name?

A: We don't have any records in Tien Fu Wu's own words that tell us about her name(s). Author Allison Hong Merrill took the liberty of fictionalizing the scenario that she was given the name Tai Choi at birth and then was given the new name Tien Fu Wu when she was six. She was illiterate in both Chinese and English when she was on the way to America. She wouldn't have known how to tell anyone the Chinese characters for her name. Since the highbinder already had fake documents for her with the name Tien Fu Wu (伍天福), it was easier for her to go by that new identity. In San Francisco, not many people knew her as Tai Choi. In both a literal and a metaphorical sense, she couldn't go back to be Tai Choi anymore, so she became Tien Fu Wu for the rest of her life. But more than anything else, she became the strong, inspiring, and empowering woman she was born to be.

Q: Why were so many Chinese immigrating to America in the 1800s?

A: After China was defeated in the Opium Wars (1839–1842; 1856–1860), 2.5 million Chinese traveled overseas in the latter half of the nineteenth century to find jobs. Due to increased taxes, the impossibility of competing against imported goods, loss of land, overpopulation, and other calamities, including devastation from rebellions and uprisings, many Chinese turned to working in the gold mines in California or the railroads in the western United States as a way to feed a destitute people.

Q: Why were Chinese girls and women trafficked to America?

A: The conditions of labor camps in America were harsh, and nicer accommodations were too expensive, so Chinese men mostly immigrated alone. Those who were married sent money home to their families. In the 1850s, Chinese women made up less than five percent of the total Chinese population in America. Traditional Chinese women remained at home, caring for the household and children, as well as aging parents, in order to adhere to the Confucian teaching: "A woman's duty is to care for the household, and she should have no desire to go abroad" (Yung, *Unbound Feet*, 20). This meant that most Chinese men arrived in America without their wives, creating a void in which women were not part of the fiber of the Chinatown culture in San Francisco. Organizations such as the tong formed to provide women for the men in the form of paid prostitution.

This played into the patriarchal culture of the Chinese, in which marriages were arranged and women "had no right to divorce or remarry" while men were "permitted to commit adultery, divorce, remarry, practice polygyny, and discipline their spouses as they saw fit" (Yung, 19).

Q: What is the Chinese Exclusion Act, and how were Chinese girls and women coming into America able to get past the anti-immigration laws?

A: Chinese women were up against anti-immigration laws from both sides of the Pacific Ocean. Chinese law forbade the emigration of women until 1911, and the 1852 Foreign Miners' Tax affected Chinese miners, along with taxes "levied on Chinese fishermen, laundry men, and brothel owners" (Yung, 21), making it even more expensive to support a family. Besides passing punitive ordinances aimed specifically at the Chinese, the California legislature denied them basic civil rights, including immigration rights, employment in public works, intermarriage with whites, ability to give testimony in court, and the right to own land.

Then came the Page Act of 1875, which prohibited the entry of a woman who was from "China, Japan, or any Oriental country" coming into America for "immoral purposes" (see https://

immigrationhistory.org/item/page-act/). This was followed by the Chinese Exclusion Act of 1882, in which the United States Congress suspended Chinese laborers from immigrating for ten years. The Chinese Exclusion Act was renewed in 1892, then again in 1904 and so on, until it was finally repealed in 1943, making this law stay in effect for sixty-one years.

Q: How did Chinese girls and women get trafficked into America, then?

A: "In the interest of diplomatic and trade relations between China and the United States, Chinese officials, students, teachers, merchants, and travelers were exempted by treaty provisions—and therein lay the loophole through which Chinese, including women, were able to continue coming after 1882" (Yung, 22).

These exemptions were the open door that allowed slave owners or members of the criminal tong to bring Chinese women into the country under false identities supported by forged paperwork. By virtue of this forged paperwork system, in which the Chinese woman would memorize her new family's heritage and claim to be married or otherwise related to a Chinese man already living and working in California, the *paper daughter* was allowed into the country. "Upon arrival in San Francisco many such Chinese women, usually between the ages of sixteen and twenty-five, were taken to a barracoon, where they were either turned over to their owners or stripped for inspection and sold to the highest bidder" (Yung, 27).

Q: Why was the Occidental Mission Home for Girls founded?

A: It wasn't until the early 1870s that women's missionary societies discovered the need to provide a safe place for Chinese women fleeing slavery. Despite facing opposition herself for helping the Chinese women, Mrs. Samantha Condit, wife of a Presbyterian missionary assigned to Chinatown, advocated for their cause until she established the California branch of the Women's Foreign Missionary Society. Not only was she up against a myriad of anti-Chinese city ordinances but finding donors proved to be difficult, with many refusing to donate to a cause that supported "depraved women" (*New Era Magazine* 1920, 137).

Condit prevailed. In 1874, she and her board rented a small apartment just below Nob Hill in San Francisco, officially founding the Occidental Mission Home for Girls. This was the beginning of establishing a place of refuge, healing, education, and Christian religious instruction for the destitute women of Chinatown. Although Bible study and attending church on Sundays were part of the curriculum at the mission home, Donaldina Cameron and her staff incorporated the girls' heritage and culture as well throughout their education. The mission home didn't necessarily expect their girls to convert to Christianity, but some of them did (Martin, *Chinatown's Angry Angel*, 153). By the time Donaldina Cameron retired as the mission home's superintendent in 1934, the number of slaves she and Tien Fu Wu rescued had reached three thousand.

SELECTED BIBLIOGRAPHY & RECOMMENDED READING

Asbury, Herbert. *The Barbary Coast: An Informal History of the San Francisco Underworld*. New York: Thunder's Mouth Press, 1933.

Cameron, Donaldina M., Margaret Culbertson, Sarah M. N. Cummings, and Mary H. Field. *Annual Reports of the Mission Home to the Woman's Occidental Board of Foreign Missions, 1874–1920.*

"Cameron House." *Cameron House* (website), https://cameronhouse.org/.

"Donaldina Cameron's San Francisco Mission Home for Chinese Girls—1906," *The Museum of the City of San Francisco* (website), http://www.sfmuseum.net/1906/ew15.html.

Harris, Gloria G., and Hannah S. Cohen. *Women Trailblazers of California: Pioneers to the Present*. Charleston, SC: The History Press, 2012.

Lloyd, B. E. *Lights and Shades in San Francisco*. San Francisco: A. L. Bancroft & Company, 1876.

Logan, Lorna E. *Ventures in Mission: The Cameron House Story*. Wilson Creek, WA: Crawford Hobby Print Shop, 1976.

Martin, Mildred Crowl. *Chinatown's Angry Angel: The Story of Donaldina Cameron*. Palo Alto, CA: Pacific Books, 1977.

Nee, Victor, and Brett de Bary. *Longtime Californ': A Documentary Study of an American Chinatown*. New York: Pantheon Books, 1972.

New Era Magazine. New York: Presbyterian Church in the U. S. A. General Assembly. Vol. 26, no. 2 (February 1920): 175.

One Hundred Fourteenth Annual Report of the Board of Home Missions of the Presbyterian Church in the United States of America. New York: Presbyterian Building, 1916.

Pryor, Alton. *Fascinating Women in California History*. Roseville, CA: Stagecoach Publishing, 2003.

Siler, Julia Flynn. *The White Devil's Daughters: The Women Who Fought Slavery in San Francisco's Chinatown*. New York: Alfred A. Knopf, 2019.

Wilson, Carol Green. *Chinatown Quest: One Hundred Years of Donaldina Cameron House*. San Francisco: California Historical Society with Donaldina Cameron House, 1931.

Woman's Foreign Missionary Society of the Presbyterian Church. *Woman's Work*. New York: Presbyterian Building, 1908.

Woman's Occidental Board of Foreign Missions Annual Reports. San Anselmo, CA: San Francisco Theological Seminary, 1874–1920.

Wong, Edward. "The 1935 Broken Blossoms Case—Four Chinese Women and Their Fight for Justice." *Atavist*, 23 July 2015, https://edwardwong.atavist.com/the-1935-broken-blossoms-case-four-chinese-women-and-their-fight-for-justice. See also https://www.archives.gov/files/publications/prologue/2016/spring/blossoms.pdf.

Wong, Kristin, and Kathryn Wong. *Fierce Compassion: The Life of Abolitionist Donaldina Cameron*. Saline, MI: New Earth Enterprises, 2012.

Yung, Judy. *Unbound Feet: A Social History of Chinese Women in San Francisco*. Berkeley and Los Angeles, CA: University of California Press, 1995.

ACKNOWLEDGMENTS

If Allison Hong Merrill gets an email from Heather B. Moore, she'll shout for joy.

If Allison shouts long enough, she'll be content enough to get to work, beta-reading Heather's manuscript, *The Paper Daughters of Chinatown.*

If Allison reads the manuscript of *The Paper Daughters of Chinatown*, she'll develop an emotional connection with the character Tien Fu Wu, a six-year-old Chinese girl sold by her father to pay his gambling debts and brought to San Francisco's Chinatown as a slave.

If Allison feels a special bond with the character Tien Fu Wu, she'll think about her for years.

If Allison keeps thinking about Tien Fu Wu, she'll receive another message from Heather concerning Tien Fu Wu. (God works in mysterious ways.)

If Allison gets another message from Heather, she'll shout for joy again.

If Allison shouts long enough, she'll be calm enough to accept the offer to co-author *The Paper Daughters of Chinatown:*

Adapted for Young Readers from the Best-Selling Novel with Heather, adding Tien Fu Wu's perspective to the original version.

If Allison co-authors *The Paper Daughters of Chinatown: Adapted for Young Readers from the Best-Selling Novel*, she'll have the honor and privilege of working with exceptionally gifted editors from Shadow Mountain Publishing: Heidi Taylor Gordon, Lisa Mangum, Chris Schoebinger, and Derk Koldewyn.

If Allison gets to work with those powerhouse editors, she'll proudly hold a copy of *The Paper Daughters of Chinatown: Adapted for Young Readers from the Best-Selling Novel* in her hands, admiring the beautiful cover that bears Heather B. Moore's name and her own, and hoping she'll get another message from Heather.

—Allison Hong Merrill

Writing a secondary story about Tien Fu Wu and Donaldina Cameron was both a privilege to focus more on Tien Fu's journey and an emotional challenge because of the heartbreaking experiences these girls and women went through. I'm so very grateful for Allison Hong Merrill, who was one of the editors on the original version of *The Paper Daughters of Chinatown*, and how she enthusiastically agreed to cowrite the adaptation for young readers.

In order to dive more into Tien Fu Wu's background, we contacted Tim Noakes at Stanford University, who gave us access to the Mildred Crowl Martin Archive in Special Collections containing the 1960s recorded interviews with Tien Fu Wu and Donaldina Cameron. It was a delight to hear their voices, and through the digital recording, we felt the love and passion they held for their work.

In addition, Allison and I felt that it was important to receive reader feedback from teenagers after our first draft was written. Many thanks to Aspyn Bond, Skylyn Bond, and Addalyn Walker. Your comments and suggestions have been invaluable.

I've been so blessed over the past few years meeting many